Praise for Nicol
YOU WHO

◆

"There is an astonishing amount of action and suspense. . . . Yet its charm is in its musings, its adroit wit, its acknowledgment of values, including love, friendship, honor, loyalty and, to be sure, justice."

—Charles Champlin, *Los Angeles Times*

◆

"The novel poses questions about responsibility: How we recognize our links with those around us, how we try to slither out of our fates . . . Freeling delivers such ideas with great skill."

—*Washington Post Book World*

◆

"Freeling, an acknowledged master, packs even more provocation and punch than usual into his 32nd novel. . . . As ever, Freeling writes with heart and unfailing intelligence." —*Publishers Weekly*

◆

"Freeling's characters are cynical, deeply intelligent types. . . . His books are always a treat—well-written, full of interesting philosophical digressions and observations." —*Boston Herald*

◆

"Nicolas Freeling is a master of his trade. . . . Another first-rate effort."

—*Sunday Times* (Trenton, NJ)

◆

more . . .

BY THE SAME AUTHOR

Love in Amsterdam
Because of the Cats
Gun Before Butter
Valparaiso
Double Barrel
Criminal Conversation
The King of the Rainy Country
The Dresden Green
Strike Out Where Not Applicable
This is the Castle
Tsing-Boum
Over the High Side
A Long Silence
Dressing of Diamond
What are the Bugles Blowing For?
Lake Isle
Gadget
The Night Lords
The Widow
Castang's City
One Damn Thing After Another
Wolfnight
The Back of the North Wind
No Part in Your Death
A City Solitary
Cold Iron
Lady Macbeth
Not as Far as Velma
Sand Castles
Those in Peril
Flanders Sky
The Seacoast of Bohemia

NONFICTION

Kitchen Book
Cook Book

NICOLAS FREELING

YOU WHO KNOW

THE MYSTERIOUS PRESS

Published by Warner Books

A Time Warner Company

MYSTERIOUS PRESS EDITION

Cover design by Lisa McGarry
Cover illustration by John Howard

The Mysterious Press name and logo are registered trademarks of Warner Books, Inc.

 Mysterious Press books are published by
Warner Books, Inc.
1271 Avenue of the Americas
New York, NY 10020

Ⓦ A Time Warner Company

Printed in the United States of America

Originally published in hardcover by The Mysterious Press.
First Printed in Paperback: June, 1995

10 9 8 7 6 5 4 3 2 1

To Renée, and for our daughter 'Nana'.

To put an end to indecent inquiry,
neither is 'Vera'.
Vera is every girl known to me.

The owl drew itself up, made itself small on
Merlyn's shoulder, shut its eyes and said,
'There is no owl.'
'It's only a boy,' said Merlyn kindly
'There is no boy,' said the owl.

Paraphrased from memory,
with apologies, from
The Sword in the Stone by T. H. White

Dun Laoghaire, Ireland

Filled with delight Castang stared straight out in front of him. True, it was cold, for all the gaily-painted sunshine; a bright, watery, February sunshine that bounced on wavelets and stung the eyes; westering there in front, low over these hills. The wind reached inside his overcoat and scarf tried to tip his hat up. He didn't want to take his hands from his pockets, but he didn't want the hat to blow overboard. He felt an instant's guilt at not calling Vera to see this. She would be cross at missing it.

The old boat, which had lurched and wallowed for three boring hours, fast now and steady as an arrow, reached for this magnetising shoreline. Now and then, one is rewarded for hating planes. All that waiting about; those horrible girls shouting meaningless messages through loudspeakers; you're sure it's for you, and as sure it's something nasty. The Irishman wedged in next him, a noticeable smell of stout, sweat, and overcoat despite the wind, was helpful. They may hate it and probably do, but won't miss the chance of a good pint of stout-frothed sentiment about the Old Sod.

"Sure the Golden Gate is nothing to it."

Castang felt pretty sure the good man had never been closer to California than Limerick Junction, but neither had he.

"Howth Head to your right. Bray Head there to the left. Above the harbour there it's Killiney Hill and the monument on top is where Brian Boru defeated the Danes, and the Dubbalin Mountains there behind, glorious."

"And where's Dubbalin?"

"Ah, it's buried down there on the right and you'd see it better in the nighttime, so you would."

Forget Dublin. What we have is quite enough to be

getting on with. It's Italian, he thought. If it were Irish it would be raining, and perhaps prettier still.

He tore himself away, rushed to get Vera, was vexed to find her at last with a much better viewpoint up on the boat deck, red-nosed but exhilarated. They were close now and the boat was slowing. Terraces in sunlit ochrey-Italian colours perched on scraps of wooded cliff. Wind-twisted growths of pine and ilex masked houses with pillars and porticos, spoiled by a large grey church in the middle, in the most vulgar of Victorian Gothic. English colonial architecture. There were even a few raggedy palm trees. "Look," said Vera, "Joyce's Martello tower." She was being literary, but he had to be a Detective.

They had brought the car all the way to Holyhead, through England on the wrong side of the road, and all those goddam roundabouts, along switchback Welsh roads, pretty and hair-raisingly narrow, and left the car: "too expensive to bring and we don't need it." A really awful old ferry, and the Irish lay about in squalid nests of beer-can and crisp-packet until a voice shouted "Past the Kish lightship, boys," and they'd all tumble out to feel patriotic.

For what, all this? Vera was a tourist, and wanted to exercise her painter's eye upon Wales, and please yes, a bit upon Ireland; both would be just as often beautiful as they were hideous and look, look, here is the proof. But he had another purpose. Horrid Lydia had cut out, and pinned on the door of the landing lavatory, an old James Thurber drawing of a bloodhound, very interested in a fly: its owner is saying, "Oh, why can't you go out and track something?" Even now, Castang has police instincts, ingrained like dirt around a gardener's fingernails, however hard and often he has scrubbed. He had a reason for coming here, though he had no reason for believing that it would do any good. A little, delightful train would take Vera in twenty minutes into Dublin, where she could be literary and artistic to heart's content. He would go rummaging about here.

Here, at the moment, was the Royal Marine Hotel, also a highly colonial piece of architecture, and yet another delight. Vera was upstairs being female; all that changing and washing and unpacking. Himself just as he was, sat in a splendid great Lounge with the bar at the far end and big seaward-facing windows. He had a glass of wine; it wasn't very nice and he asked for a pint of stout instead. "What a good idea," said the barman hospitably. All his whiskers quivered, antennae waving away madly: here were his first clues.

Strange; a couple of unmistakeable horsey-Irish were propped against the bar, but everywhere else around the tea-tables it was English. Elderly and most of it female. Harrody tweeds, Harvey Nichols hats and Liberty scarves, solid bridge-playing Kensington, high clear voices easy to overhear and eavesdrop upon. It was borne in upon him that this was a Darjeeling, a dear-old-Ooty, fifty years after the Raj and surely here eighty, but in this pleasant corner the natives were well out of sight, Dun Laoghaire had become again Kingstown (the garrulous man on the boat had been full of potted history) and the former colonists were quite at home and much at ease. Just like uh, Torquay or uh, Bournemouth. He had never been in either, but had much broadened his education since coming to live and work in the Community, in Brussels. This was one of the pleasant seaside places where the English came in retirement. No longer "theirs", but a little detail like that isn't going to worry them.

Vera appeared, packed with useful information like maps and timetables. "Can you do that, here?" slightly horror-struck at the enormous glass of stout. "Can I have a small one?"

And with evening coming on, and rain to reassure him that he was really in Ireland, a walk along the seafront to the point at Sandycove, Vera still going on about tedious-James-Joyce, but himself pointing the whiskers at all these tiny seaside "villas". In one of these, perhaps, lived the gentleman he had come to see. There was not much to go on. A casual remark or two let fall. "My father lives near Dublin." "Maurice is a comic old bird" – had these been important at the time? Castang could not remember. One of the odd things – afterwards – was that Eamonn had kept a few papers, and no personal letters. The details had been in an address book, a thing in itself slightly odd. Did one put one's father's name and address in an agenda along with useful people like the plumber? Wouldn't one know it by heart? There hadn't been a phone number, but rather formally *Mr Maurice Devaney. Sandycove, Co Dublin*. There were a few other Irish addresses but all in the north. The name was different – well, there had been more odd things about Eamonn, and the manner of his death not the least of them.

They found a restaurant on the seafront and went back to it for dinner. It wasn't bad at all and Castang ate a lot, and asked a lot of questions.

The seaside railway line ran in a cutting below the hotel, and the ornate tiny station was just across the road. Vera boarded saying "back tonight", all aglow with anticipated delights, and he turned his collar up; the rain came in sharp windy gusts, blowing as it does on the streets of Brussels. Well, it would be the same rain, wouldn't it, blown by the same west wind. Just a bit earlier, even on the small European scale Ireland is not far from Belgium. Only a matter of being an island. He could have taken a plane and been here in an hour. But he'd been right not to, he thought. The history is not the same. Whatever else it had been, Belgium had not been an English colony, as Eamonn had liked to point out, with emphasis.

"These Brits, they still all talk about leading the world."

"But you're a Brit, aren't you?" said Castang teasingly. "United Kingdom."

"Rather a vexed subject, dear boy."

He rounded the point – when they came on the market these little houses would cost a packet. Most were very small, and looked both damp and dark. An English feel, at once prim and faintly raffish. Tiny, post-Georgian terraces, minute post-Regency cottages, grandly pillared porch and on either side one window, small and sorrowing as an Irishman's eyes after four pints and a defeat at Lansdowne Road. The roofs hidden by a cornice, crowned with a pair of topheavy urns or a plaster eagle – oh, grand stuff altogether. However minuscule, plenty of colonial self-confidence; however snug, a good dash of British braggadocio. Some were smartly painted, the rosebush cared for and the hydrangea pruned. Mr Devaney's, when he found it, looked dilapidated. He could hear the bell ring, within, but nobody answered the door. Dingy curtains drawn. Hm. He did a bit of circling round. Chap had popped out perhaps, for bread or milk? Or did they get brought to the door, here?

An old man was coming, along the pavement with a dog on a leash; there was the simple answer. A good seventy – yes, that could be the father. Tall, thin, a retired military Brit look, with the tweed hat, the Burberry, the silver moustache and eyebrows, the bright blue eyes – those looked familiar.

"Looking for me?" amiably; the ringing English voice. Castang made conventional mumbles; um-colleague, er-friend, uh, your son. Happened to be in the neighbourhood, thought I'd-uh. The old boy seemed unsurprised.

"Really? Better come in then, Mr Castang, hadn't you?" Spry enough; got his name right, straight off. Cottage bigger than it seemed outside. Dark low-ceilinged English living-room full of worn Persian rugs and dingy leather furniture. Smells of clean old man and damp dog, lots of junk and lots of dust. No trace of a woman's presence. The old boy perched, cavalry twill knees sticking out; these chairs were too low. Snapped his fingers and the dog went to a basket; old, like him. Reached for a pipe.

"Too early, for a whisky?" There were several on offer, some very nice-looking Irish ones and some single malts, too, which weren't Irish.

"Not just yet, I think." Both the question and the answer were a bit wistful.

"So; a colleague, mm, a friend. Of my son's. Indeed. But you didn't come all the way here just to offer condolences." If anything, rather too spry.

"No. Well perhaps I won't say no, to a shot."

"Water? Just as it comes? Quite right. You see, Mr Castang, one is both Scotch and Irish. Either will do."

"So I always understood, from Eamonn."

"You did? And what else did you understand?"

"Oh, jokes, mostly. We got to be quite friends, there in Brussels – perhaps enough so that I didn't feel happy with the way he died."

"With, or about?"

"Super stuff," said Castang to the cutglass tumbler. "Both, really."

"You're a policeman, are you?" It was direct enough to take him aback, and there was no point in shuffling.

"I used to be," sadly. "I suppose there's some remnant of the manner left."

"Something of the look. And something of the sound. So you must tell me now in what way I can be of service to you."

"In the old days I could have said, would you answer to some interrogation? I have, of course, no official standing."

"Just curious, is it? I was curious myself. Didn't seem much I could do about it."

"How did you hear?"

That question like others went unanswered. Saying that the Irish were devious is like saying the French are pinchpenny; it may be a national cliché, but so often it's true.

"I don't mind being interrogated. Rather like it. Gingers one up. Change from all the sleepy heads round here. Not much point though. Knew little of my son. Saw less. Exchanged Christmas cards. Why come to me?"

"He died a violent death. The police enquire, but the enquiry as they often do petered out. When gravelled like that they're filed with a note, saying alive, but on the back burner. Unless there's something new, nothing will be done. He was my friend, when all else is said."

"Parallel police are you? Political?'

Now why should he ask that? "No, I'm the man who kept saying "I want to know". A sediment of professional dissatisfaction."

"Mr Castang, I'm an old man. People die. It affects me, since I'm human. But I've been a soldier all my life. I don't ask why they die. Life continues for as long as it is given us."

"*En effet.*" Castang was used, now, to speaking English, but still fell into French without noticing. A Brussels habit. "In an unexplained death, one likes to look at family background. It could be something from the past. People lead complicated lives."

"Really? I've led a very simple life. HM Forces, retired half-colonel. Small pension and small private means. I am as you see me."

"Hickey was his mother's name?"

"My dear sir, I've lost sight of her these thirty years. You could have asked the boy. He had some government position here. They're all Catholics you know, Republicans, I'm indifferent to them. Fill in my forms, pay my taxes. Ireland

– England – Europe – at my time of life it's all the same, isn't it? Delighted to have met you, but desolated that I can be of no use to you."

He would try for a little more before being chucked out. "He came to see you, now and again." He got a sharp look. "Now and then, yes. We were not sundered, if that's what you're getting at, by any bad blood. He'd have consultations with his officials here, briefings they call them. I don't know and didn't ask. He'd drop in to see how I was getting on. A whisky, a chat. I'm always here. Politeness, would you call it? I'll miss that. Always glad to see him. Now, I get people like you, instead."

"Has there been anyone else, asking?"

"No, no, I only meant, most interesting. But you'll forgive me, dear man, if I have to see about my shopping. Not the day for my kind cleaning woman. Make do for ourselves, don't we, Tinker old boy?" The dog rapped with its tail and so did Castang.

But that old sod knows more than he'll say.

Castang withdrew, to meditate upon the streets of Dalkey. Feeling energetic, he climbed the hill, and had some lunch in Killiney village. He didn't think the obelisk had anything to do with King Brian Boru. People said things and they didn't have to be true. Hm, the rich lived up here; nice for them. A lot of modern building had gone on, but one could still perceive, perfectly clearly, the old pattern. It was his job to look for the patterns in things. In the days of the Raj, down at the bottom lived the small people, the great army of clerks and mechanics who filled the minor posts of the empire. Distinguished from the natives by imperial symbols on or around even the tiniest of imperial dwellings. An engine driver was socially a long way above the Irish huddled here in the village. As one climbed the hill, status increased. Above what was now the bus route were the squares and terraces of middle management; the businessmen and bank officials, who would in England be nobodies but who here enjoyed status, as representing the occupiers, the power in the land. They had a word for it here – the Ascendancy. He giggled; it was a world he understood. Madame Chose, whose man was in the Secretariat, would scarcely deign acknowledge the salutations of la mère Machin, whose husband was only in the Public

Works Department. And that all came to an end in 1921, and what had changed, since? Not, he dared bet, so very much. He remembered Eamonn giving him history lessons. The Republic had been very poor; free at last but economically backward. Only in recent years was there new money – you could see it around here, clear as day, speculators' money, flashy money. People in big Mercedes whose parents had only had potatoes on the table. And the English lived on unperturbed, alongside.

Footsore at last – policemen's feet were of a long-lost past – he got back to the hotel to await Vera. Teatime! A nice little Irish waitress (wearing very odd clothes but all smiles) brought a tray. Mm, in times gone by, and even outside his territory, he'd have run a discreet tape-measure over Lieutenant-Colonel (Retd) Maurice Devaney. Not, heaven-forbid, a neighbourhood enquiry – they'd all be gossiping like a flock of starlings, and within the hour the man would be feeling the pressure. But one had one's ways and means.

Near him in the window embrasure there was an old memsahib, giving tea to a younger woman whom she hadn't seen in some years, perhaps. The perfect type; tall, cool, aquiline, *racée*. The replies were low-pitched, inaudible, but the questions were all he needed.

"Do you play bridge? No. Nor do I any more. Are you keeping up with your painting?" And a little later "Did you ride, when you were young?" Only Americans talk about 'horseback riding' . . . When the younger woman left she sat on, taking a packet of cigarettes from her bag, glancing at her watch; she plainly had time on her hands. Castang was tempted to play the benighted stranger. "Do please forgive me, Madame, I'm a bit lost hereabouts." She would welcome the distraction, apart from the inbred courtesy and the being sorry for poor foreigners. "But of course I know Maurice Devaney." This was a community which held together, in a solid front towards the natives. The golf club, the ritual changing of library books, the grocer who had Gentleman's Relish and Cooper's Oxford marmalade. Would it do him any good though? He felt unusually sure that what Mr Devaney did not want known would stay unknown: he had a perfect front to present to the world. A son who had gone native? Worked for the Irish government and called himself Hickey? But he had Eamonn's word that things were not as crude here: he could remember the subject coming up over other glasses of whisky in Brussels. Amid roars of laughter.

"No, no, you're thinking of the curry colonels down on the Devon coast or in the Algarve. The Anglo-Irish aren't like that; they're genuinely Irish and being Protestant doesn't alter things at all. A great many of them work for the Republic and are proud to. If they were English, no — Childers was never really trusted and got shot for it in the Civil War. Oh, they made honourable amends and his son ended up as President. But they couldn't get over his being such a newcomer — whereas some of these families have been there hundreds of years." But you weren't, thought Castang now. You're Scotch import, and where does that leave you?

And now, here was Vera, rather travel-stained.

"Rain pissed down all day in Dublin."

"*Tiens?* Cleared up quite soon, here."

"But it was lovely!" She was loaded, bursting to tell. All right, they'd go and have a shower, find somewhere to eat, and he would get another small step further forward in understanding. Now she had seen for herself, she too would remember bits of Eamonn's conversation. Devious? Yes, but also very direct.

"Good case to be made," his lovely voice with Scottish and Irish notes in it, as well as cavalry-English, "for finding, say, 1880 to 1910 the best of times in Dublin. With of course an income within reasonable distance of expectations; one should always be a little poorer than one would wish. One would live perhaps in Mount Street, upper end, by the bridge — oh dear, you should see it now. The girls lived in hopes of seeing a lancer — splendidly mounted, the horse sliding a little on the cobbles — come to deliver an invitation to a vicereine's ball . . . Medicine of course still exceedingly crude, but you mustn't think in terms of today, dear boy, but in the context of the Crimean War. Remember the surgeon who said that chloroform was a disgrace and should instantly be banned because pain is the most powerful of all stimulants, I do so love that. Whereas Irish doctors were then the finest in Europe."

And Castang's mind slipping off now to the other voice, the father's so similar, softening after a shot of whisky.

"Fact is, my boy, the English did everything that's worth keeping. Made great nonsenses too, of course – patronage of the lower classes. The Peepuls' Park, where nobody has ever set foot nor ever will. The Vicereine's Home for Poor Children – you'll find it to this day, up the hill on Tivoli Road. Dun Leary indeed, call it Kingstown if I want to, though nowadays Dun Roamin would be more to the point."

And yes, Vera's delighted pilgrimage through Dublin had revived recollections.

"I passed Trinity College – oh there are still some fine things there in the centre, they haven't quite dared knock down yet. Don't you remember Eamonn setting us into fits telling how he was a student there and there wasn't a lavatory in the place and all the students peed out of the windows?'

"Now you mention it, yes, indeed."

A young, romantic Eamonn. "You can't imagine how beautiful Dublin was in those days – they were the first years of the war. No cars of course. Oh, there were buses – the nine or the ten, Trinity to Baggot Street Bridge for a penny-ha'penny. Special way of getting on – time it nicely and it needn't even stop; point of honour to get off before it stopped for all the old ladies in Pembroke Road; and the trams, ah ... Fourpence, from Admiral Nelson in Sackville Street, always known as the Pillar, to Marine Road Dun Laoghaire and twice as fast as it is now. The Swastika Laundry – no, I swear it – and the Tel El Kebir Dairy bringing your milk. But above all, you walked, you walked ... O'Nolan was the great guru, Myles na Gcopaleen, it was a daily column in the *Irish Times*. The jokes about the Brother and the Glimmer Man."

And what was the glimmer man? Vera had wondered, fascinated. "Gas was rationed, only on at peak hours. They couldn't cut it off: altogether, air in the pipes or something, so in between there was a tiny bead, known as the glimmer; it was strictly forbidden to boil a kettle on the glimmer, and the myth was that the Glimmer Man would knock at the door and catch you, and then of course you were for it. Which lent an extra relish to doing so."

And then to the old Army tune of "Bless 'em all" he'd sung:

"God Bless de Valera, and Sean MacEntee
Who gave us black bread and a half-ounce of tea."

"Oh, you don't know that? Where were you children educated?" And properly juiced now, in a surprisingly good tenor voice, indeed formerly known as a "pub tenor",

"They say there's a troopship that's leaving Bombay
Bound for old Blighty's Shore –

and how long is it since a British troopship left Bombay?"

One would have to ask his father, Castang thought sentimentally now. He would have served there. The Connaught Rangers. The Black Tyrone!

"Since you tell me it was no good," said Vera "I suppose you won't want to stay any longer." Female; pretending to be diffident and really being provoking.

"Who said that?"

True, he hadn't got the oyster open. Police jargon; a criminal enquiry is often like having nothing but your hands to open an oyster with. So one hunts about for a tool which might serve. Have you tried with a penknife? It's much harder on your hands than on the oyster. For the Irish are very like the French, or any peasant, anywhere. Russians, let's say. They had been very keen on their Tsars. The Irish would be no different. They rather liked the English monarchy – what else brought them into the Army's Irish regiments? It was the title to their land that made revolutionaries of them. The English stole our land!

A day or so more. Perhaps then he would start to understand Ireland, which had to be the key to someone called Eamonn Hickey.

Vera was not very good at walking. Never mind, she would look at Kilmainham Jail, now a good museum, she was told. And this house of Parnell's she talks about, out there in those mountains one sees on the skyline, and very beautiful too.

"Who's Parnell?"

"Statesman, in the last century. A great man and a very odd one. Got into trouble with a love affair with a married woman. The Irish were very puritanical, and they disowned him." Castang was pricking up his ears. "He loved this

11

house; it's a forestry school, now. But there was a story I liked: an English writer was there looking, and an Irishman told him 'I see him out walking sometimes, but sure it's only an illusion.' Isn't that good!"

Lymington, Hampshire

This was another of the places the English retired to, but not at all Italian! No mountains – quite the contrary, dear little wooded inlets full of dear little boats; a dear little harbour – and across the Solent in Yarmouth just such another. Cosy. Here the English played at being Admirals. And here Jane had come back to live with her mother, who was probably an admiral's widow. 17, Broadwalk, a desirable and very expensive piece of English Georgian cottagedom. The point was that Jane hadn't left after Eamonn's death but before. A strong-minded, tenacious woman – Castang had been fond of her, and Vera close friends with her – she had simply upped sticks and gone one fine day, without a word to anyone. So that he wanted, very much, to talk to her. And here she was, popping out of this preposterous doll's-house with the enormous eyes he remembered, much surprised, and the delight not altogether faked.

"Hen-ri! How nice. Vera too!" and with genuine affection. "But is it for me you've come?" Jane's "little smile", self-deprecating, and just a touch embittered. "Or for him?"

Castang answered in a hurry, before Vera could get her mouth open. "Both, but, may I say, you first."

Jane as usual is a portrait of virtue; the modest expression, the rather dowdy clothes, the gentle, nigh-inaudible voice. Appearances are deceptive. There was plenty of steely stuff underneath. Right now "much embarrassed" and gone a bit pink. "It's lovely to see you both," with obvious sincerity, "but will you mind awfully if I don't ask you in. Because I think Mother will get into a stew."

"No, we were going to the hotel anyway."

"Oh, not that horrid Trust House. But there's quite a nice pub, and it's just down the road. I'll just pop in and explain matters."

And the Ship is all a pub ought to be, log fire and Windsor chairs polished by Hampshire bottoms and brass polished by the hands of Courage, or is it perhaps the Strong Country? "Two pints of bitter," said Castang happily.

Jane appeared, in a fluster. "I'm sure they'll have a room this early in the year. I'll go and ask them shall I, d'you want pork pie or something, they've quite good cold beef, I feel ashamed, you see my mother doesn't want to know, I know it seems absurd, oh all right, a small shandy."

Politenesses were exchanged, and gossip, and "exclaiming" and talk about children; and Jane ducked her head in a remembered way saying, "I'm not going to talk about it."

Poor old Jane, much more vulnerable than cunning Maurice Devaney, but just as obstinate. Castang had thought he knew all about interrogation methods. He cajoled, irritated, provoked, was kind and cruel. Not a trickle could he get and he was in the middle of picking his words carefully when Vera suddenly said, "What you don't know and what you wouldn't know how to say is that Eamonn was the Good Soldier."

It meant something to Jane all right: it gave her a shock and the shock turned on no trickle but floods of tears and imprecations.

"That's exactly what he was. The nicest possible person; kind, generous, considerate. The best of friends, the man you'd have trusted anywhere, and with your wife—and you'd have been wrong," added in a startling vomit of bitterness.

"Wrong!' Castang, stupefied. "But I don't trust anyone with my wife. I mean I trust my wife."

"Good for you," said Vera acidly. "Did you really never see it?"

Apparently he had been very stupid, and he tried to pull himself together. "I'm not anyone's wife," an effort at sarcastic humour which fell extremely flat. "But why didn't you say?"

Vera said nothing, but pointed to Jane who was still trying not to cry in public.

"I suppose I understand. I mean I suppose that you were being loyal. Now I've made a fool of myself." Damned Vera! "But still . . . why did I never see this?"

"Because you never looked," kindly now. "Nobody ever

saw either with the Good Soldier. You don't know about that, but it's quite a famous book."

"I don't know any books, I'm just a dimwit," thoroughly cross.

"The man," said Jane, nettled at her own stupid tears, "was exactly what I said, kind, generous and unselfish. High-principled. A gentleman, my mother said when she met him. That's what upset her so badly you see, that she was wrong. That I was wrong was beside the point. The Good Soldier was all those things, and also utterly unreliable with women. I also see perfectly that Vera didn't tell you because she didn't want to humiliate me."

"I'm sorry," said that lady apologetically, "but, you know, *Banane!*" It is one of the children's words for Thick.

"I suppose I never saw because we were friends."

"And I suppose I saw," said Vera, "being hers. Since at least he knew better than to try it on me."

"He would have, you mean?" As a police officer one didn't have friends much. And look what happened when one did. So that he pitied himself for a second and then cheered up. Because now for worming it all out of Jane, who was clutching her hanky and staring at a pretty picture of unnaturally white yachts bouncing about in unnaturally blazing sunlight; the Solent around 1867, when perhaps the greatest pest known had been Sir Thomas Lipton, and there were no leaky oiltankers.

"I think you're reading it wrong," said Vera who was watching Jane. "I don't think he saw it as a betrayal of friendship, and the idea would have shocked him. I imagine it comes naturally to people like that. You're hungry, you reach out for a piece of pork pie."

Having at last wrenched the cap off the bottle – the poor girl must have been brooding about all this for months with nobody but Mum to talk to (one did see now why Mum should feel no enthusiasm for meeting Mr Hickey's friends) – Jane was ripe for spitting it all out. She was even resolute. Floodgates opened.

"He didn't even see it as a betrayal of his own wife," taking a gulp of her drink and finding it failed to brace. "Might I have some whisky or something?"

Castang felt a bit comforted when the explaining started. It wasn't really a French – in the sense of Latin –

phenomenon. The French would go to bed with anything on two legs and call it love: they liked to feel that love came into it somewhere, even when quite aware that this was the most transitory of illusions. It wasn't the vanity of conquests either. The chap would, it appeared, be quite humble about it and even ashamed of himself, inclining to crawl about tail down, and slinking rather. No, said Jane, she wasn't being contemptuous or vengeful even now; she'd become exceedingly embittered but now factual and nothing more. He liked to chase kitchenmaids.

No trappings of romance: One wasn't to think of any Iseult drinking magic potions and sinking into a bower of bliss. They got bedded, and as far as Jane knew, with the least fuss possible. No Brangäne to sing from the battlements *Habet acht*! because he did look out. Five minutes afterwards it was as though it had never been. So no Celtic or indeed any misty northern romanticisms.

Castang remarked that he found all this a bit odd. Protestant or Catholic, the Irish surely are prim about sex, no? All right, he was beginning to see that this was a character much more complex than anything he had seen or known – and that is a lesson the police officer has to keep relearning, not to oversimplify things merely to keep his paperwork to a minimum. Here is a great big area in this man, he was thinking, which I did not know. I realise that I did not know him at all well. It is quite likely that there are more large areas still to be discovered. I must learn all I can here, while the going's good.

This wasn't easy because Jane herself was a prim soul. There was all the humiliation of talking about a situation she'd known all about for a long time. She had adopted the good old method of 'stout denial'. The best way to fight anything is to say it doesn't exist, and go on behaving as though it didn't. But women like this – Vera is much the same, and "prim" is not quite the right word, too pejorative. What they are protecting here is their own personal female dignity. Vera too dislikes that easy male talk, comfortably coarse because the men are not taking it personally, about getting into some girl's knickers. He'd had to learn at the start, with Vera, to avoid turning round in the street with even the most casual of remarks about some fine pair of tits just gone past, because she did not like it At All.

And perhaps there'd been a streak of puritanism in Eamonn's Irishness, because come to think, he couldn't remember Eamonn ever making that sort of joke. It had been natural to think that he was not that sort of man. While he himself could leer, and often did, and Vera still didn't like it.

Jane, he could see now, was drinking whisky deliberately to loosen her own tongue. And to be able to talk at last with some detachment. About a man who is dead. She is now wanting very badly to purge herself of the long-contained misery. Probably she'd find it easier without Vera here (however silent, withdrawn, a sort of tact; pay no attention to me I'm not even listening). Jane was still very stuttery. Huge blushes came and went. Was it right to push her, even to force her to go into detail? He had to go by instinct. Some crude questions might be what was needed, to disinfect.

"It would be in some public place, at first I saw nothing. Later I got so that I would dread looking, in case I would see. He'd have gone silent, and quite immobile. A hawk circling, and it sees something? No, a crocodile. Drifting along, there isn't a ripple, you wouldn't know it was there unless you were looking out for the eyes and the nose. As I learned to, and then I had to learn to force my own eyes away. The eyes would focus, and then they would devour. It wasn't hidden at all. It was even quite unself-conscious. No pretence or hypocrisy. The crocodile would drift up closer, very quiet and patient.

"I mean you know how fashions are nowadays – I mean the womens' clothes, they're very revealing, I won't even say the girls want that, they don't even notice half the time. Even quite elderly women, a skirt you can see through, trousers you can see the whole outline of their knickers, heavens you can even tell the colour. Shirts so thin you see the entire modelling of their breasts, shorts so tight they might as well be naked because of their labia, their nipples practically knocking the glasses off the table." Jane peered round guiltily hoping there was no one to overhear even if one could scarcely catch her voice while sitting next to her. "I don't wear clothes like that. Nor would Vera. But a great many do. That's the way things are. A lot of gnus for the crocodile," bitterly.

"Kitchenmaids! Oh yes, I know I'm not supposed to talk

like this, it's snobbish and racist and everything one mustn't be, and tell me then, how am I to speak about those empty-faced girls, there's nothing vicious about them, they're probably deafened and blinded by that pop noise they have with them wherever they go, and they chew and it's all to them as simple as a cow lifting its tail, you feel they're not even going to wait until the door is shut – God, I hate talking like this." Her voice had risen and she looked around again guiltily.

"Let's go out and find somewhere we can walk," suggested Castang.

Low tide, along the Solent, and a considerable stink despite the wind. Wind sharp enough to bring water to the eyes, so back to the car to get dark glasses; a relief for Jane to talk about King Charles the First. Hurst Castle, which was not castley enough to please Castang.

"No, one has to cross over to the Island and there's Carisbrooke, he was in prison there too, that's rather more like it." But she was not free of her torments. "One could sit there on a terrace and see him mentally stripping them, feeding his obsession."

As now you are feeding your own, thought Castang, but not about to say so. "I don't know," dully.

He had to push her a little way further, still. Had the police found out about this in their enquiries? Not that they were under any obligation to tell him, as indeed they hadn't. "He was killed," said Castang gently.

"I mustn't leave my mother too long alone. Yes. Yes. Don't think I haven't thought about it. And felt it. One will always think one was wrong, that one handled it badly, that one should have . . . A man came to see me, Detective Constable Something from the Hampshire CID, and he told me what had happened. I suppose it must have occurred to them that I might have murdered him. I could show them of course how long I'd been here, and I think he understood that I'm really not that sort of person, I mean to run away and then go back after a deep-laid plot to kill poor Eamonn. He must have seen it was a fearful shock. They phoned afterwards and I had to go up to Winchester and make a statement. By then I was feeling nothing much but a sort of immense apathy. One says things at the time. When I left Brussels, you know, I just could not stand it any longer,

18

I daresay then I did say hysterical things like "I could kill you." But one doesn't, I mean one says things like that for some quite trivial motive — leaving the soap under the shower. Doing it is quite different."

"What was it that tipped the balance, that caused you finally to leave him? Was there some crisis?"

"Oh, I remember now, you were asking me before. That perpetual philandering with typists and kitchenmaids, one could pretend it didn't happen as long as he was relatively discreet, and then I came back and found this one actually in the house. He swore blind of course it wasn't so, it was a business thing. My eye, I said, that's it, I went upstairs, I packed a bag. That must have been a good fortnight or three weeks before . . ."

"Can you remember her name?'

"It's funny, isn't it, that social conventions are so strong, one doesn't make a scene in front of a third person, there might have been two minutes of well, strained talk before I made an excuse to go upstairs and then I heard the door shut and knew she was gone. But the name, yes, I'm not sure I caught it. Cordelia? That doesn't sound right, no, more one of those odd French names, could it be Ottilie? But it's gone, I'm afraid."

"But you could describe her?"

"Very vaguely, I suppose, short curling hair, a chestnut brown. Bright, dark blue eyes, striking — but she was wearing a lot of make-up. Earrings; I rather think a lot of jewellery. The clothes I don't remember. Something of an Italian look."

"But not a kitchenmaid?"

"No, not the usual type."

"Tall, short, slim or rounded?"

"No, just medium as I recall, I'm sorry but — really Henri, I've got very tired and I'm feeling the cold, I came out without a proper coat."

She could not be persuaded to come out to dinner; no, she really couldn't leave her mother. And Vera was treading on his foot, but he could see that Jane wanted to get rid of them now, and that she was thinking she'd said too much already. Witnesses go dry, and it's of no use then to squeeze the sponge. She would sleep on it, and the oyster would shut tight. It didn't matter much; he felt pretty sure

19

he would have come to the same conclusion as the CID in Winchester.

Dinner in the pub — a glance was enough to show that Jane was right about the hotel's food — was unexpectedly grand. He had a partridge, English style. Crisps which one ate first while admiring the rest, and bread sauce! Delicious, and he could lord it over Vera who was only having boring old pork-chop. But a lovely tender one she said, and nice apple sauce for once not sweetened.

"She makes sense though, doesn't she?"

"Well, I'm sure she didn't kill him, if that's what you mean. I never thought she did. But the Hampshire Constabulary will have made sure of it. She was in full view here, doing the shopping for Mum and whatever, and the butcher would remember seeing her."

"It would be one of those very old detective stories," said Vera, "which get one in a dreadful muddle about timetables. Freeman Wills Crofts — I found one in the passage and took it to read in bed; lovely."

"I'm going for a stroll by the water."

"Don't pick up any kitchenmaids."

The tide was in, and the wind had died down. Water lapped and chuckled. Pretty little boats swathed in tarpaulin nodded patiently, waiting for people to come and be nautical. There was nobody about but a few seagulls; television is no treat to them.

Curly hair, made-up eyes, Cordelia or possibly Ottilie, it didn't add up to much, did it? I saw those harbour lights, and they only told me we were parting.

He found Vera in the bath, stretched out being luxurious, letting her toes float, sailing a plastic soapdish, generally being childish. When one comes from far-flung European shores, baths are peculiarly English, like milk on the doorstep, and she enjoys them instead of saying dreadful-insanitary-thing. This being so he poured some cold water on her while brushing his teeth and was rewarded with a howl before going to look for another detective story and only finding a very old copy of the *Reader's Digest*. He then became aware that she was pottering about with a lot of perfume on and not much else, and drew the conclusion that she was feeling uxorious.

Brussels, January

In Brussels is the Berlaymont Building, for many years the expensive, not to say extravagant, heart-and-centre of the European Community. It has been very suddenly, not to say ominously (and one can't help feeling belatedly), discovered that this lordly pile is inefficient, insanitary, and even dangerous. It is full of asbestos, so that all the Commissioners in their large offices upon the eleventh floor are about to succumb to silicosis. Further it has been discovered that if the place did catch fire it takes far too long for the rank and file to be saved, so what good is all that asbestos anyhow? The r. and f., who weren't consulted, say Bloody Good Job, because the lavatories are a perfect disgrace.

It has nothing much to do with this story, and Castang who works in another of the Community's buildings – they are numerous – could not care less, but is moved at the thought that right opposite is a building of great importance to the Community, where he frequently has occasion to set foot, and he hopes these habits will not be unduly perturbed.

Kitty O'Sheas is a just tolerably scruffy pub got up to look Irish with old Guinness and Smithwick advertisements, it isn't only a place for the Irish to stop feeling so damnably offshore: it's also a watering hole for all those hard-drinking journalists. In Brussels they are powerful, and not just thirsty. Castang liked having a jar here with Eamonn Hickey.

Eamonn was not all that hard-drinking and nor was he all that Irish, and was not to be found here for all eternity propping up the bar. He'd pop in, have a jar, pop out, but this pretty regularly, so that if, say, he didn't answer his

phone you might be fairly confident of catching him on
the wing, around here.

Here too Castang got English lessons, songs such as
"Hallo Patsy Fagan you can hear the girls all cry", or
"There was a wild colonial boy, young Castang was his
name"; a great deal more improving to the vocabulary
than English-language summaries of Community direct-
ives, which are largely incomprehensible whether or not
one's native language happens to be English.

On one chilly draughty January evening, Castang had
whipped in with his coat-collar up and injunctions from
Vera not to lose his scarf which is silk, pretty, and a present
from her. Eamonn was not there. A journalist was there, a
pleasant chap with a little naval beard such as were worn
by those who gallantly blocked Zeebrugge harbour in
HMS Vindictive; English but been here long enough to be
part of Bruce local colour, who hurried over with a
circumstantial face. There's this thing about journalists;
they're all sitting there boozing but the grapevine is
quicker than anywhere else.

"You've heard? Eamonn's dead."

"Oh Jesus. Car accident?" For Eamonn's cars are old
and decrepit and bought off junkheaps for fourpence-
farthing, but have been known to go too fast.

"No, and this is the thing. Destroyed by a shotgun blast."

"Oh, holy COW."

"There was that thing, his wife buzzed off a couple of
weeks ago. Jealous husband, you'd say, lurking there in
the bushes?"

"I wouldn't say, it sounds most unlike him."

"That's what I'd think, too, but all rather hole and
corner."

"You people going to make a thing out of this?"

"No, no, shouldn't think so, just a couple of lines in the
squashed-dogs column. Obscure functionary, pure coincidence in the same service as you and Mr Claverhouse of
fragrant memory. Be frowned upon by editors to make
anything of the likes of this, but wanted to say I'm sorry
because he was a friend of yours. What would you make of
it?"

"Nothing at all and certainly not to print. Friends but
not intimate, and I've no information on the jealous-

husband brigade, but I feel close enough that I'm profoundly upset."

"Sorry – let me – what will it be?'

Yes, that was horrid, and the next day no better. News of violent anything and including death had been a rudiment of Castang's professional existence for so long that the habit of disinfecting all emotions is still strong in him, even though it was three years and more since he'd had a criminal brigade to run. Shove a bedpan in a nurse's hand and she'll hardly notice: she won't utter cries of delight, though. Before deciding whether or not to tell Vera he looked to see whether it was in the paper. It wasn't, so he didn't. That in itself was rather odd, because a shotgunned Func, however obscure, is more mouthwatering than a squashed dog. He assembled his scarf grimly and went off to the office.

And yes, he got buttonholed in the passage by Mr Suarez lurking and wanting-a-word. Doors shut; private word.

"I've some startling, and I'm afraid melodramatic news."

"I know; the journalists had it last night. But it's not in the paper. Television I haven't looked at.'

"No. It'll be in the local paper down in Namur. We got it stopped for twenty-four hours to cool it off. There they got the bare facts and no more. We want to keep it that way, obviously. It's highly embarrassing especially since it's only a year since Harold . . . Now you're – you were a friend and you're a police officer."

"No longer and I hope not ever."

"No, well, we're working on that but these things take time to go through channels. I'm aware that originally you were only seconded, but I think I can say, call it a semi-official certainty, that you can view yourself as having tenure; your qualifications after all, and your work . . . and it's unlikely, to put it tactfully, that they'll be roaring to have you back in Paris . . . Thing is, you know the police here, and you remember that at the time with Harold . . ."

"I do know Commissaire Mertens, slightly," said Castang, hoping that sounded chilly.

"Very good," to squash this lack of enthusiasm. "It might be as well to find out, quite discreetly, backstairs as it were what they make of this. Especially after the Claverhouse episode, the last thing we want is gossip. What we'd like is an accident." This is very French. Mr Suarez is in fact Spanish, but Castang has known several French government servants of high seniority explain away compromising disasters with the blandest disregard for fact. He was cleaning his gun, you see, and fell down with a heart attack, and his waistcoat buttons caught in the trigger; goodness how sad.

"Better, a heart attack," as though reading his mind. "That's harmless and merely sets people thinking of their own cholesterol levels and a vague notion they themselves haven't got enough golf in lately."

Nobody had ever suspected Suarez of humour. He had a stationary bicycle in the office which he rode while mentally formulating precise legal language: Eamonn had been accustomed to calling it the wanking machine. He was suspected of having a thing at home one sits in and rows upstream of the bathroom floor.

Castang nodded.

"Of course Harold was brilliant, but one always did feel there was something fundamentally unsound. I always had the impression with Eamonn of something rather sinister, d'ye know what I mean?"

"Exactly. And the less time lost, the better." Sighing, Castang started reknotting his scarf.

"Your permanency, Castang." Mr Suarez had picked up his fountain-pen and was examining it closely. Was there a microphone hidden within? "The department welcomes it. I have so formulated my written recommendation. You know how the French are, dragging their feet because they never like to say a definite yes or no to anything in case they might like to change their minds later," he added in a much more human sort of voice.

Mr Mertens, Central Commissaire at the Kripo in Brussels, looked just the same as when Castang had last seen him nigh on two years ago. He still had his enormous ashtray, a great slab of stone as though containing an interesting fossil, in this case a human skull. His giving-up-smoking technique is to light his pipe and then put it into this. Castang, whose more childish technique was to leave his cigarettes behind on purpose in unlikely places, quite liked him.

They got on well, cop to cop, largely because Castang

could not be regarded as a threat, surreptitiously undermining another senior cop's position: his (very French) situation as a senior commissaire sent to help drive the phrasing of legal protocols in Bruce with an eye to the tender corns of the Keeper of the Seals in Paris, allows Monsieur Mertens to feel sympathetic as well as amused.

"Hallo." Getting up and shaking hands; a polite man. "Bet I know what brings you here.'

"Bet not taken. Know all about it, do you? Good, because I've been sent to spy. Everybody's imploring me to be tactful."

'Yoh, I'm willing enough, I'm always tactful." Getting up and taking a folder off a shelf. "You're a bit premature; this is still very thin. Let me make myself clear, your main problem is going to be Delahaye down in Namur, he's not a bit tactful. He has jurisdiction, you see. All according to Cocker, local cops notified the Proc, Proc designated an examining magistrate, who rightly concluded this is likely to make everyone shit and has ordered a full judicial enquiry from friend Delahaye, who promptly goes underground with it."

"Aren't you his superior?"

"Technically yes, on the ground no. There's a chap who's jealous of his prerogatives, hates the idea of being messed about by a lot of cheese in Bruce. I have a concern, naturally, since your Mr Hickey was domiciled here. So I'm like the Queen, I have a constitutional right to be kept informed, which is why I get photocopies of whatever Mister Delahaye might like me to know if he's in a good mood. Which will arrive late, get lost in transit – not yet but that'll come – be illegible, have page three missing, fall down in court because not properly countersigned; and so forth. You know all about this, for god's sake."

"Yes. We'd rather like this to be a heart attack; what are our chances?"

"Not very good. Chap got blown apart with a shotgun."

"Caught it in the door. Fell on it."

"Trouble there is ballistics says the range was a good three metres."

"Well, ballistics got it wrong. They nearly always do."

"A'Ha yes, your two cops in Paris who shot the thirteen-year-old boy in that very dark cellar! Was it the one who got the door pushed into his poor nose? Or the one down the passage who saw that threatening dark shadow? So we'll have their two guns test-fired. Then we'll have to fall back on that old gag of the guns weren't properly labelled. No way – photos show the gun lying there three metres off. Even if he flung it *despair*ingly there as he fell it won't wash; his prints aren't on it. Here," passing a bunch of photos across.

"This is very odd." It caught the eye straightaway.

"You said it," said Mr Mertens relishing his nasty surprise.

"So not his shotgun," said Castang; a remarkably dense observation.

One of the scene-of-crime photos – they aren't supposed to be artistic, just very clearly lit – showed it with brutal clarity. A sawn-off shotgun. The two triggers taped together; pull one and you get both. A 'lupe', so-called because it is thought of as the classic Mafia weapon. Calabrese, south-Italian. Not Belgian.

Another of the photos showed the result. In past times Castang has seen more like these. But one never got used to them. Hair-raising, sick-making? – Empty words for stomach-emptying visions.

"I suppose they're sure that it is him?"

"Well yes, Delahaye does know his job, say that for him. Identified by the dentist." The two lines of dialogue give one all we need to know, thank you, about these bloodstained pictures.

"Well . . ." said Castang. "I suppose you'd have no objection to my pottering off to Namur, little chat with Monsieur Delahaye?"

"Good luck to you," said Mr Mertins stolidly.

To abolish, or at least slightly disinfect those dreadful photos Castang's eye has been roving around the office. In the corner was a sort of pie dish.

"What's that?"

"The cat's dish," surprised. "Visker."

"*Visqueux*?" Perfectly good French word; means something between sticky and slimy. Not very nice. Not like a cat.

"Visker," irritably. Making a big effort, heavily apirating, "Whhiss-kah."

"Oh, sorry," now the penny's dropped. He was over in the corner, studying the artwork. written neatly in nail-polish "wisker". Belgian police orthography.

Castang had only a postal address, and that the laconic Chemin-de-la-Something known only to the villagers, but of course they could point out his way with relish: a Crime had taken place there. Nothing like a bit of blood-letting to liven up the neighbourhood, and what a disappointment not to be on television: the village would then have ranked as a tourist attraction for at least a week. As it was, a little Ardennes cottage, one of two or three along a path hardly more than a woodland ride, a bit rutted from car tyres, weedy in summer, dead-leaved and muddy in winter. Simple stone-built places, humble and pretty, picked up cheap by the bourgeoisie for weekending, but in summer. Only an eccentric, like Eamonn, would come here now, where patches of old snow lay in the shady bits. A little house in the woods, with a pretty view across the valley; stocky, shapely, with the traditional pile of split logs weathering under a lean-to, doorway and windows of dressed stone, a little box-hedged garden, the brook, behind; shuttered, closed, empty, with nothing to tell Castang except that a friend of his has died here.

Music is sounding in his head, strongly, so that he almost hears it. He is no musician; what can it be? Something intensely banal, so much so as to be whistled by the butcher's boy. Something Vera sings, a simple joyous melody which he knows by heart but cannot put a name to, which he is himself whistling softly as he paces round the cottage – really he should have brought gumboots. Eamonn has left it quite primitive, even the outside lavatory. One could modernise here, "build out" on the sunny side. Terrace, patio, glass it in, modern conveniences, very nice. Perhaps he had intended to but the shears had snipped a life. Oh, what is it?

And then it resolves itself; a Viennese teenage girl, innocent and wicked, ingenuous and disingenuous, knowing nothing, teasingly pretending to be experienced the tempo must be alert, while remaining measured, steady-paced. No conductor but Kleiber has ever got it quite right, keeping the simplicity; Cherubino's love-besotted little song.

Who is it sung by? Who is it for? Written for a light lyric soprano but she's no lesbian; it's the pageboy, madly in love with both Susanna, who is barely out of her teens, and with the Countess who is thirty, a woman ripe like an apricot against a sun-warmed wall.

Not that Cherubino cares! Horrid little boy! Purely — that's hardly the word, is it? — sheer sexual obsession, of the teenage boy, growing into virility. Castang, like Eamonn, belongs to a generation that knew the intense pain as well as the horrid frustration, of growing up. Is that why nobody, now, can ever get it right? The music is for Susanna, a ferocious carnal greed to get her clothes off. But the words are for the older woman because only she can understand them. *You, who know, what a thing is love.*

Any woman will do him, really — he'll settle happily for Barbarina. Susanna would be terrif, but she's been captured by that bastard Figaro. Since the Countess is both neglected and frustrated — what harm can it do, to make a try?

Does it only make us laugh, now, the greedy little hard-breathing boy? Is it possible to start from an eighteenth-century comedy of manners, and find there a tragic outcome?

He was standing with his hands in his pockets, his mouth making the ghost of a whistle; staring at a closed house. It didn't tell him a damned thing. He had wanted to say goodbye to a friend, no more. Had Eamonn been a bad husband? Simply, this makes no difference. One is not about to start passing moral judgements on one's friends; there aren't enough of them.

Eamonn was tall and thin, with the face of an old horse. He had a lovely speaking voice; not the trained voice of an actor, more that of a poet. When we moved into our house — which he found for us — he did Louis MacNeice's "Bagpipe Music" (another Scottish Irishman). When a bit drunker, Noël Coward's "Parties" (it wasn't a party but he made it so.) A gifted mimic, who could do an Ulster or a Glasgow accent as readily as imitate John Gielgud; he possessed perfect pitch. Harold had a preposterous name for him — "Columcille Mac Corquohodale".

Vera asked him what he stood for. He laughed. A united Ireland, and since that is impossible, the cause of civilisation in Europe. What else are we all doing here, in Brussels? He would talk about the Irish monks who had done their bit in the past for that cause. He could unroll Irish history, with passion; the Wild Geese, the Flight of the Earls. But with no narrow fanaticism; he spoke of Scotland with the same love and knowledge. "I cannot write poetry. I do legal injunctions instead." He wrote a fine English prose; like, said Harold, Jonathan Swift. Castang had not the pleasure of Mr Swift's acquaintance, but could tell the praise was high.

Perhaps he was a poet after all. He had had plenty of secrets. Castang said now that he wanted to know. He had said goodbye to the friend. He would like to know more about the secrets. They played a role which seemed likely to increase, and be important. He walked slowly back to where he had left his car. He had stopped whistling.

Namur, February

Oops! One is surprised now and then by the unaccustomed speed of reaction. Knocking over a wine-glass, catching it before it spills; hadn't known one could be that nifty.

Castang approached the Commissariat of Police ploddingly, with no enthusiasm. He would have to tell a lot of lies. Mr Delahaye was touchy about his prerogatives, no friend of Brussels (Vera, quoting Joseph Conrad, talks about "the sanguinary macacques in Santa Marta"). So that he had three or four stories, all cock and bull, and is mentally practising to get them a bit consistent even if none is convincing.

Mr Delahaye jumped up from his desk with a big beaming smile. "Why, hallo, Castang!" And gave him an enthusiastic clap on the shoulder. So that the mind had to work like Lightning. In fact, Greased Lightning.

It was the face which brought instant recollection; long sideburns and gold-rimmed glasses. How many years ago was it? Four? Five? He had still had his criminal brigade, on the confines of Picardie and the Pas de Calais. It wasn't unheard of, a bit of business over the border in Belgium . . . Slap a bit of grease in, and boy, aren't his synapses rapid when he least expects it. Why hadn't the name warned him – it had meant nothing whatever. Castang had no recollection of being in Namur: no no, wasn't it Dinant?

"Siddown then old boy. Like a drink?" Young Louppes, that was it. He had gone across after a sly fellow dealing in narcotics who had slipped over the frontier. Made a balls of it, Castang had had to go himself – a boat on the Meuse, those steep twisty valleys of the Meuse at Dinant . . .

"Still over there then – where was it, Arras?" Now he remembered the man perfectly. A bit cracked on politics; the attach-Wallonie-to-France programme, to get rid of those detested Flamands! "Belgium doesn't exist; what's wrong with the old Department of the Ardennes, hey? All right in Napoleon's time; be perfectly feasible now, hey?"Decidedly boring, but apparently he'd been polite, made the right noises.

"So tell me what you've got on your mind," jovially, "and what brings you our way." A lucky hit. One could do with a bit of Francophilia, right now.

"Well, no – not actually Kripo any longer." That wouldn't do; too easily verified; one phone call and he'd be exposed.

'Aha. Sideslipped, eh?" But one could let the fellow think he was RG. The parallel police is by nature more discreet and he could find some cover there. It is not in reality unheard-of for a Police Judiciaire officer to do a crawl sideways into "Renseignements Gen" (the rather sinister political police corresponding to "Special Branch") And it could be made to fit the present circumstances.

"Well," says Castang with that air of someone in RG (like the classic baby, brought in "falsely genial in a knitted coat"), "it's a small affair, and one of those things one would rather do in person. Without a lot of signals traffic, you understand me." Enthusiastic nods, and a bottle of cognac on the table with two glasses, gold-rimmed like the spectacles. "It's just that a fellow, who I don't know, but who seems to interest my masters in Paris, fellow seems to have been found dead in your district, donchaknow, and was wondering vaguely whether there was anything a bit funny about that?" So now he is a spy. That was fair enough because yes, he *was* a spy . . .

"Sure, sure sure." Better and better; Monsieur Delahaye was thinking there wouldn't be any harm at all in being in the good graces of the French government. In a discreet way, and one need not mention it in Brussels. "Why not? I mean, when it's handled right. Informally between us, if you've got any dossier on the gentleman in question, it would be appreciated."

"I've nothing myself – as yet. It would be a complementary thing, no doubt – any light you shed we'd return it. Might turn out chocolate, you'd giftwrap that for your people. If it's zero all round, no harm done, because who's to know? You see why I wasn't making a lot of phone calls. Or going to Bruce first," traitorously.

"Right you are. Might as well say, from the PJ angle, we've a lemon, the investigation's pretty well stalled on the start line. So tell me, what exactly you want."

"Oh, you know, a looksee at whatever you've got, just so I don't put my big foot in anything you're cooking, and I'd guess a shuffle through the house if you'll give me permission. They've been pretty guarded, so my guess is they don't really know what they want but they might know if they saw it, huh? All I know is that he was a Communauté functionary, Irish as you know, prob'ly they just want to open the cupboard, make sure there's no trapdoor inside. As you remember, they got awfully burned about the IRA men in Vincennes, planting weapons and arresting them, big deal which went wrong because chap gets stroppy about the cans he's left to carry. So my guess is, it's a sensitive region, any shit that might fly they'd like to catch on the wing, right?"

"Give you what we have," said Mr Delahaye with such generosity Castang felt confident that he had nothing. "Nothing much really except the sensational job. Highly professional; bang, drop the gun, walk away. Signed but who by? IRA? Could well be."

"Gun?"

"Nothing about the gun. Straightforward model, like dozens around here, made in France, Saint-Etienne, fairly well-worn, could have been his only he wouldn't have had it sawed. No, chap knocks at the door, t'other answers. "Hallo, good evening, here's yours," pop, straight in the face, both barrels of buckshot, from just far enough away not to get blood on his coat. There was some snow, snow melting, no decent footprint, tyre-tracks, eff-all. Nobody saw or heard nothing because nobody was in any neighbouring cottage that weekend. Nothing inside, chap was alone, nothing except What a Big Surprise. Sure you'd say political assassination, and I don't see what I'm to do with it, because who by, unless one of your chaps finds a lead. Made my report to Central in Bruce, and washed my hands."

"Okay to see the house?"

"Right now if you like. Everything's as it was. Proc walked about, sniffed. Judge got nowhere; wife had left him but she's in England, that's proved. Beyond that, not a sausage to show for the trouble."

Castang had to agree. Eamonn was a tidy man and kept things tidy. There was a desk with drawers. A few papers, stuff like electricity bills and repairs. A few books, a few clothes. Why had he come up, alone, that weekend? Was he expecting anyone? Nothing to show. A few old photos, including some of Jane. And of Eamonn himself. Holiday snapshots. Three or four showed him smiling, in a funny old hat, and these were different, because there was a background of mountains, with snow. Sharp-peaked jagged mountains, Alps by the look of them. Castang shrugged.

"Take these, can I? Nothing there I can see, but just for luck."

"Oh, I suppose so. We can have them copied, back at the ranch."

Bruxelles, February

The United States is not, to be sure, part of the Economic Community, but is present in Brussels, very, and what does it do there? Spying on us, obviously. Even for Castang that's a bit too superficial, but the truth is he's pretty vague. Asked what all those trade delegations are, clinched in rude discussions about unpasteurised French cheese, he hasn't the least idea. What's Gatt? Nobody knows. There are enormous numbers of them in orbit, going round and round Waterloo.

Still, everyone knows about Nato. This immense, impressive fortress is now so full of tubby Russian generals being jovial in flying-saucer hats and managing to appear simultaneously over-shaved and hairy, that nobody is quite sure what its present purpose may be. Or so Castang's argument runs; that they're all in mortal terror of Senators saying "America First" and posting them all to Arkansas, to defend General Motors against the Japanese.

With this in mind he is brunching with a friend in Rick's Bar on the Avenue Louise, on a sunny Sunday morning, laying into the muffins and the maple syrup, and conspiring. The friend is also called Rick. Vera, who likes him, says he ought to be called Burton G Cordwainer IV because he looks very Yale and dresses very New Haven, but he's a gentle man with a soft voice, good for conspiring here, where bright-faced American students bring you weak coffee and clean-cut American food.

"Let me see them again." Castang passed his snapshots across and splendidly, Rick took a magnifying-glass out of his breast pocket.

"Alps," he said.

"Yes, but what Alps? There's a lot of Alps, right? Uh,

Carinthian and Carnatic and uh, thousands of the buggers."

"These were taken with a pretty good lens," said Rick, meditatively. "Blow them up, you'd get quite a lot of fine detail."

"That's what I thought. Can I have the glass a sec?" trying not to get either ketchup or maple syrup on it. "This looks to be pretty high up, judging by the background. Sort of a railing here and what seems a footbridge, and all that water, like a lake but looks kind of man-made."

"What exactly d'you have in mind?" asked Rick patiently.

"Well, you have this bloody great collection of satellite photos. I don't know how good they are, nor how close they get. The French go about boasting theirs come a lot closer and are a lot sharper. But you have them."

"Inexact, but basically accurate. We don't have a close-up of you sunbathing on the balcony."

"No, that's not very strategic. But you do have things that are *thought* to be strategic."

"You're edging a bit into the forbidden area, there. Can't compromise military security."

"What I was thinking was, suppose it were a reservoir? Water supply for some big town. Wouldn't that be strategic, or do I mean tactical? Catastrophe scenario; Russians swoop down, no, not Russians, lets say mad ayatollahs, and drop poison in the water."

"Balls."

"Yes, but there are people in Nato who worry about their balls; drink the wrong water and you're impotent. I was wondering whether . . . maybe if you put these through the computer for me it might come up with where it is. You see, I'm wondering who took these photos."

"This guy," tapping the snapshots of Eamonn in his funny hat, "this is a wise guy."

"Undoubtedly. We're thinking, maybe he's in with some other wise guys."

"Who would that be?"

"We've a wide splendid choice. IRA, Mafia, mad ayatollahs, you name it. I'm getting very interested, I'm hot in pursuit."

Rick put his knife and fork in a "finished with it" pattern

amid the ruins of the muffins, snapped his fingers at the waiter, was mysteriously obeyed: he had authority. "I'll say this; we're also interested in the wise guys."

"I'm only asking for a cross-bearing right now, to fix the position. I've no right to suggest more I'm saying this much – this is a very interesting man. Beyond that point, all I can do is ask the favour."

"Leave these with me, okay? I don't guarantee any goddam result whatsoever."

"I have always wanted to be able to say that!"

"D'you know, you're a pretty good guesser? Ran that through from entry-point reservoir, and the thing lit up; you hit it! And as a result, we've got quite interested. Understand me – not the North Atlantic Treaty Organisation. But we're fairly close you know – no, you don't – to a number of security services. They're getting a bit curious about your wise guy."

"Tell," signalling for another two beers.

"All right," producing some extremely mysterious photographs of an infra-red geological-survey nature, meaning nothing to Castang.

"This here's the Valtellina, okay? Valley of the River Adda. In Italy. Alps."

"Alps. . . ."

"Up here at the top, Bormio. Winter sports resort. Above that, a pass. Important pass, not greatly used nowadays because it's steep and it's shitty. The Stelvio. Historic, okay? Now up here there's a lake. Nice, pure, clear Alpine water. And what-d'you-know, yes it does supply the city of Milan with water. Eventually."

"Very eventually."

"Correct; what your wise guy is doing up there is sort of a rhetorical question. I wouldn't say we were greatly interested, but who is – wait for it – is Brits."

"Brits?" Numbly.

"Little lights lit up with the Brits. You better take it from there, because this is where my sun gets hid behind a cloud. But I'm grateful to you, because I just happen to have gotten a good mark out of this. alert perspicacious Jake put his finger on a sore point."

"Please elucidate if you can."

"That I wouldn't know, wheels get cogs into wheels and one never does know. Guessing, anything might be IRA, that's an awful thorn in their foot. Okay? The rest is up to you."

Mr Suarez was sceptical, not to say querulous.

"I never wanted us to get involved with the Brits – of all people. A vast amount of unneeded and unwanted paperwork. Time is one thing, Castang; money quite another. If they'll pay, of course, and I mean pick up the whole bill, so that I don't get involved in these ghastly quarrels about expenses – then I can give you a month off. Just don't come to me with an expense account for your wife, your mistress and your five dependent minors."

"No," said Castang.

Vera was displeased but resigned: the ways of bureaucracy.

"There you go, wallowing around the Lake of Como, just what I would like best. Is it Como? I can't tell the difference."

"Neither can I, they're all so squiggly. Alps!" said Castang distrustfully. "All looks a god-forsaken part of the world to me. Peasants talking Austrian and nothing to eat but polenta." In fact he hadn't the least idea because he'd never been there, but wanted to be tactful.

"I'd like it," said Vera sadly, "but the children, with their examinations and everything – I'll just have to stay behind."

"I'm not sure you could, even if it wasn't," confusion in his syntax bespeaking muddle in his mind. "I'm far from clear what's going on. They're sending some sort of ghastly bureaucrat to whom I'll be answerable, described as an Observer."

"Who are?"

"I don't know – does one ever? The World Health Organisation? Suarez fixed it. The whole point is, people with pots of money. Nato with millions to spend to protect us from being invaded by Albania, and the Communauté without a brass farthing. For me, that is . . ."

"What do they need you for, then?" The sort of question that shouldn't be asked, and which Vera does ask.

"Aha, cunning Mr Suarez. An Internal Investigation, and it's cheaper to send me, whom they don't have to pay for, than some security man, whom they would."

"But I don't understand."

"They think Eamonn may have been some sort of mole. IRA, perhaps."

"Oh, it's not possible!"

"I'm afraid it is," said Castang.

Zaventem Airport, March

Castang had had a lot of trouble with packing his suitcase. Northern Italy in March; in the sun it might be boiling hot. Or might one be plunging about in snow up to the bloody waist, and in need of warm woollies? He'd been to Venice and places like that, meaning the frontier post at Domodossola; it wasn't a lot of help. He picked up his ticket at the desk, with a grievance about being nursemaided. And this infernal Observer, who would it be? Some piss-vinegar functionary, no doubt. Or some abominably cheerful young man, athletic . . . keen on skiing . . . Castgang, sunk in gloom, sulked in a corner. It is true that the Brussels Airport, even more than most, induces sinking feelings; that wherever one is going it will mean changing at Atlanta . . .

"Mr Castang? Voice of educated English, officer class. Decisive, commanding tones. And oh-my-god, female tones. Prefectorial. He looked up. *Dio merda*, as they say in Italian and it's nearly all he can say, it's a games mistress from Cheltenham.

"Margaret Rawlings," A crisp, and extremely cold hand. "and there's our flight being called. So I think we'll leave the explanations till Milan, don't you? Planes are eavesdropping places; we'll begin as we mean to go on."

Much oppressed, also by the wearing of mountain boots for which there'd been no room in the suitcase, he refused deep frozen croissant vaguely microwaved, refused Nescafé, drew *La Chartreuse de Parme* from a pocket. It had comforted in many bleak surrounds. "Spinach and Saint-Simon have been my only staple diet," as Monsieur Stendhal (that great man) sagely observes. His Spanish was a mix of French and Italian, and he got on very well with that. Castang will do the same, with his pretty-indecent Spanish. Oh, *porca madonna*. Miss Rawlings, beside him, crackles forbiddingly with the morning's *Times*. Going to put him in his place by being Brit, huh?

Surreptitiously, he examined this dread fate sidelong. Fortyish. Or more; it is the sort of hair which goes from fair to grey and one scarcely notices, and cut very short. Long ski-jump nose; from his days with fraudulent art come memories of portraits by Modigliani. Mouth pursed, reading. Large bony chin. Fine forehead. In no sense pretty, but formidable. Perhaps a lawyer? His spirits rose a little. Come, one can cope with this.

When the flaps clanked and the retrothrust came on she put the newspaper away, neatly folded, spoke in a pleasant voice.

"Stendhal – good man in a pinch. Pick up our bags shall we, and then perhaps elevenses?' Glancing at a man's wristwatch, a good one and gold, but she wore no other jewellery.

"Coffee? Or as I gather, you start drinking early." A pouncer.

"A Carlsberg," he told the waiter unperturbed. "Finish early too, as a rule."

"A capuccino will hold me till lunch. Very well, Mr Castang, we're companions. The expense account's mine, anything you want, just sign for it."

"Is it Mrs Rawlings or Miss?"

"It's Mrs, but for our purposes it's Miss." Cool if not refrigerated but silky polite, so that one couldn't be offended. Now that the nose was opposite him there was a saddle in it. A nice mouth but the lips too thick, an odd diamond-shape.

"I'm not going to ask your permission to smoke, I'm afraid."

A slight smile. She'd be nice when she laughed. So make her laugh. "I don't want you to feel edgy; that would be unprofessional. I'm a good observer, Mr Castang, I'm thought good at evaluating what I see, I'm here because I speak Italian. Now you."

"I'm an ex-officer of Police Judiciaire. I was friendly with Eamonn Hickey. I speak no Italian." She did laugh.

"You have a Czech wife named Vera who paints, you

have two teenage girls, you speak four languages rather well which is one more than me, the Police Judiciaire is frightened to employ you, you'll stay in Brussels with plenty to occupy you. But what interests you?"

"Love, I should think."

"Really?" One tries to sharpen ones ear to English usages. Rilly? Reely? Rehilly? It is very difficult.

"You know, crimes . . . the boring ones are about money. The interesting ones are about love."

"And *La Chartreuse*?"

"Is just about the best crime novel I know."

"I've a book in my luggage that might interest you. We've a car booked, here, shall you drive or shall I?"

"I should think you, and then you can shout at Italians who feel aggressive. We're going to . . .?"

"For today we're going to the Lake of Lugano. There are places too on Maggiore, on Como. At this one, the food's good, does that please you?" Good teeth for an Englishwoman. "And I seldom shout," putting a fairly respectable Alfa into gear. "It's then the more effective when I do."

She drove well, decisive and unaggressive. Castang is not a good driver and – says Vera – is getting worse. The lake country is very beautiful still, when one can get off the roads: the traffic is simply awful.

"The Nato people think they've identified that place in your photos. That's way up the Valtellina, above Bormio."

"They told me that much. It doesn't have to mean a lot, does it? I should think it was quite pointless asking who you work for."

"That's a sensible attitude to take. Indeed there are moments when I wonder, myself. Of course we're interested in the IRA, how could it be otherwise? Have you views about this?"

"Ambiguously worded, that's a great English talent. It's a tempting thesis. Northern Irish or is it Scotch? Works for the Irish government which detests the IRA. Nothing in Ireland is ever what it seems, not even the Constitution. That's all quite lip-licking but I can think of fourteen reasons for Eamonn being up here. I'll make a little shopping list and we can compare. Let's go for a ride on the boat."

"Good, this whole frontier is fairly dotty, and ever since the Austrians people have been adept at slipping about on it for – I agree – a great many varied purposes. We're going to look at a few of these. Here's the book I mentioned. English-language edition."

Fogazarro, *Little World of the Past*. "The Valsolda," said Miss Rawlings after eating neatly and swallowing, "that's right here where we are. A bit later than your Mister Stendhal, this is just after the 1848 – Risorgimento, know anything about that? Austrians still in command, very much so. Place stinks with police spies, corrupt customs officials – greed, power – nothing much changes really, around here. Be interested to know what you make of this. Lovely people, these. So one wonders what Mr Hickey made of them."

They know something, or they think they do. Or they wouldn't spend money sending her here. They don't know what it is, but she's thought bright enough to sniff it. I might be a loose wheel or I might be a connecting thread, and I've always been suspected of having French governmental ties. Remember Miss Huntingdon, Harold's admirable secretary? She didn't like being a spy and was no good at it. This time they send a pro, and allow me to be aware of it, which is very English. We'll let them work at it, and sweat a bit. I only want to understand, apart from soothing Mr Suarez's little worries, and that's really only to ensure a favourable hearing for tenure in my job. Complicated, isn't it? But me, I want to keep the separate sides of my head. And distinct, too.

Lugano, Evening

He was pleased to have put a suit on, because Miss Rawlings appeared for dinner in a high-necked jumper and a long skirt, rather smart and altogether the cultivated tourist lady in comfortable circumstances. One was reminded of a Procureur in his scarlet robe with ermine. Or perhaps an Academical lady on a formal occasion, at some mediaeval university. He got up politely from his chair, and she said she'd have a gin, with tonic water. There was a fire, but it's chilly by the lake shore, of a March evening. Castang was determined to get a good dinner out of her paymaster's pocket, and said so.

"Quite right," she said. "We aren't proposing to trudge about with sleeping bags on our back."

"What are we disguised as?"

"Disguised?" The word pronounced as though faintly indecent, and a small lift to the eyebrow, which was formed in a handsome arch.

"One is generally pretending to be something else. These pretences should not be too extravagant, so that if penetrated, as they often are, one does not appear over-ridiculous. What are we doing here? Should we be seen together? Come to that, what are we looking for?"

Her look couldn't be called condescending. Perhaps a little indulgent. "I don't attempt a front. I am a government official on holiday; that in itself is commonplace enough to be discreet. A middle-aged lady whose occupation is sedentary, who breathes too much dust in offices, who likes to walk in the hills. There are several thousand English women very like me. I may carry a camera, and binoculars. Neither attract attention; the English are interested in birds.

"I might perhaps say too that I have a number of contacts, in Milan, and elsewhere. Perhaps I shouldn't say too much about that. I am sociable, polite, gregarious, I like to exercise my fluent if rather academic Italian; I quite like a little chat with the customs officials and the Carabinieri. Quiet, respectable family men. They don't take it amiss when I ask after their wives and their children.

"I am also a cultivated lady, keen on art. I potter, in antique shops, in village churches."

She was boning her fish in a competent way, understanding the anatomy. "You are also a government official. We have a nodding acquaintance. It is quite a pleasant coincidence to meet. We are to some extent company for one another. We enjoy having dinner together and comparing our day's activities, and sight-seeing. Should we meet, in the hills, that would be nothing untoward. I have a car, I offer you a lift, since the bus won't be along for some time, there is no comment from anyone. Is that enough of an answer?"

Castang ate his veal and nodded. Agreeable, this Swiss white wine.

"There is not a great deal, it might appear, of work in the technical sense. That is by no means certain, since you are a trained observer, but you have no police authority or standing. However, you were a friend of the late Mr Hickey. This I understand was quite a stamping-ground of his. Fond of the region? Nothing untoward about that. It is possible that by tomorrow I can give you one or two starting points."

She ate fast and neatly. She had the English sweet tooth, and allowed herself to be tempted by a concoction of chocolate and chestnut, with cream on top, unafraid of adding pounds to those slim bony hips. Castang made experiments with the local cheese and went on saying nothing.

"What I propose – from what I know of you it might not be disagreeable – is along the lines of a reversal of conventional roles. A man – I dislike these hidebound attitudes – is expected to adopt a technical, intellectual, deductive approach towards an enquiry. A woman, it is thought, is more at home among looser, less structured

44

ways of thinking. The emotions? I'd query a good deal of that and so, perhaps, would you. Do you want a coffee? I'm going to have some tisane, orange-flower perhaps. You've quite a pronounced feminine streak, haven't you? No bad thing, in a police officer, however ex. The remark is of course no reflection on your maleness, which comes out the more prominently. I don't think you are offended – these dualities in a personaity interest me.'

Castang had begun to laugh. "Sorry. No, go on. This also interests me."

"Well then, to be brief, you made a remark about love. I'll give you a literary quotation, such as your wife is fond of."

"You've done your homework on me, haven't you?' Castang giggling. "I'm impressed. I'm listening attentively."

"Anthony Powell – a good writer. 'All human beings, driven as they are at different speeds by the same Furies, are at close range equally extraordinary.' "

"That's well put. And asks me to give it some thought. I'm inclined for a stroll, perhaps, along the lake, and then I think I'll be ready for bed. Shall we meet at breakfast? Fairly early? Fresh for a day in the hills? I should have an answer for you, by then."

"Fine. I've some telephoning to do. And a bit of paper-work. Seven too early for you? Here? That should indeed give us a good start. I'll say goodnight, then. Oh, and my bedroom's next to yours. But I don't think the mountain air goes to your head, does it? Apart from literary quotations, we're here to work."

Castang walked. After a while, he turned in at a café for a little cigar and a grappa. His notebook – it is really a child's school exercise book – sits in the inside pocket of his raincoat. He doesn't as a rule bite pens, but does fiddle with them between his fingers.

E. stamping-ground. R. has good reason to suppose this. Has "contacts". Promises, coyly, 1-2 starting points – places or personalities? All along here, frontier region, & much trafficking Switz-It a self-evident propos. Obvious examples, a) narcotics & b) antiques. Either provides strong money-power motive. That, isolated, in classic sense, seems out of character, initially. Thus, source of occult finance for ulterior need?

R. evidently has strong ground for IRA supposition — or is that a front for kidding me along? Are all terrorist groups interconnected? Political motivation is a religion — does that chime with what I know of E? Marxist? — Stasi, Stani etc. — could that stand up?

To narcotics, antiques, add arms. Either in Switz or It, illegal exports highly lucrative. Islam, at all? E would not be interested simply in the money. Outward cynicism a front for deep convictions of ?religious nature.

Look, hell he was killed. Why killed? In mafia world, for getting out of line. Treachery selling secret info. Or diverting money-washing chain into own pocket: both highly out of character.

Something else altogether . . .

A secret personal thing — esoteric, occult? a possible.

A psycho thing — event. blackmail. Sado-mas, sex games minors? Strong enough to lose him job? — not to be ruled out, I suppose. Wouldn't Jane have known or suspected? Could this good-soldier talk be a front? Something very powerful, to cause her abrupt flight. Really IRA? Ex-Col-Brit-Army Devaney. So fundamentally unlikely as to be very clever indeed? — but extremely artificial. Avoid spy story scenarios.

No, not a second grappa. Bed!

At precisely two minutes past seven Rawlings was there eating müsli. Well, she would, wouldn't she. Castang pottered round the service table at some length and got back to find her with China tea and a pained expression.

"Sorry. There's always far too much of everything. Like supermarkets. One doesn't Want seventeen different kinds of sardines."

"Oh, I do know. Like South Africa. Porridge, fried fish and bright orange tea."

"Room twenty-eight. Coffee please. You know, I'm no really any sort of agent. I mean of the French government."

"Mm?" Meagrely marmalading rye bread.

"Yes, I'd say that even if I were. Not though with this tone of voice. Or perhaps not at breakfast."

"My dear man, I know that. Before leaving I had a nice chat with Miss Huntington. That sort of very low-level espionage was there only to stir you up really. Give me credit for professionalism. Why d'you say this, does it worry you?"

"I'd like to feel that you were trusting me. I'd like to hear what you yourself feel, or know, about Eamonn Hickey. Whom I thought of – is it right there to say whom? – as a friend. I scarcely knew him at all. That's being – one moment, I've the phrase – steadily borne in upon me. If he was IRA then I'd be surprised. No, it's the old joke about the husband and the wife's lover – you are surprised; I am astonished. So I want to know what you know and whether you're surprised by it."

Rawlings, who had been holding her teacup in both hands on propped elbows put it down with a clank.

"I've been in too much of a hurry. Have some more coffee, finish your breakfast in peace, we've plenty of time. We'll go over to the Italian side of the lake. We'll look at the Valsolda. We were going to Como but this is more important.

'The good old abbot of Thingummylock
Has put a bell on the Inchcape rock'

"Not something for Vera – whom I begin to know quite well. Sort of poem one learned in elemenary school and never quite gets rid of. The point is that despite the good-old-abbot the ship goes full tilt into the Inchcape Rock and sinks with all hands, and I mustn't let that happen. I'll pay the bill and do some phoning while you're collecting your traps."

She got up, long and slim, displaying corduroy breeches below a Lapland-ish pullover and above boots; a Swiss tourist. No handbag today, but she caught up a little, brightly-coloured nylon knapsack. A day in the hills, and one wants the arms free.

She did not speak before they were on the ferry, when she leaned over the rail, watching the water. There were not many people. There was a wind on the lake, the *breva*. Castang looking at a fine rolling cloudscape felt unpleasantly soft and urban huddled in his raincoat He would like a day on the hill, to shake the slackness off. He felt some envy of Rawlings, who looked a bit blue around the hands and the nose, but like a woman who would show a cracking pace on a stony path.

"We'll leave the car and the luggage down on the shore. Buy a bit of sausage and an apple to take with us; okay? Any albergo will give us a jug of wine when we want a rest.

"Franco and Luisa lived here – you haven't read that book, yet. *Piccolo mondo antico, the Little World of the Past.* Sounds rather Proust but it's the little world of the present too, as I think you'll agree. Look, there's a baker, I'll whip in, and you get sausage."

The whole day was like this. Conversations interrupted by looking at the view, by pauses when he got breathless, which he did much quicker than her; by eating or drinking or going for a pee, which she did after lengthy and cautious withdrawals into bushes. Even Castang, blatantly French about peeing anywhere – a thing of which Vera complains – subjugated himself.

"Shocking as it may sound, I do think he was IRA. In perhaps distorted ways. But they're complicated people, and that's why it's hard to get exact lines on them. They worry us a good deal. In your own criminal investigation experience you'll have found it much too easy to slap on labels like 'psychopath'. No, I haven't proof. I don't think it very likely we'll find anything like direct proof. We're here to acquire what French judges term an 'intimate conviction'. We may find some circumstantial evidence: there are some rather odd people up the Valtellina. Yes, where those photos you found were taken, they were perhaps the missing piece in a puzzle which has been obscure for many a day. I can say that the fact you found them made me determined to ask, no, to insist that you come with me. I may find out some material facts. But you were the colleague and as much as he had friends you were the friend.

"To my mind it's a psychological thing; that you might see, hear, or experience, and it will go click in your mind, because you'll recall something he did or said which meant nothing at the time but means so now.

"I think I know who took those pictures. She's a woman who uses a camera skilfully, a good photo-journalist. That's her hobby. You'll know her if you see her; tall, thin, dark, my build but even skinnier. Nice girl. She's well known locally, wife of a local notable, very animated, tears about in a beat-up Fiat and causes smiles among the local gendarmerie for some hair-raising driving. And she's Irish . . . Oh, she looks Italian enough. They often do, hm? Speaks the local patois with great fluency . . . highly voluble. And great fun . . .

"Wouldn't you hesitate too? – I know I should – before using a word like cat's-paw. We don't know enough. Get a description, extrapolate from that; isn't it too easy, to make it fit a preconceived notion? Warm-hearted, noisy, tactless, given to gaffes and easily forgiven since so patently spontaneous; what d'you make of that?"

"Good synthesis," said Castang. "I'd look at the husband, if there is one."

"And you'd find something equally interesting. Young-ish, a lawyer with left wing sympathies, much liked locally for giving good advice and not overcharging for it. Tax, successions, boundary disputes, divorces, anything you like, settle it in a friendly way and avoid litigation. Good man to have in your corner if the administration is heavy-handed or obstructive. In fact talks very little, and then soft-spoken, conciliatory. Always being pressed to go into politics, and says he can do more good outside. You'd know him when you see him. Ferrari man, rockets about in ziggy-zip machinery. Good-looking, too. And there's a circle of friends. I'd quite like to know more about these people. Even though we don't have anything at all to connect them to your man.

"Traffics? – any supposition you care to make is easy. These people stroll across the frontier to buy a ha'penny stamp; literally because the Italian Post Office is casual and unreliable. Nobody needs suitcases full of money. You go over to St Moritz for an icecream or to have your hair done. Antiques, you know, don't take up much space."

Castang knew a little bit more about this subject than he cared to say, right now. Miss Rawlings' enquiries into his personal life, which seemed to have gone back far enough. That's perhaps one of the handicaps for these espionage people. If they wish to take the trouble they can isolate every aspect of your life in the present, turn it inside out like an old raincoat, shake it thoroughly; the dust which comes out will tell them everything they wish to know, from your taste in ties to your occasional tendency towards constipation. But it leaves out your past, your *piccolo mondo antico*. Rawlings was not seemingly aware that they had spent a year in the *Beaux Arts*, prudishly entitled the Office for the Repression of Fraud, hunting both art objects and the transactions in same. That year had been far too short to learn more than the most superficial rudiments of this world (and of his dear Carlotta Salès with whom he had been a little in love); but he knows how very easy it is to walk about with a little picture in your shopping-bag, worth a million francs when you know the right people.

He had not got far with Mr Fogazzaro's lovely book, because he had fallen asleep over it. But – right here – he was in the Valsolda. He was treading the stones of Albogasio and Cressogno, of Oria and Casarico: from the lake shore he had looked across to the Doi, the Mount San Salvatore.

He had barely reached the moment where Franco and Luisa marry, in the teeth of the horrible old Marchesa who has all the money. But something of his thought must have filtered through to Rawlings, because she suddenly said, "Tell me about love."

Yes, he recalled making a "jocose ellipsis" in answer to a fairly silly enquiry about criminal investigation. He'd said that when interesting it would be a story about love. Quite right . . . so it was. Love is also a story of sausage and the local wine, but so be it.

"Love? Yes. I stick by what I said. Love is disconsidered nowadays – no, that's not English. Has a bad press. Nowadays people believe in sex, and it isn't quite the same thing. Frustrating for everyone. Thought themselves frustrated, going mad for a bit of tit; nothing to what they feel, even when awash in it."

Miss Rawlings' expression showed some distaste for this police language while according approval to the sentiment.

"Awfully sad for them," concluded Castang cheerfully, not thinking it necessary to go further into the matter, while mentally rehearsing the probable result of a kind offer to help her out of those forbidding breeches.

"Base this upon the teachings of religion, do you?"

"Base it upon commonplace police observation," he said a bit curtly.

"Traditional teaching implies restraint," in a strong-minded academic voice. This was a sunny day; this was an Italian hillside; he didn't feel much inclined for talk about morals.

"Look. I've met ministers of most religions for whom I could feel both liking and respect. I'm only saying that I myself would put responsibility where they put restraint. People do things without caring about the consequences, and believe me, that filled a police officer's day. What's that stuff growing there?" This time she took the hint.

"Wild garlic."

So that he would, after all, look back on it as a pleasurable as well as a memorable day. Castang, the townsman, who wouldn't know wild garlic from a bunch of chrysanths, was delighted to get lessons in elementary botany. Morality he could get on the streets of Brussels; ethics like politics – or football – tastes better in a smoke-filled room. Miss Rawlings, put upon her headmistressy mettle by his simple delight, found wild daffodils for him. Cyclamen. The minute flowers of the Mediterranean spring; God what heaven.

"I'm an ignorant lout," said Castang sadly.

There is nothing much to say about that day, except that ravenous from all this fresh air he overate on risotto at the end of it.

He remembered, afterwards, that she had been a good, even an amusing companion. He had made the joke that if he were to be in her company much longer his morals would become quite good. He had an impression that seduced, as he was, by the countryside, she had been quite content to loosen the reins for this day and let her mind run free upon wild flowers. Next day would be time enough for work.

The following morning she was businesslike. She had, she said, affairs of her own to pursue. Why didn't he take the car, go up the valley of the Adda from Como, up past Tirano, climb up there, and see for himself whether he could pinpoint that map reference; the place where those photos had been taken. It was important to get a picture of the ground, because satellite photos have their uses, but from now on . . . He quite agreed. He would be a tourist and go sight-seeing. In the Valtellina there would be more wild flowers. And, perhaps, people.

Como, for traffic, is a hell-hole. At last one gets back to the lake but the road is narrow, difficult. The beginnings of the Adda valley are both dreary and dusty. Sondrio is a dump, Tirano little better. He stopped here, and prowled about with some interest because here is the frontier; the main road goes over the Bernina into Switzerland, and here too is the little railway to St Moritz. Nothing to see, the usual customs post with a couple of bored agents of the Dogana hanging about scratching themselves; the Swiss just up the road looking a bit more martial.

Further up the Adda things became more countrified, narrower, crookeder, more interesting, and the road emptier. The little town of Sondalo was attractive, and he stopped for something to eat. What was that monstrous building, sprawled out above? A hospital? Wasn't that very big for such a small place? Mussolini, they explained, a clinic for lung tuberculosis, wheel you out on the balcony, lots of fresh air. Well yes, the magic mountain, just like Davos. Castang has seen similar places in France. One had forgotten what a scourge TB then was. But every generation invents its own. We've AIDS now, and stress, and mysteriously it has become dangerous to smoke, and our spermatozoa count is only half what it used to be. Quite, thought Castang, and who the hell knows what we're breathing? Why are there no birds any more? Toads. Butterflies. Be very grateful indeed, mate, if there are still some wild daffodils. Who knows how long before they, too . . .

Bormio is a winter sports resort; modern, trim, and dull, with the old village drowned now in nasty little apartment blocks. The road goes on from here up the Stelvio, but the other road . . . he knew he was on the right track when he found a Spanish fortress. Very bare, very square, very grim. That Spanish infantry, which had tramped everywhere in Europe, like the Roman legions and had been as single-mindedly sullen, stubborn, iron- and leather-hard. Blow it hot, or blow it cold, and hereabout you could get both, and both as tough as they come. It lifted his heart, obscurely.

Further. . . and a reward. A plateau – and water.

Unmistakeable. A few holiday chalets were scattered across the meadows, but nobody came here save in summer. There was not a soul to be seen, but plainly that was the reservoir "in question": one source of water supply looks, it can be claimed, very like another, but if you have a photo of it from the right angle, no alpine peak looks like another. He tacked about until he had the exact emplacement of Eamonn's footsteps pinpointed. Well and good, but what could they have been doing up here?

He was in a natural, shallow bowl or depression within a ring of nasty jagged alps. The water filled the bottom of this, gravity-fed by the melting snow. From the lower slopes the snow had melted, leaving a wide expanse of alpine meadow. On all of which the grass was cropped short, telling even the townsman detective that in summer there would be cows up here. There was a farmhouse at no great distance where the herd would live in summer, busied with cheese and hay. A couple of summer chalets, closed and shuttered were the only other man-made artefacts. The reservoir, the simplest possible structure, needed no attendance. Further down would be some sort of filtration plant, no doubt. It was all innocent, peaceful. Castang pottered around, sat down on the jacket he had taken off gratefully in the March sunlight, and wondered whether some clue would be apparent to a more educated eye. From somewhere behind him sounded a sharp cracking boom. A whole volley of echoes rolled and reverberated from the surrounding peaks, but it wasn't thunder.

Castang sat up, relaxed again in recognition of a high-powered hunting rifle. That had been quite a large calibre. The frontier could not be very far away. Probably within easy climbing distance to a local knowing the paths. Sun-drugged, he thought vaguely that there was a national park on the Swiss side. Game reserve, quite likely. Patrolled by foresters, rangers. He wondered what sort of animals lived up here. Marmots and things, you'd hardly take a rifle to them. Chamois maybe. He scored zero in natural history, but there were things like chamois with different sorts of horns. The ranger would cull a stray, some old male going back. Conceivably a poacher – were chamois good to eat? Like any other goat, he supposed;

good when young. But the shot had made a hell of a racket. Chap would get pounced on unless unusually cunning. Must be frontier guards not too far away; tough afghan sort of hillsmen on skis. He sat back again on his elbows until they got cramped, and shook himself. Wouldn't do to fall asleep, however sunny and quiet. He'd make a tour around, take a look at that farmhouse, plod back down to where he'd left the car. He didn't quite know what he'd come for. Yes, he'd verified the informed guess made back in Bruce from aerial photography, but did that do him any good? A bit of a puzzle. Miss Rawlings, eventually, might "connect it up" – was that correct English?

The farmhouse was a simple affair, one-storied, low-eaved; one could get buried up to the roof here in snow: they'd been built like this for hundreds of years. Primitive enough. Jakes out the back, human as well as animal manure would go to a little vegetable garden, a fruit tree or two; some vitamins to go with the polenta. A hay barn built at the side, come mid-October, when the shadows from the peaks began to lengthen and cut the sun from the meadows, they'd get the wagon, assemble the cows, get back down the hill to winter quarters. A hard and a lonely life. A well, with a little paved area to stop the ground getting muddy – winch and bucket work, but the subsoil would filter the water to purity and a flavour you couldn't get elsewhere. The farmer had left an old table and a crude bench on the little terrace. Frugal, simple, monotonous meals, but good. The wife would bake bread once a week. Nowadays, he supposed, she'd take the car down to Bormio every so often. Yeast, paraffin for the lamp, a few luxuries like batteries for the radio. Her staples, like oil, salt, vinegar, she'd bring up in the spring – probably in another fortnight or anyhow by mid-April. She'd have a row of maize to feed a few chickens; onions and carrots, summer vegetables and of course tomatoes; she'd make her own cheese, her own air-dried meat and sausage. If she took the trouble to churn she could make her own butter. Salt it, bring it down, sell it on the market – no, whoa. Castang, stop. In the first place you know nothing whatever about it. In the second you're just another imbecile townsman, sentimentalising.

But it still sounded good. Wasn't that a fine way to live! He turned the corner of the barn.

And that was a fine way to die.

He had found Miss Rawlings.

One can't blame Castang. He had always been, for a cop, handicapped. Never make a really good one, Divisional-Commissaire Richard used to say. Too much sensitivity. Too much Fucking Imagination.

He'd got over being sick, fast. One couldn't be sick – at least, go *on* being sick – on the street in Paris. Older cops took the piss.

But now I've been out of the Police Judiciaire two years and more, and I've gone soft.

He remembered Eamonn – yes, Eamonn! – making a joke about drunks being sick on the street in Glasgow. "That's what we call Pavement Bolognese!"

Castang was sick again. Then his head cleared, and he got a grip on his stomach. Because the voice rang in his ears; Eamonn could do the Glasgow accent to perfection. "That's not the whisky. That's the fault of the Diced Carrots. Eat the fast food, man, fast through you is the word."

Castang entered the privy which smelt now only of stone, sun, and earth. After a space for thought he buckled his belt.

One had better not get too close because the ground is soft from the thaw. The sun has only dried and hardened a surface crust. So mate, if you don't want to get involved don't get too close.

It was borne in upon him that he bloody well was involved. No chance of dodging this one.

He made a determined effort at self-command. He'd heard the rifle shot. A ballistics man would only make a rough shot, sorry, effort, at angle of fire, because a big high-velocity cartridge spins you round and sends you flying.

Pretty good shooting. Range of five hundred metres? More, maybe.

He was not an expert but even if you aim chest high – no, head high for a chest shot. The bullet, even if copper-jacketed would make a smallish entry but an exit as big as a Metro tunnel. It had thrown maybe a tiny bit low and right. From the front it took the liver straight out of the body.

You would die instantly. You wouldn't feel a thing. Your entire blood supply, all the little network for veins and arteries, even totally disregarding the major internal organs, simply explodes.

The face is more or less recognisable. The corduroy breeches, rather more so.

Castang, make tracks out of here. The whoever could pick you off right here as easy as a chicken.

Castang retired again, feeling subdued, but the word does not adequately convey the action.

Big pool of blood. He had forgotten how many litres of blood, precisely, the human body contains. Don't want to know either. All there. But once it begins to coagulate in the sunshine, it can nearly all be picked up in a spoon and put, if desired, in an evidence bag.

Don't want evidence bag. Thought self-emptied, still a bit of sick to throw up. Guts hurt.

Finished now?

Castang toiled – very wearily – back to car. One kilometre had become ten. Fellow won't shoot me. Long gone. Rifle buried or otherwise disposed of.

Go to Policía – what the hell do they call it, Questura, in Bormio; mut be some sort of police post there; hell, big winter sports resort, month of March, plenty-plenty tourists. I'm one. Went for nice walk, found highly unpleasant surprise.

Damn it, drive on the righthand side of the road. Why does this pissy Alfa keep wandering over to the left: if there's anybody round the bend coming *up* there'll be a nasty accident.

Policía plenty fed up. Quite enough to do with these bad-mannered skiers who bash into one another. Insurance companies, whose view of the world is cynically chill, cut it all in half anyhow.

The Policía accepted the news with fatalism. A dead woman makes a change in the routine of tourists who have lost their passports, their jewellery (that rather valuable brooch with the slightly shaky clasp they have unaccountably chosen to wear while out ski-ing) or complain of sexual molestation in the lift. They spoke Austrian

German. They wrote it all down at great length. It was exactly as it would have been at home, very dull and very slow. A Carabinieri lieutenant had to come all the way from Sondrio, which is the administrative centre. Remember, if you are thinking of finding any dead bodies, don't, because your civic spirit will come under heavy strain after about six hours of hanging about. Luckily for Castang, he knew all this. He had to drive all the way down the valley in the dark, with nothing to eat but some Alpine fried chicken courtesy of Colonel Sandosi, and didn't get in much before midnight, with a severe instruction to come to Sondrio in the morning for a lot more bureaucracy; the threat of having to say it all once more in Como, and quite possibly again in Milano the day following.

The very first thing the next morning was the damned hotel manager.

"Ah, Signor Castang, the lady who was with you —"

"Lady, what lady?"

"The lady hasn't come back, her room seems to be empty —"

"Her business, I should think."

"But I understood you were together?"

"I'm right here, I'm afraid. About to pay my bill —"

"Perhaps if I could just have a word in private?"

"You're welcome."

"I'm sorry if I caused you embarrassment."

"None whatever, let me reassure you."

"I must apologise for the misunderstanding. You see, she made the booking, and as I understand, her credit card —"

"Yo, one of those things. I made the lady's acquaintance and mentioned that I'd been stupid enough to leave my own card back in another suite in Milano. I'm settling your account with a personal cheque, if that's all right."

"To be sure, to be sure. You do see how my mistake arose."

"These things happen. The lady and I found we'd mutual friends back at home. A chance companionship, you follow me?"

"Of course, of course. Simply that if the lady doesn't turn up —"

"Then I imagine you'd do whatever you usually do in such circumstances."

"The tourist Board can be very fussy. I might have to mention the matter to the police."

"Let your conscience be clear, Herr Direktor, whatever you think is appropriate."

"I'm so sorry to have bothered you."

There would have to be a rather lengthy telephone call too. Best made from Como.

"Morning, Suarez, Castang here. Bad morning, I'm afraid," and related the news of Rawlings' demise.

"Oh God."

"I'd say, let the Brits know, smartish, cover up your end, I may not be fatally compromised here, but I'll have to get hold of some senior officer and explain matters – and ask for discretion."

"I must rely upon you, Castang."

"Just so's you know what to say, if the Carabinieri come checking on me in Bruce."

"Quite, quite. How very unfortunate."

Como, Morning

The lieutenant of Carabinieri was a pale, twitchy young man. He had the sort of beard that shows in black dots beneath the skin however closely one shaves. His uniform cap was on the desk; it is a becoming uniform and he had some claim to be called handsome in it. He had white, oddly feminine hands, but looked male enough for the girls to want to eat. He also looked tired and cross, but an unexpectedly sweet smile would sometimes break through across a long, lippy jaw and uneven teeth, belying the mask of bristly officialdom.

He showed some bad temper. Castang, when behind the desk, had often done the same.

"Yesterday you told a lot of nonsense. Today you've a chance to set that right. We'll start again, with the truth this time, and no evasions or concealments.

"Name? Permanent address? Occupation?"

"Civil servant. Generally known as Eurocrat. I think it was Churchill who said they would no longer be civil, and no longer be servants. Some truth in that, I'm afraid."

"You're a cop," wearily. "It's the only reason we put up with you at all. Otherwise I'd have your arse in jail."

"I used to be."

"You're a PJ man. You hold the rank of Divisional Commissaire. But here on my piece of paper you're another clown trying to throw mud in my eye. There's no way you can get any leverage out of Paris or Brussels or anywhere. You're a pro. Behave like one."

"Well, since technically I'm your superior officer — no, wrong, since humanly we're two pros together, let's be polite for a start."

"I've been up all night."

"I know the feeling."

"You're very lucky. General Bonacorsi says I should listen to you."

"Bobby a General now?" Castang had met Colonel Roberto Bonacorsi nine years ago, at a police conference in Munich. A good drinking companion; he could hardly claim a friendship.

"Commands the Bologna district. Technically your superior officer," with the first of those Italianate smiles.

"Shall I talk to him on the telephone?"

The lieutenant thought about this. There was a green one as well as a grey one. The narrow clean fingers punched buttons. Three figures for the district, two for headquarters, two more for the boss and one for a personal line.

"Ex-Commissaire Castang of the PJ prays for a word with the General," all of it sarcastically underlined.

A remembered voice said, "Castang old friend, how are you? Nice cup of coffee? Little intrigue with Nato? Little pankiwank with Brits? I'll tell you how you are – in the shit. Not just raining on your head, chum." It was the old-fashioned English of the educated foreigner, with the phrases of forty years ago.

"I hope you appreciate the depth and specific-gravity of this shit. Quicksand, my boy, you're sinking at the rate of a centimetre a minute. So tell my lad there all; I calculate you've ten minutes. Sorry to be a bit abrupt but I'm rather busy. We'll jack you out, you have a shower, we'll manage a drink eventually. If it isn't going gloo-gloo over your head by then. Give me back my Lieutenant, would you?" Who listened for thirty-seven seconds and said, "Yes sir."

"Hear that great long rawhide whip go crack," said Castang.

"Stop fucking about," the Lieutenant blinked his eyes against the sand of fatigue. "I'm prepared to let you go. Quoting the General, better to have you inside the tent pissing out than outside pissing in. So I'm giving you a choice. Either you get straight on the next plane across the frontier, or you surrender your passport and any official document identifying you as a PJ officer. When you want them back you come to me here. You then give me an exact account of your saying and doings. If you do something illegal on your own you can expect no protection or indulgence. Which is it to be?"

"What about wearing a yellow star?" said Castang agreeably.

"What's funny?"

"You don't expect me to be impressed? The pieces of paper are meaningless. I'll do as I please, and tell Bobby Bonacorsi I said so." The young man flushed angrily, and then broke into his smile.

"He did say you were an undisciplined bugger."

"If I do find anything I'll let you know it. You can persecute me or even arrest me, but you'll do yourself more good by leaving me alone."

"So tell me something," drawlingly, "were you following her or was she following you?"

"Yes, that puzzled me. I thought she was in Milano."

"Perhaps she didn't altogether trust you."

"Possibly, but I'd have expected her to have more sense. My present trouble is that she knew a good deal more than she told me and now I've no access to her. I'm very much in the dark."

"Suppose you tell me what you do know."

"No more than a working hypothesis," all too aware that this would be one-way traffic.

Unfortunate, said Mr Suarez. No Error!

Castang, driving along this awful road out of Como. In all the world women are the most exasperating, incomprehensible, awkward and utterly marvellous of inventions.

Two recent Vera-examples:—

"I've got to go to the dentist so I'm just having a quick cup of Nes. I'm making you some proper coffee." And, "I've got to go to the airport, so I'll also have a quick Nes."

"But you hate Nes. I'm making you a real —"

"I don't need it. I don't want it."

"You have to have a proper start to the day."

"Why can't I have a cup of Nes and not all this fucking argument?"

Vera much vexed.

Only the week before . . . he'd been moved to complain.

"Those are awful flowers."

"Yes."

"Banal, vulgar, and quite hideous."

"Yes, indeed."

"Perhaps we could throw them out."

"No."

"Or put them where they'd be less offensive."

"No."

"They're in the worst of taste."

"Yes, and no."

"That silver paper left inside the vase. That shiny plastic string curling about. Why?"

"Because . . ." Why do my wife and I quarrel all the time? And why is that such a silly question?

Our ancestors, to be sure, found Electra, Antigone or Cassandra alarming girls. Phallocentrics of the world, go cower in the corner. An unfailingly comic spectacle.

It is peculiar to start with some minute variation in chromosomes and to end with this magical female being, the basis of all art. Unbearable it may be in character and behaviour, it is full of glories and grandeurs. The sexual pleasures are transient if (thank heaven) renewable. Art however is long, unaffected by a grumbling prostate.

What am I doing in this goddam car? What's this I'm whistling? Why?

Rawlings' hired Alfa, and he was stuck with it. The Gendarmerie needed no hotel manager to make the connection; had only to ask in Milan's car-hire firms. Whose signature is on the paper?

Mozart again; catchy number, top of the pops this last two hundred years. You who know, what a thing is love.

Yes, indeed: he'd have to think about that. Unless of course he got shot. A detail to be borne in mind. For the chap with the rifle could have potted him there, sleepy on his hillside. Didn't. Hadn't perhaps worked out what he was doing there. Had perhaps lost no time in hurrying away. Wanted to see what he would do next? Chap thinking "one thing at a time".

But by today, perhaps, chap might have added more ideas. Or had them added up for him. Could be, a decision was arrived at that Castang was an inconvenience. There had been talk of Mafia. Well, when mafiosi want to make a public statement, hold a press conference you might call it, they bomb people. When it's run of the mill, mostly they just shoot you.

So that this is no time to be thinking about art. One has never the leisure to enjoy it because before you've turned around a calamity has you by the tail. Another crime. Another death. Hurry, hurry, and it might be for the appointment with his own death. He had done over twenty years of police work. Homicides are fairly rare, although in France gunshot homicides are not infrequent. But add accidents and suicides, and violent death is never far away. Castang has learned a thing from this; to treat his own death as a familiar spirit, lurking just out of sight but close by at his left hand.

Likewise lurking, and making him no less vulnerable, would be the Carabinieri. He was at best a stalking-horse, the sort of "loose cannon" a police force hopes to turn to its advantage. At worst they'd be following him; a faded green Opel had been sitting just-far-enough back this last twenty kilometres. It didn't have to mean anything because this was no road even to pass trucks. Well; here was Tirano. He'd get out and walk. One might see things coming, then. Equally, one might not. One would try and use the terrain.

The Valtellina is never better than narrow, and frequently steep-sided. A smallish climb took him beyond urban and even suburban building projects. His path was suddenly bare hillside and he didn't know whether there could be somebody sitting there with binoculars, chuckling. Above him was a stony terrace, and a stony cottage, and a "peasant" pruning his row or two of vines. Both of them raised their head to look at one another, to take the other in, and both smiled and said "Good-day", and "Sorry," said Castang in Spanish (idiot), "don't speak any Italian!"

The peasant (after all, the word means countryman) straightened, smiled again, stretched from the hips to ease his stooping back, and said "*Bisserl Deutsch*?", "Less bad," said Castang, because this was an oldish man with a fine face. Not the crooked dwarf that has made *paysan de montagne* one of the worst of French insults. He was handsome, and had princely manners. Castang would learn that in northern Italy this is normal.

"D'you mind my asking what sort of grape you're

63

growing there? A white, d'you make, or a red?" The old man thought about this, while choosing words in his rusty German.

"You know, that's a complicated question," laughing. "But it's warm. You've climbed. You're hot; perhaps tired. Come into my house and then you can taste it, and that will be better than my talking about it."

This too, Castang was about to learn, is the simple hospitality of the Valtellina. He demurred, but only for a second. "Come, come," said the old man smiling at urban awkwardness, clownish stiffness at being asked into a home. In the house, a brown, beautiful old woman made a sketch at a curtsey, the arm movements that say "my house is yours". Castang felt shame at his own barbarism and sat at a linoleum-covered table.

"She speaks no German. But it doesn't matter," producing a bottle of country wine and two glasses. "The vines can wait. They take patience." The woman vanished into the kitchen from which the smell of coffee came within a minute. "No, take it. Please her. You have time."

Yes! He had time! All the time one could wish for. For art, for love, for living. "Your prosperity, happiness, and a good season for the vines."

"Prosit," clinking their glasses together.

"I'm a lucky man to find you speak German," said Castang. Police officers, in order to be good, have also to be lucky. Napoleon, it is said, before promoting a general, would ask whether he were lucky. Those must have been his younger days and before he began to rely upon toadies, because it is a sensible remark. Castang had not always been lucky but when he had been so, generally he had been successful too.

The old man smiled. One can still meet these old men who have lived lives of hardship and love for something worth the having.

"My parents spoke German a little. Austrians, you know, were our overlords. Myself no, but in this last war we were again occupied. There was some hardship; there was no barbarity. Those troops were quiet, oldish men. They wished only to arrange matters. No persecutions and no assassinations. They looked for a few comforts. So that like ourselves, in the question of a few small illegalities across the border, they looked the other way. We used to stop and talk to each other. There was, even, a certain respect."

Castang was answered, but he also had a cue. "And I suppose these arrangements over the mountain still continue?"

"Times have changed. Those soldiers wished us no harm. They were not happy with the zeal of their Führer: we felt embarrassment at the bad manners, the noisy mouth of our Duce. They were lonely men. One made them a little present; they were content. The officials now are hard and greedy men, who care only for money.

"You want something," gently, "brought across the border?" A soft voice but a shrewd one.

"No," said Castang, "though I may know of those who do."

"There are young men who will do so. For fun. They look for adventure. I, you understand, am a bit stiff in the joints. They do no harm. But there are city people." His smile said he did not want to talk about that. "I do not know them. I do not wish to. People to piss upon."

Castang didn't want to be betrayed as a cop.

"Any hunting?" tactfully changing the subject.

"If one knows where to look. Small for the most part – a bird, a hare."

"What would you take? Small shotgun? Four-ten?"

"That, or a small rifle, twenty-two. Some people set snares," he shrugged as though in self-deprecation.

"Nothing for a big rifle? Boar, say. Twenty-two wouldn't stop that chap."

"You'd do better close up," gravely. "Load a shotgun with ball. They keep to close cover. A goat – but if you used a big rifle you'd have no goat left. What do you want," smiling now "a big fine antelope perhaps, with splendid horns? Some get them – but no rifle was used. Only a woman. A little more coffee? Luisa," he called, softly.

"No, no, I'm abusing your hospitality. It is good to walk."

"It is good to walk," agreed the old man. "It can also be a risk. Yesterday, as I hear, in the hills up yonder, a walker was killed."

"Really?" pretending to be startled. "I couldn't read the paper."

"An accident. They didn't say, but it's said – with a big rifle.

"Such as we spoke of." Clear old eyes looked at Castang with serenity. The neck was scored with deep lines, like the bark of an old tree; the jaw was shaved clean of that soft silvery stubble of old men who economise on razor-blades.

"Let's hope it doesn't happen here," said Castang, laughing.

"It was, my friend, no accident," holding out a hand that was warm and unexpectedly soft but raspy, like a sawed pine. "Come again. I am always here. I am Franco."

"I am Heinrich, and I am honoured."

"Luisa, our guest is leaving us." He kissed her hand and her face broke into amusement but he could see she was pleased, too.

"Tchuss," said the old man exactly as though Castang were a German tourist. "*Et bonne promenade*" to show he knew perfectly where the funny accent came from. But Castang was still feeling lucky.

So that after working up a good appetite he came back down into the town for something to eat, and the sun was warm enough for them not to mind serving him outside, so that he ate rabbit and sat watching the good people of Tirano. And was lucky in a way he had never expected but which comes sometimes. Like drawing a card at vingt-et-un and getting a natural and knowing there'll be more: the winning streak. They happen, but the snag is in not knowing when it will stop.

A bashed old Fiat car drove too fast up to the greengrocer three doors down, and a young woman ran in to do her shopping; the motor gulped and died with the car halfway up the pavement. Castang, who had paid his bill and was enjoying a cigar in the sunlight, sat and waited. She ran out, flung a crowded basket in the back, banged the driving door, turned the ignition key, and the starter motor made a small weary sound. She did it again. Castang got up. He had plenty of time to scrabble in his trouser pocket, sort out a tip for the girl, walk slowly towards the open window just as she said, "Oh, fuck." She looked up, stretched her face in mechanical apology. "Sorry, not meant for you."

'Let me try," he said gently. "If I may say so, you're too rough with it."

"Be my guest. Playing me up all bloody morning. Stop for a red light, the motor dies." She got out; he got in. Pushed back the choke, let everything rest, turned the key without accelerating. The motor caught and idled stuttering. "Well, a miracle-worker. Thank you."

"Let me drive or it'll stall again."

"Mister, I don't know you."

"No matter. Just a tourist. Live far?"

"Far enough," studying him, dubious, with her index finger laid along her jaw, "for it to be a goodish walk back."

"I've nothing special to do," nursing the motor with little touches. "Don't look like a bandit. Right enough; ain't either. New plugs, is what you need."

She made up her mind, gave him a smile, got in. "Straight down, and right at the crossing." It was about two kilometres, not too strenuous for an afternoon walk. "This'll be okay."

"What we do is back in a little, up the slope. If she won't go you let her roll, put her in second."

"Or phone you to come and push. I'm grateful. I suppose I'd better ask you to have a drink, at least." Still a bit wary; plainly she was alone in the house.

"I wanted to talk to you," he said, simply. She looked up from the heavy shopping bag.

"Did you now? Why then, I wonder."

"Because you're Irish."

She smiled and frowned together. "And if I had just driven off?"

"The place is not that big. I'd have found out, I suppose, without too much pains. Saved myself some trouble. Didn't want to accost you in the street."

"It's not much of a reason. But you saved me trouble too. Come on then," unlocking the side door into the kitchen, dumping her vegetables on the table. "Sit down. Like a beer?" opening the fridge. "Must be more of a reason," with her head inside it.

"You take good pictures." She came out with two beers, straightened up and laughed. "Still not much of a reason," scrabbling in the table drawer for an opener.

Castang noticed two things. That she sat down with the table between them, and left the drawer open; and that she had some sturdy kitchen knives there handy: prudent girl. And that she had the camera, loose, in with the vegetables. She posed it negligently on the table, pointing towards him. The lens cap was not on.

"You take it anywhere, everywhere, don't you. Hobby of yours. But," reaching out, "careful, your lens might get scratched," turning it to point upward. "cheers, and here's to the clock over Mooneys," remembering a phrase of Eamonn's. She was looking puzzled now.

"But you're not a Dubliner. Look, I think you'd better explain.

"So I will," feeling in the inside pocket of his windbreaker. "These are yours, I rather think."

"Why . . . how d'you come to have these? That's Eamonn Hickey. We were out on the hills with Coralie."

Cordelia or Ottilie – not a bad shot, Jane, though.

"Of course they're mine – I took them – but that's meaningless. What I'm asking, is, what are you doing with them? What's all the mystery? Last autumn, that must have been. Snow already on the peaks but it was a lovely day. You can just see her arm, in that one – taken a bit crooked. Please do explain."

"You mean you didn't know? That Eamonn is dead?" Her eyes and whole face flooded with shock. And fear. The eyes clouded, troubled. They don't really cloud, but it's quite a good phrase for the play of light and shade. Irish eyes? A hazel-brown with green bits. She was not "pretty", but the face was alert, bright, highly mobile, and now much discomposed. I am a camera, with its shutter open, thought Castang cornily. She drank some beer, to cover confusion, but the fear stayed there, unmistakeable.

"Eamonn was killed," brutally. "Cut down with a shotgun, at his own front door." Now when she was off balance was the time to push her.

"Dear God," faintly. "I – I – didn't know him well. She's a friend of mine."

"The police are wondering who would have done that. As well as why."

"Are you, are you, some sort of police?"

"Eamonn was a friend of mine. So I want to know about Coralie. And you too."

"Dear God," trying to pull herself together. Her lips

were shaking. Trembling is the word in English. Yes, they do tremble. "I don't know what to tell you. Coralie is a friend. She lives up the road in Sondalo. She used to work in Brussels. She met him there, I think. He likes, he liked, the valley here. They were together then. But we just went out for the day, I mean, it's meaningless, where did you get these?"

"Yes? Go on about Coralie."

"She's just a girl I know, just a friend, she has this house here, her parents died – this is all perfectly innocent, what are you trying to make me say?"

"Why are you so frightened?" She rallied at that. "Frightened, who's frightened? You're trying to make me frightened. You come storming in here telling me some tale he got shot, it's a shock, how do I know it's true even? Naturally I'm upset, but I hardly knew him, he was Irish so we made jokes together, what are you trying to do? I think you'd better go, I don't like having you here in my house."

Castang slapped another photo on the table. "You don't believe me? This was Eamonn Hickey after he got shot. Not one of yours. Police photo. Nasty, isn't it?"

She got up and rushed away. He could hear her being sick, in the lavatory next door. He hunted for the lens cap and found it under the carrots. She came back in with the dignity found in putting a towel under the cold tap and wiping one's face clean.

"I don't want to be rude but please do go now, you can see this has upset me, I'm going to phone my husband but you'd better understand I'm able to protect myself and I can phone the police too and say you're harassing me.' She had a pistol in her hand, a 7.65 Beretta popgun but quite able to pop intruders; stashed in the downstairs lavatory, not bad. Violence is a fact of life even in the peaceful Valtellina. "I won't say anything more, just leave, please."

"Certainly. I mustn't have you thinking I'd try to abuse you. Call the Carabinieri by all means. Down in Sondrio, they'll be interested. But don't phone Coralie. I'll be going up to see her, and if you were to tip her off – that would be thought an obstruction of justice, and it would link you directly to a homicide investigation, and then, you see, you'd really be in trouble."

"I won't." Her lipstick clung to the corners of her

mouth. It is said that lips "go white". A cliché of krimi stories, but she had gone very pale; result of being sick. She had courage, though. "I suppose you must be some kind of cop. I took those photos, I take lots of photos, of anything, I'm not involved in this, it's pure coincidence, you can ask Coralie, this doesn't affect me at all, it just made me sick hearing about it, now fuck off. I won't phone Coralie," struggling for control, "because it has to be clear I know nothing about this."

"But you're very frightened, and I think the Carabinieri will want to know why."

"That's natural, you come here with a beastly story, you show me beastly photographs, I'm a woman, you're an obscenity, get out of my sight. And walk," with a little spurt of spiteful delight that he'd have to walk.

"Coralie's exact address, please. And if you're out of this, my advice would be to stay out."

"Twenty-five via Roma. Now go," waving that pistol at him. Had she worked the slide, had she got it cocked? They go off awfully easily, you can't push her further. Phone your husband by all means. Does he know what it is that has you so shaky?

"Thank you, Madame, I'll trouble you no further. It's to be hoped that the Lieutenant down in Sondrio, the Captain in Como, will agree. They have a criminal enquiry on their hands. They might think you're just a casual witness, a woman who likes to take photos – or they might find a connection they'd like to tighten.'

It is outrageous, this abuse of non-existent police powers, but it's also common form. There's something here. An intrigue? A fiddle is better.

There's a French phrase, *virer son cuti*, which means to change one's skin as snakes do. It gets used to describe a more fundamental reversal of attitudes, over perhaps a longish time. Snakes are said to take some hours, women while drawing a single breath.

"Sit down again. No, please. Monsieur – Monsieur?"

"Castang."

"Would you like another beer? Or I could open a bottle of wine. Or a cognac?"

"Fine as I am, thanks. But you were saying?"

"I made a mistake. You see I feel frightened – are you

really police?"

"Officially? No. I wondered what my friend Eamonn Hickey found of interest here in your part of the world. I suspected it might be more than a walking tour. I loiter about, I look, I listen. And lo . . ."

"But you're an official?"

"Just a cog in our Brussels bureaucracy. Eamonn was rather well thought of, up our street. Who'd want to kill him, we wondered. Odd occurrence."

"Did you by any chance hear that some woman got shot, up the hill yesterday? Some sort of a hunting accident, it was said.'

"I found her."

"Oh . . . So you went to the police?"

"They think it rather a coincidence, too. They're a little upset about it."

"I'm frightened." It hadn't occurred to her to ask how he had known she had taken those photographs. She was well known around here – a harmless example of personal vanity, and which might be useful. She saw signposts everywhere pointing at her!

"I think I'm going to have some cognac."

"Then I might join you in that," always anxious to be friendly.

"If you're only really interested in Mr Hickey, I mean suppose I were to tell you some things a bit personal – could I trust you not to tell the police? Because while it's quite harmless, it could turn into an embarrassment for my husband. You see he has a certain position and one wouldn't want that compromised. People are so malicious. This is a small place – people gossip so."

"Quite truly." And so it was. Originally.

"I can't help feeling frightened because this seems to – I mean I never dreamed . . ."

"That's the way of things," encouragingly.

"My name's Siobhán. Shavána people call me round here. I'm Irish." Castang can remember the exact moment, in Kitty O'Sheas, when Eamonn explained a peculiarity of the Irish language. "You've a b. Pronounced as such. It can be aspirated, shown in writing by an h behind it. Then it becomes a v."

"Like in Spanish? The b-burro and the v-vaca?" he'd

asked.

"No, a real v, a soft one."

"Pretty name," said Castang helpfully.

"There's not a lot of Irish people round here, so as you can guess it made a bit of a bond. Well, there's a few friends of mine, it isn't me personally, but I sort of know about it, it's a sort of game really, they've sometimes done a bit of smuggling, like you know, the odd bottle of cognac."

"Paintings, was it?"

She was taken aback enough to get confused. "That has been known. But I mean, just for fun. I mean Coralie's a friend and I haven't sort of cross-examined her, but she was a bit mixed up with this. I don't know about Eamonn. I just want to make sure there isn't any trouble. I mean if he got killed — no, but hearing about that woman yesterday, that upset me. I don't know anything about this, but you coming out of the blue with those photos, that frightened me."

And up the road again, the Alfa now dirty , which didn't make it inconspicuous. This local grapevine worked well; he had a nasty sensation that the whole countryside was ringing with his exploits. There didn't *seem* to be anyone marking him over this twenty kilometres stretch of twisty and relatively unfrequented mountain road. Or was there somebody who didn't need to, who was well aware of his purpose.

The little town, hardly more than a village, was quiet and sleepy in afternoon sunlight; the grandly-named via Roma was a narrow street of old houses climbing the steep hillside. He knocked discreetly, and again louder, unpleasantly aware that the foreign personage was attracting attention, that eyes behind the openings in shutters were memorising his particulars.

But the moment the door opened a little way, grudging and suspicious, he knew it was no false trail he had followed. This was the young woman with the curly hair and pretty eyes, the "girlfriend" glimpsed by Jane, the woman who had been important to Eamonn; there might be enigmas there, but first there were questions here. She stood on the threshold with her chin thrust forward aggressively, a white-knuckled hand gripping the door.

He produced the winning smile, the lifted hat.

"I'm sorry, I only know you as Coralie."

"I should have known it," she muttered. "I guessed that sooner or later . . . you had better come in, rather than stand there blaring on the street."

"I didn't blare," said Castang, quite vexed at the idea. "Didn't phone because how would I have explained myself?" Not saying that he finds phones of little use: he wants to see people.

"What odds, now?" She led the way; a short passage, a country kitchen, a country living-room, in one large and very pleasant space. The country smell of old houses, of old stone and old wood. A floor of tiles, there for a hundred years and still good; a big sideboard of locally carved fruitwood; all warmed by a massive old stove with a cooker top. A round table was covered with oilcloth . . . it was the house of a former generation, all untouched, unspoiled. The sideboard was full of painted china. There were pictures of landscapes in marquetry, there were wax flowers under glass, a row of battered old copper pots; on the stove a kettle singing . . . but the young woman was altogether modern. She sat listlessly at the table, signalled to him to do the same, watched him as he looked around with admiration.

"Do you live here by yourself?"

She took her time, studying him, listening to his accent, and then she answered in French. He didn't think Shavana had phoned her.

"*T'es flic, ou quoi?* You're a cop, aren't you?" He was getting used to this and gave his usual answer.

"Used to be. But a friend of Eamonn's."

She nodded. "It's my house now. My parents died. Quite recently. My father was taken off with a cancer. My mother took sleeping pills because she didn't want to live any longer. Does that answer you? I came back here. I thought I'd get some peace at last. I was mistaken."

She was wearing country clothes, corduroys and a hand-knitted pullover. She got up, moving lithely but with no spring. Thick socks, sandals. Went to the sideboard, came back with a bottle of grappa, two glasses, but no enthusiasm. The conventional offer, to the "guest in the house" of village hospitality. She filled his glass without asking, filled her own, drank it off in one.

"Bruce? You've a French accent though." Her own was slight, her French easy, fluent.

She was like the old man up the hill, very good-looking indeed. But she was still a young girl, and this meant that she was beautiful. A beauty of maturity; she was twenty-five or -seven. There was a long-case clock on the wall which he stared at. Country wood, walnut but so beautifully grained, so lovingly cut and finished one would take it for the work of a sophisticated Paris eighteenth-century ébéniste: Castang had an eye for fine joinery, likes himself to have a lathe in the house, like George Orwell, says Vera, kindly. This was native wood but better than anything exotic. And she was like that. He tasted the alcohol, which was of excellent quality, and made a face of appreciation.

"It was my father's," she said, expressionless. she watched him, so that he watched her. He offered her a cigarette, which she accepted.

She was durable, not fragile. Under the lumpy clothes she looked to be solid but finely articulated. But the face was remarkable, magnificent in cut and modelling. Intaglio cut by some fine Renaissance craftsman in a stone – what stone is that, harder than amber? An amber colouring. Fine-grained skin but too pale to be called olive, and with the blood in it showing. The sapphire eye was in an orbit of extraordinary beauty, the eyebrow in a natural arch, high and perfect, the brow itself most exquisitely modelled, the ear the same. In the fine shallow curves of jaw and cheekbone there *was* something exotic. Some distant ancestor had set foot in a port – Venice, Genoa – who had come there from a Slav land, from deeper in the Orient than Vera's Czech looks, and had left here its mark. This much, at least, of Eamonn's fascination was readily understandable.

Her bad feature was her hands, reddish and heavy; peasant hands. She knew it because she wore no rings. It might have been better for her to say the-hell-with-it, and wear sapphires: she had only tiny gold earrings.

On the cornice above the stove were twin photographs in a leather frame.

"That's your parents? D'you mind if I look?" He got up.

74

They were peasant faces, yes, but of unusual distinction, the woman prematurely aged as country women are but with the same fine skin, the lines in it etched as finely as though by Rembrandt's needle, the old man full of feature and magnetism, a splendid Etruscan face; the young woman in front of him embodying the best in both, and both outstanding. "They are quite magnificent."

"I loved them both, very much. And when they died I was not even here. I was in Bruce. And I'll never cease to mourn that." He had said something right. She poured herself another glass of the grappa.

"You were with Eamonn, here. And in Bruce. And you want to know how it all comes about. So I'll tell you. As far as I know, which isn't much. If you can then fill in gaps, we might know where we stand."

She nodded dully, with a sort of fatalism. "If we both live," she said.

"Eamonn was shot. On his doorstep."

She nodded again. "When you knocked, I thought it was my turn. And then I told myself no, not in broad daylight, not here, with half a dozen old biddies watching behind the shutters. So I opened the door. How did you get here?"

"I worked at it. In Eamonn's house there were some photographs. Your arm appears in one. Did he keep it for that, I wonder, because you were there, with him? Up the hill here, beyond Bormio. Beyond the old Spanish fort."

It was familiar ground to her. "One of those huts there was my father's. We used to go up there in summer. When I was a child . . ."

"The waterworks, the reservoir, that's recognisable. Above all, the mountains in the background. These are identifiable. There are people in Bruce who have aerial photos, satellite photos: they pin-pointed it. All I had to do was to go up there and identify it.

"A bit of deduction. It wasn't difficult. Shavána took those photos. She's known hereabouts for her skilful camera."

She nodded, again. With hindsight it is all so easy.

"A woman came with me, to look about. An Englishwoman, some sort of Intelligence Service. I didn't know her, I still don't. She got wished on me in Bruce. She was interested on her own account. Eamonn and Shavána both being Irish. Maybe . . . she didn't tell me. She was a bit too clever, it seems to me. She wanted to use me as a stalking horse.

"Pushed me up here to see what I would find. But I'm only interested in Eamonn. He was my friend, I knew him well, and I find out I didn't know him at all. Good, people are secret. But for reasons of her own, which she doesn't tell me, this woman followed me, and that was a big mistake, because she must have thought herself covered, and through some leak I haven't fathomed and doubtless won't, the leak gave her away: she was followed. And when an opportunity came, she got shot. I was sitting a few hundred metres away, peacefully enjoying the first spring sunshine I'd seen this year, and thinking about alpine flowers . . . Kind of a shock.

"Well now, I had to give some explanation to the Carabinieri: they weren't born yesterday. And for all I know, somebody followed me here. I want to know what Eamonn and you had going. But somebody else is interested and that somebody has an itchy trigger finger. We're at risk, both of us.

"If you can tell me about it I can arrange, more or less, for some protection. But I think we had both better get out of here."

She started to cry. Will one say that it is purely self-pity? Will one be harsh with her? Be a cop? More generally known as "the filth". But she wasn't giving way: she was trying to control sobs of desolation.

"I've made such a mess of things."

And Castang wants to throw back at her "*Et Nous?*" What about us, we, me? D'you imagine I've never made a mess of things, never done anything wrong?

Et nous? Les petits, les obscures, les sans-grade.

And footsore on the streets of Paris Castang had quoted them in irony. He had ended as a chief, commanding men, but knows how little it means to wear an officers uniform, carry a sword: he has no opinion of generals.

He has listened often to those he had to arrest. They all say what a mess they have made. Like the bureaucrat general, pitying himself, "But you see, we became so tired . . .' to be answered by the old servant and former soldier. "and us then?"

A marriage, for instance. People find it an unbearable constraint. They tell one they have fallen in love with another. Really? And then? After that?

Vera, the over-sensitive, tormented out of her skin by the doltish antics of the Man. While he – he – no, shut up. He can get torn too; it can get rough.

God, said Lydia the other day (she is seventeen, with the pain in front of her), how is it possible that you can be so *thick*? He had not bellowed even if he had taken refuge in sarcasm.

"I'm afraid that upon occasion everybody is thick. However bright they find themselves." Oh yes, he has snarled at his stupid, obstinate Czech peasant. Who has too often told herself that she has been the destruction of his life.

So that he says, quite gently, now to this young woman, "Yes? You, who know – tell me then."

She does too, but about love, not a lot. For that, he'd have to ask Eamonn, who is no longer there.

Vera would say that all too plainly this imbecile Eamonn knew nothing about love – had said so! "Adultery is only sex, after all." Castang, who does not agree, said so, with some sharpness of tongue; as she grows older, then, does she become a village bigot, complaining of the young girls' licentious behaviour? Stupid, yes, of someone like Eamonn? Did it not show how tormented he must have been, to search for love in this helpless, hopeless way?

'Whoremongers,' Vera had said furiously. She had been much upset; Eamonn was her friend, also.

"Bigot!" Castang had shouted.

"Tell me more," he prods Coralie, gently. She is sodden and silly from crying.

"I wish I were lesbian," she burst out, "and so bloody obviously I'm not. Christ what a shambles!" Castang laughed. The girl means, presumably, that if you love a woman and a woman loves you, there isn't all this abuse of emotional generosity. Since women are caring, tender, unselfish. Only on occasion, Castang would say, out of his years of police work. A vociferous argument, now that the gay brigade is so fashionable.

"I don't think you're very les."

"Do you want to go to bed with me then? Here? I will if you'd like." And smiles, unwillingly, when he puts on "a voice" to say "A little later."

"You see, I met Eamonn in Brussels."

"You met him how?"

"I've pretty good secretarial skills. And several languages. Instead of going to Milano I thought I'd try for a better job in Bruce. With the Community, you know? But that isn't so easy. So I did get good jobs, though for one reason or another they folded. And then one day I took a crook job. I'm not proud of it . . ."

'Look – I've things too I've no reason to be proud of."

"All right . . . I thought myself clever; superior, don't you know? And it was a lot of money. More than that . . . I had responsibility. It's that, now, I'm not proud of.

"Oh, all right. My job was to get girls for modelling work in Milano."

"I can guess. There wasn't any work in Milano. Not modelling."

"My only excuse is that *I* was so green I didn't know that at the start. I don't have a modelling figure, you see. I'm sort of squat."

Castang is aware that this wasn't the reason. A question of mental rather than physical measurements. They want girls who'll be biddable. This one would have altogether too much backchat.

"A good many girls who have – or think they have – go for the glamour notion. So I was here to interview them, get them to pay – you know, agency fees – put them on the train . . ."

"To be prostitutes in Milano."

Her eyes were dry by now. "That's a bit harsh, you know. I face it; some do. Joy clubs. It wasn't white-slaving. If they didn't like it nobody stopped them going home."

"Be honest. Vanity stopped them. Didn't like to go home and say they'd been made fools of. Not much asked of them," acidly. "Tall blonde, good presentation, 'likes to work with people'. No model openings just at present. Bit of photo work, a walk-on here or there – just enough to keep going and make them hope for more."

"Well, you've said it, just about. It's the end of the month that the pinch comes. They get suckered step by step.

Show your tits, nothing in that, sex is fun anyway, no harm and you can even get paid for it. Security, comfort, not much work, and they write home saying they've got modelling jobs."

"And you're not especially proud of having steered them there. Since you knew, perfectly well."

"No, I'm not," said Coralie bleakly.

"Go on being honest. There's a man behind all this."

"Only just. My contact was the lady in Milano. I'd put adverts in papers, and get office space in Bruce. I look reliable and sympathetic, you see. I'd get girls from all over, German mostly but Norwegian, Finnish – Bruce is a magnet of course. So one explained that we had expenses, office rent, phone calls. I got commission on the girl, of course. Five per cent on the agency cut."

"And you paid the expenses. He did better. What's his name?"

"Thomas Lhomme. I hardly know him, really. I've only seen him twice. He's a television producer, in Germany somewhere, gets about . . ."

"The girls who came back?"

"They hardly did, you know. The odd one, with a lament, and I'd say oh, bad luck, but I'm afraid I told myself they were a pack of silly sheep, and if they got made into hamburger, that was their bad luck. There was one, then . . . Maybe she had parents to kick up a fuss, I don't know. The Belgian police didn't arrest me, didn't even charge me, just said *Raus* within the twenty-four hours. I phoned Milano, they just said too-bloody-bad, they weren't worried."

"You got a phone number for this man Lhomme?"

"No. But he wouldn't be worried, either."

"We haven't got to Eamonn, yet."

"He knew . . . he'd say he was looking them over – he used to call them the kitchen-maids. He was absolutely honest about it. He'd talk about his escort agency. But it was me he fell in love with." An effort, at pride.

"You fell first?"

"I don't know," trying hard. "I wasn't about to get upstaged by the kitchen-maids." You see, Vera? Not just black on white, like your drawings. There, you are right to simplify.

"You've no idea how stupid they are," said Coralie pathetically.

"Oh yes I have." And added with regret, "Pack a bag; I've the car down the road. I don't know anything but I don't want things getting complicated."

She looked at him and he could have sworn she was getting ready to say that she was a big girl but didn't take up much room in the bed. And then she decided that after all she had some self-respect left.

A level, clear stare. "You want me to go away with you?"

Yes, that was what he wanted. To take her off to one of the little lakeside hotels. "I told Shavána not to phone you, and she didn't, because I think I threw enough of a fright into her. But she may have been very busy on the phone to other people."

"Shavána wouldn't do anything to hurt me."

"You were frightened when I came."

"Yes . . . I don't know why. I was upset. I didn't know who to be frightened of. I didn't know who you were. That woman who was killed; that frightened me somehow."

"This man Lhomme?"

"No-o. He's frightening in a way, I suppose; he's a gangster. But what would he want to hurt me for? I was just a piece of business that went wrong. He'd shrug and find another."

"Of somebody else? Someone round here? One of Shavána's friends?"

"I don't know, I tell you. She has lots of friends. Some of them a bit shady, maybe. It's meaningless, it's nothing to do with me."

"I still want you out of here. Two people have been killed and I think it's no coincidence."

Her look was a little too sad, a little too knowing. "Where to? It's because I said I'd go to bed if you wanted? But I'm not a prostitute. I'm not even a joygirl even if I did steer a few girls that way. Still, if it's what you want." She stood up and began to unbutton her trousers.

"Coralie, stop."

"You mean you want to undress me? Okay."

He'd had time to spit on his hands, to tell himself to be professional. Well yes, there was this question of Vera. It is central. Was that enough to hold him? He'd like to think so.

He had a picture of Eamonn, who had been his friend. This was the girl Eamonn had loved. Lusting after her was not only adulterous: wasn't it a bit incestuous into the bargain? The idea made him laugh. Anyhow she looked ridiculous there with a winter sweater on and her knickers sticking out underneath.

"Coralie, put your trousers back on. I'll find friends who can put you up," with a vague idea that Bobby Bonacorsi ought to be of some use. "A couple of days while we get this business cleared up.

"Weekend bag. We'll go back down the hill." Not the moment yet either to tell her that the Carabinieri would be interested too.

Well, let the old women – of either sex – of Sondalo think whatever they liked. Ooh, there's the Tompkins girl with a bag packed, going off with a strange man; up to no good that's certain.

The car was where he left it and he didn't think anybody would have wired up the ignition to a bomb, because it was coated with dust, and little boys had written slogans on it. *Forza Juve; ACM vincera* – was that spelt right? And on the door *Porco* – not really deserved, that. There were long silences on the way down; both of them with thinking to do.

"Errand here, won't be a minute," at the Carabinieri office in Sondrio. "Not here," said the duty dogsbody when he asked for his Lieutenant. "He's down in Como, I think." Driving along the lake shore he had no time to be regetful about waterside idylls because the road was too narrow. He left the red Alfa insolently on the police parking lot and was told that the Teniente was in conference.

"*Urgente, importante.*"

"Yes yes, it always is," but they were sufficiently curious to take his card, and quite soon his officer appeared, shook his head sadly at this infernal trouble-maker, and beckoned him into the sanctum, where there were two men he hadn't seen before, but who knew all about him because they both looked with a sceptical eye before turning it on Coralie; with rather more pleasure.

The man behind the desk was plainly a superior officer because he wore his smart civilian jacket as though it were a uniform. His open-necked shirt was beautifully pressed. He had that enviable Italian hair, shiny-dark and sculptural; all straight out of the advert for Men-of-Distinction whisky. But the features were alert, intelligent. The other man looked more interesting although he was a lot smaller and his shirt was both limp and crumpled. Thin, light, and looking to be quick both on his feet and behind the eyes. Very tanned. Longish wavy hair between brown and grey. Amused expression. He spoke first, and he spoke English, and though he didn't look English his voice, which was superior-officer, told Castang that he couldn't be anything else.

"So this is the famous Mr Castang. Notable stirrer-up of wasps' nests. Notice too, Colonel, in charming female company." Castang felt no inclination to yield to anybody in cheek.

"And who the hell are you?" he enquired politely, drawing a broad smile.

"You're a considerable pest, you know that?" remarked the Colonel in a light pleasant voice, and also in good English. This wouldn't do, especially in front of Coralie. One would have to put out more flags.

"And bringing with me an important witness. Whom I want treated with consideration. In the first place shelter, safety, and comfort for as long as may prove necessary."

"I'm afraid that we're not here to squire girls around – however pretty," with a little glance of gallantry at Coralie, but she had sense enough to keep quiet.

"I think your officer may have told you that General Bonacorsi is a friend of mine." The lieutenant broke out into a low gabble, too fast for him to follow the Italian, but it sounded like a Milanese patois. The Colonel looked unimpressed, then glanced at a watch on an elegant brown wrist and said, "He'll still be in his office. All right – call him." The lieutenant did the telephone rigmarole again. The Colonel took it, spoke a few words in patois, smiled nastily and held the phone out to Castang.

"What the fuck you on about now?" said an irritable voice.

"Hallo, Big Tit," sending the Colonel's eyebrows up. It was a schoolboy joke at best, "robert" being a French argot word for a girl's breast as well as the General's name. But it defused the explosion.

"Tell me what you want and make it quick."

"A safe house for a witness I've taken away from her home because I think she's at some risk, and I wouldn't be bothering you unless I thought it serious, would I now? Oh yes, and your Colonel thinks I'm a conceited French prick."

"So you are," said the voice. "Pass me back to him." The Colonel listened straight-faced, breaking gradually into a grin. There was quite a long exchange. Castang looked at the thin man.

"I still don't know who you are."

"Your companion gave you the name Rawlings, am I right? You can say I'm Mr Rawlings." Pleasant, tenor, now formally polite. "And by the way, that car of yours – she hired it, right? It's got a bit conspicuous. I'll see the bill's settled."

The Colonel had put the phone down and was looking amiable. "We'll give you a lift, down to somewhere nice on the lake shore – Bellagrio, Menagio, what does it matter? Take his bags and see to that," to his subordinate.

"But she comes with me."

"No, she doesn't," still smooth. "She stays with us. Not to worry, we'll make the signorina comfortable."

"Don't feel bothered at all," Castang told Coralie. "I'll get this sorted out," flipping a finger towards "Mr Rawlings" who was all reassuring smiles, "and I'll stay close. I'll be in touch in an hour or so," aware he was being shunted out of the room.

"And so will I," said Rawlings. "In fact, with your permission, we'll have dinner together. Okay?"

And the Carabinieri drove him to the shore, ferried him across the lake, and left him with much elaborate saluting on the terrace of a rather smart hotel amid a lot of sub-tropical vegetation, where a smooth-faced manager said, "Yes yes, Monsieur Castang, it's all arranged and your room is booked." Fuck this, thought Castang; I'm getting railroaded by that bastard Bobby.

It was nearly dinner time and good smells were coming from the kitchen. He went upstairs for a wash, pleased that they'd given him a nice room. French windows opened on a balcony, with a view of the lake. Very pretty too. He went down feeling tired and hungry, like a good tourist.

"Rawlings" was sitting peacefully on the terrace with a glass, and beckoned hospitably.

"What will you drink, and this is on us, by the way, we owe you that. The girl is valuable; that was a find. Don't worry about her, she's well looked after"

"I'll stick to the local plonk, red for preference. I'm starving too."

"So am I. We'll eat. One eats well, here," – almost a French remark and it made him feel better. "Margaret was the expert. Knew the terrain. Spoke much better Italian than me. She's a great loss and it saddens me much personally. But we'll do what we can."

Castang then began to take a liking to this lined, smiling face full of humour. A toughy though. Looks like an ex-paratrooper. Which was smart of Castang because the man didn't look like it, but that is exactly what he was.

"I have to fill you in, don't I? In fact it's you mostly who has to fill me in. Margaret didn't have time to put anything much in writing, so I'm largely up in the air. I need to know what she said and what she did while in your company, and as precise as you can possibly make it."

"I've one preliminary question. I want a serious answer. Do you think – seriously – that Eamonn Hickey was an IRA agent?"

Rawlings stopped with an artichoke halfway to his mouth. "No, I don't. Margaret wasn't so sure. I told her there was no hard evidence. To some extent, I've come here to verify. Why do you ask?"

"Because I don't believe it. Very well. We went first to Lugano. She told me nothing, you know. Didn't stay long. I got the impression she was a bit puzzled."

"True; there's something in Lugano we haven't quite fathomed: skip that, it's this, the Italian side, which interests me most."

"We went just a little way, about twenty minutes in the car, along the lake; just across the frontier. The Valsolda. She had an interesting book about it which she lent me. Fogazzaro. Good book, I'd like to keep it. Souvenir . . ."

"Do so. Means nothing to me. She was rather literary. But continue." They had octopus, the white kind, very good, plain charred on the grill.

"There are tiny villages along the lake. Very narrow, the hillside goes up steeply. Place a bit like this. Oria, Albogasio, I'm not all that clear. She went out at night; she knew someone there."

"I wonder. She was over-secretive. Field agents are like that; they cherish their own little private networks and get paranoid at telling one. The point, I should think, is that lots of Italians travel that lakeshore road daily, they go to work in Switzerland and back that evening, it's perfectly impossible to oversee that frontier and if you have someone who passes it daily, you could bring anything across you bloody well fancied. Into Lugano and from there on . . . there's the rub. Antiques, we think, mostly, there's a lot of money in it. Do go on."

They'd progressed to pieces of pork. Flavours of sage, of lemon-peel, of capers. Of anchovy? In Italy cooking is quite as subtle a business as smuggling. Maybe more so. There was fennel. There were potatoes . . .

"One thing is plain, I think," said Castang, "she wasn't feigning an interest in this part of the world, stirring up dust to cover a real conviction that the centre of affairs is over there in the Valtellina. It took some planning to kill her, some hours of preparation. It was known, surely, that she'd go up there. Why shoot her and not me? That's easy; she knew something and I didn't. But since I had the car, how did she get up there? We found no car, so somebody drove her. That somebody may not have been the one who shot her.

"The Irishwoman knows something. But she's married to a local notable, friends with all the notables; I can't see our police pals getting anywhere much thereabouts. In fact I'd be ready to bet they were all far away and thoroughly alibied when the accident took place. That they're all dipped in illegal traffickings of one sort or another – yes, but who's to prove it? But as for this IRA suggestion, I've nothing to offer there, save that all these groups, Rote Fraktion in Germany, Red Brigades here, have links with one another and the financing is important. And cross-border fiddles are a handy source of finance."

Rawlings never said anything. Went on nodding from

time to time. And eating. Castang was aware that he himself was drinking a lot. Well, he'd had a busy day.

"I'll ask you to tell me one thing," putting his knife and fork together and deciding he had no room left for pudding. "What gave you the notion in the first place that Eamonn Hickey might have been in the IRA?"

"He was denounced," answered Rawlings deliberately. "and the denunciation came from a source that sounded pretty well informed. We were able to match a few items with stuff we considered sound, so that it might have been a true bill. Might still prove to be so, at that."

"Mind telling me the name of this source? Since Eamonn – that's really the only bit which interests me."

Rawlings smiled. "No, I don't think any purpose will be served by your hanging about further," he said. "You're burned anyhow, every way you can think of; by being there when she was killed, by having been seen in her company around here, by your own subsequent activities; you name it. Oh, don't think me ungrateful, it may turn out to have been a lot of help, but what I want is for you to make tracks for home, smartish tomorrow morning. Milan airport for the first Brussels flight; you'll do no good here any further, for yourself or anyone else. Leave it to the police, and leave it perhaps to me. I'll settle your expenses, which will make your office happy. And I'll tell you that I now think it quite unlikely, in fact most unlikely indeed, that your friend Eamonn was culpably mixed up in any terrorist dealings. He may have known a few people who are. As for your name – he seems to have ducked out of sight but if you come across this in any of your circles in Brussels, he's a Belgian chap called Paul de Man. That might not, of course, be his only name."

"Why is it familiar?" puzzled.

"Oh, there was a chap in America, well-known academic guru of the same name – a common enough name in Belgium. Chap died. That's probably who you're thinking of."

"Seems to ring a bell."

"There was a fuss because this very simon-pure philosopher turned out to have a Nazi past – collaborator-cum-journalist during the war."

"That's it no doubt. No, no coffee thanks, I'm yawning

my head off, I'm going to bed."

"See you at breakfast," lazily. "Sleep well."

Castang found a girl in his bed.

Very well; what would you do? Turn her out? She's a Russian honey-trap? She's Carmen Sternwood? She's infected? You had turned down the offer earlier for perfectly proper motives? You're at the end of a hard unpleasant day and are very tired, but no, thank you? Or, having drunk a tankful of Valpolicella, you aren't really up to a high-class effort? You're afraid she'll scream, make a scandal, cry rape? Or just begin to cry and won't stop? However confused you are, it's still vanity.

The cold alpine wind had dropped. A warm mild night. The French windows to the balcony were open. It is possible to suggest that Castang stopped being French, and hence vain, on the day he first slept with his windows open. It is spring on the shore of an Italian lake, the little wavelets made a pretty sound. Mozart entered into it, for Coralie does not know what a thing is love but she's trying to find out.

So – on such a night as this? Shakespeare. Rarely much good in French, save to illuminate the dirty-double-meanings. Castang's English is inadequate to the original. He'll do no better with the splendid German version and he knows no Russian at all. But he gets a lesson in love, and for this he's grateful, quite humbly. He learns to conjugate Italian verbs. I, thou, he and she, we, make love beside Lake Como. There is a lot of traffic, but at enough distance to minimise disturbances.

Some vanity still in his thinking. He's being "set up"? Who by? A Colonel of Carabinieri? Mr Rawlings' English sense of humour? Coralie herself? She wishes only to forget her miseries. And yes, to enjoy herself. She wants to get her self-respect back. Mister, how does it stand with your own?

He would try to avoid hypocrisy, and is not going to creep about burdened with guilt. Coralie is one of those girls gifted with unusual physical presence, whose strong powers of attraction are the cause of much unhappiness. She has a vague idea that he has got into some trouble on her behalf, is even running some risk, but he has shown her kindness and she wants to make a generous gesture; take it in the same spirit. Anything else would be insensitive.

Political considerations? No, no no, five times if need be. Mr Rawlings knows, is tactful enough not to mention it. The Carabinieri might be pointedly straightfaced about it, but they don't have her wired; it isn't supposed to compromise him. Coralie herself does not think, like Dumas' Madame de Chevreuse, "what a pleasant souvenir it would be in her old age to have damned an abbé" So that he slept – as far as is known – soundly, and felt next morning much aesthetic admiration for a magnificent body on its way to the bathroom.

And in the plane from Milan to Brussels, "Well, that's over, and a good thing too." He has grown out of what his former PJ chief used to call his morbid taste for complications. There is nothing much he can do about Eamonn Hickey, that good drinking companion who became a friend. He can go back to Mr Suarez (a careful man whose fault, perhaps, is to worry overmuch) and say "It's pretty certain now that Eamonn wasn't anything at all to do with the IRA. Since it's nothing to do with us, we're well off all round knowing nothing."

The Holy or Benito Suarez wouldn't be content with that. He'd continue to worry; he'd go on asking why. Castang could frighten him, then. Well, there was this girl. I've met her, she's a nice girl. Unusually attractive. (Mr Suarez hates stories about girls. Girls had got his predecessor, Harold Claverhouse, into big trouble and the Blessèd-Benito, virtuously married to a Spanish lady of really staggering plainness, won't want to know.)

Even if he did . . . "Got tangled up through her in some obscure traffics over the Swiss-Italian frontier. The Carabinieri," a type of Guardia Civil for whom Mr Suarez feels a respect perhaps exaggerated, "are going to tidy that up. The tricky bit is that there is or was an IRA connection through finance, and someone seems to have known about that, enough at least to make the Brits sit up and pay heed." Repeat: – We're well off knowing nothing about it.

For Mr Rawlings – "kindly" – had driven him to the airport, Castang aware that he was being seen-off.

"No trouble at all; I have to be in Milano anyhow. Least

88

we can do after snatching your nice Alfa." And yes, Coralie had been a lollipop. "You can see for yourself that she'll come to no harm. Your friend Bonacorsi agrees to keep her out of harm's way while they clean up that antiques fiddle, since she might get viewed as an informer." And, while sitting still for a moment in heavy traffic, short of the airport, "No one can say when an IRA cell might shift from being merely a collector of useful intelligence towards the centre of a conspiracy bent on havoc, but we think now your man's involvement was fortuitous."

There remains what Vera calls a metaphysical area.

What had impelled him to go all the way to Ireland? Not that she should understand all that stuff tedious ol' James Joyce kept on about . . . Going out of their way, on the road home, across country to an obscure corner of Hampshire; that had not been just in order to be "friendly to poor old Jane".

There was a pattern. He was part of it. Vera is part of it. Coralie is part of it.

In fact, it is possible, going to bed with Coralie has a significance that has nothing to do with moral or political affairs. She was not just a little treat, given to him to lick.

Voi che sapete, que cosa e amor. He still doesn't know whether when mouthing his rudimentary Spanish he might not be talking Italian. At nearly fifty he does know a little bit about love. Not enough; not nearly enough.

Brussels

Extraordinary: Zaventem Airport, that hell-hole, but he was home! The smells, hardly to be called invigorating, of the shuttle back to the Gare du Nord, itself another hell-hole. The taxi, smelling so northern, so familiar, so delightful (sod taking that tram!) – he was home! Oh, the joy of finding the hill above Schaerbeek drenched in sunlight. The trees in bud, so heart-rending. Vera, in an overall, "sculpting".

Not real sculpting. She was not hammering at stone. She was not proposing to cast some monumental thingy into bronze. Quite apart from other considerations she hadn't the money. Big pieces of stone are most attractive but wait till you see what it costs heaving them about. Not to speak of the mess it makes. No; Vera had started to collect "pieces of wood". She took over his "carpenter's workshop". She put her pieces of wood in his big wooden vice, with lumps of poly-this & that to prevent their getting bruised. Then she sat and stared at them. Then with his hammer, his wood-chisels, she started chipping at them. Sculpting? He had taken rather a dim view of this, accustomed as he was to Vera in her personage of a "Czech" artist; very graphic, very silver-point, very pen-and-indian-ink: very clean. This new mania for the Shapes of Things, for Forms, for cutting, scraping, Chiselling – this is something altogether new.

Vera is a professional, even when she slips into the semi-professional, even back into amateurism. She sells her work – not often, and for no great sums, because she is never fashionable, can never and will never be the darling of a gallery. She has stopped working with oils. "I'm not a Gwen John and I never will be," (in London, in the Tate, spending an interminable time in front of "Dorelia by lamplight in Toulouse"; sailing past Vanessa Bell saying, "*Scheisse*"; pursuing William Blake while he muttered saying, "Stuffy in here".)

Odd that it should have been here that the passion began; Vera is odd, as well as embarrassingly rude: Henry Moore was pronounced, "exactly right for putting in front of the Chancellery in Bonn," while poor Eric Gill — "Dominicans and incest; could one imagine a lewder combination?"

"We better get your Czech arse out of here," said Castang glancing round nervously. Surely it couldn't have been those pieces of wood by Barbara Hepworth? Her last Christmas present had been a nice book all about Matisse bronzes.

She was in cheerful spirit now, wanting to know about everything in close detail, like Mr Rawlings.

"Yes, there were one or two slightly cockeyed details," not anxious to put too much emphasis on Miss Rawlings getting shot a bare hundred metres away from where he had been sitting, "but the main thing was I got into trouble with the police and was rescued by Bobby Bonacorsi."

"Le Grand Robert!" (a French joke since the "petit Robert" is a dictionary). "I hope you gave him my love."

"Over the phone because I didn't see him. Now a General and extremely grand. But I got told off for doing some police work of my own; thrown out of Italy in disgrace. The essential fact in all this is that the Brits no longer think Eamonn was IRA."

"Oh good," said Vera staring at her piece of wood and picking up a knife. "And is that the end of it?"

"I don't know, have to see what Suarez thinks."

"Well, if you have to go anywhere else tell him I'm coming too," scraping. "What was Eamonn doing in Italy, anyhow?"

"Oh," said Castang, "mixed up with some girl."

Mr Suarez was in a fussy, executive frame of mind. "What's this you're telling me? I don't like this at all."

Castang realised that he had said both too much and too little.

"If this scandalous IRA suggestion can now be seen as

definitively scotched . . ." (Harold would have become interested in the word 'scotched' – "Tells you something about the English, that, and 'welshed' just the same", but Mr Suarez is not conspicuous for humour), then that's to the good and your time hasn't been wasted. But then you reappear with this tale that one of my staff is tied up with a woman running a call-girl business! We must get to the bottom of this. From what you tell me, the police should know about this story; exactly the kind of rumour that spreads and grows and loses nothing in the telling, all around Brussels, just imagine, the next time I have to go to some official reception and everyone is grinning at a juicy titbit. You weren't away a couple of days, that's to your credit. Take the weekend, but I want a report that will make it perfectly clear, that nobody in this office is or was engaged in any sort of criminal misbehaviour . . . It's very good, Castang, to have got the Brits to pay your expenses."

"I can't stop girls getting on the train to Milano," said Commissaire Mertens, "and I don't even try; there's nothing illegal. Of course," heavy sarcasm, "If you want to have Belgium annexed as one of the United States, then I daresay we could invoke one of those marvellous pieces of legislation they have, like transporting girls across state lines? There are always half a dozen of these phony agencies. We unstick them and three weeks later they pop up again under a different name."

"Talking of names," said Castang, "does this name mean anything to you?"

"Thomas Lhomme? Not to me; sounds commonplace enough. In this connection? We'll ask the computer. One will remark in passing that it doesn't take much to put the poor weak-minded thing off – no, nothing there, any further information?"

"Said to be a German television producer."

"Then don't ask me, apply to Westdeutsche Rundfunk, have you got any producers running callgirl rackets, and the bloody computer will drown you in them."

"Oh, all right, just asking," said Castang crossly.

He was long home before it struck him. Vera, deaf to

plaintive enquiries as to what was for supper, suggested that he might perhaps like to go and do some shopping, and it was while meditating about onions – onions? but so much for the feeble-mindedness of computers – at the greengrocer (who is called Lejeune, and in Flanders would be called De Jong), that a stray particle struck him somewhere in the synapses: one alliterates in moments of emotion.

Rawlings had said that the chap who put in a rumour to the Brits that Eamonn Hickey was dipped in some covert IRA activities was called de Man. A literary reference, some way above Castang's head. Brit jokes, about the Deconstruction industry, and that very English form of humour, a clerihew, about Jacques Derrida, that great guru whom even Castang, being French, has heard of. De Man is a common Flemish name: Castang, back with his onions (Vera being Czech, and an artist, is a great consumer of onions on both counts) got on the telephone.

"Oh, that's a very old story. It was a fellow during the war, wrote for '*Soir*' at the time it was under German occupation influence, glorifying various Nazi hegemonies, Jewish Bolshevik conspiracies. Well-known collabo. Became a big shot professor of philosophy in America and got into hot water on this account, but who's this de Man of yours, some relation?"

"As far as I know, only an association of thought, but thanks anyhow."

Nor did one need a computer to penetrate the television industry; Germans like to have great serried masses of fact in orderly availability and there is a man Man. Quite well known, lives in Baden-Baden and is believed at present to be under contract with SüdWest Funk. That's right; right there – if I'm making myself clear.

And police instincts satisfied by these laborious computations, "You said you wanted a couple of days off," while peeling the onions.

"Badly. My piece of wood doesn't go the way it should."

"Would you like to go to Baden-Baden?"

"The name's familiar but where is it?" Vera asked, puzzled.

"Down in the Black Forest. Between Karlsruhe and Freiburg." Castang has been there before, has indeed some hair-raising memories, but these were not told to Vera at the time; it was not an episode to feel at all proud of. In fact he wondered what the German police computer would say now, if someone were to tap out his name . . . But like that of Paul de Man it would be very ancient history.

"Oh yes, please," said Vera eagerly. "You've no idea how jealous I was, your going off to Italy. The girls will get on very well by themselves, in fact they'll be delighted. Is it still this business of Eamonn's?"

"We don't know the half of it yet. Suarez wants to cleared up. Probably won't be more than a couple of days. The weather in Italy was sort of patchy. But if we go south now – well, pack your bag and take some warm things too; we'll take the car."

Interlude, a few hours on the Autobahn

I don't know that I think while I drive. Stream of consciousness, call it.

I told Vera about Coralie. Most of it . . . Eamonn chased the kitchenmaids. This "Good Soldier" type is not all that uncommon. They were necessary to him. But Coralie was different. That is Love. Vera will accept that.

" 'Love consists in this, that two solitudes protect, and touch, and greet each other.' That's Rilke." Even I have heard of Rilke. But then Yeats. A poet she found in Ireland. Pronounced Yates. All right, Lejeune is Dejong in Flemish. And de Man is Lhomme in French. We won't quarrel about names.

" 'In true love, desire awakens pity, hope, affection, admiration, and every emotion possible to man.' "

"I won't quarrel with that either."

"Yeats doesn't date." (A Harold Claverhouse sort of joke.)

He went in for magic, it appears. I don't dismiss that. I am a coarse materialist, but I have an artist wife.

"He was studying Japanese art. He speaks of an animal painter so remarkable that horses he had painted upon a temple wall slipped down after dark and trampled fields of rice. Somebody came into the temple in the early morning, was startled by a shower of water drops, looked up, saw painted horses still wet from dew-covered fields, but now, 'trembling into stillness'," entranced.

"Means just that it was a fucking-good painter,' said the coarse materialist.

"Oh, Bra-vo." Very crude Czech sarcasm.

"But wasn't that the way Eamonn saw Coralie, trembling into stillness?"

"Less bad! There's hope for you after all."

Belgian autoroutes are lit along their entire length. That unending line of gaunt gallows lamp-standards is like an early surrealist movie. All too easy to imagine a corpse, pinioned and hanging from each, the "strange fruit". But beyond Liège is Aachen and Germany, the Ruhrland one will not see from the autobahn, and which Vera loves; the Piranesi ruins left by the bombers; huge Gothic fragments of tower and chimney, the abbeys and cathedrals of nineteenth-century industry: it is on the tram between Dortmund and Essen that one will begin to understand Germany.

But from the autobahn and its ceaseless ballet of shark and barracuda you must not lift the eye for a second; not if you wish to avoid being eaten. Not until brought altogether to a standstill by the big sign mounted on a truckbed, the four letters picked out in winking lights saying *Stau*, where the sharks have struck, and lives have trembled into stillness, but there's precious little dew hereabout.

A bad one it had been. Quite under control before we reached the patient, accustomed police flagging us into single file, inching us past at walking pace. From the car in front, children as well as adults were hanging out of the window to gawk at the twisted metal, the broken glass, the blood. One cannot blame them; it is a deep and a terrible thing in man. I do not forget that I have been a police officer.

Only Vera does not look. Her eyes are shut and she is speaking.

'Turning and turning in the widening gyre
The falcon cannot hear the falconer;
Things fall apart; the centre cannot hold;
Mere anarchy is loosed upon the world.'

"That's your chap Yeats, is it?"

"Yes, – the growing murderousness, our unending paranoia. And that was back in 1922; he was upset about the Civil War. What would he say, now?" We were gathering speed; she could look, again. "You seem rather fraught. Would you like me to drive?"

"I could do with a beer. But I can hold out, up to Frankfurt."

And when, after lunch and that much-needed beer, I got back from a pee, she had written out two more lines on her scratch pad; tore them off and handed them to me while she went to explore impressive, extensive German plumbing. What will it be – a hundred, two hundred thousand pees a day? This patient old European soil of ours.

'The best lack all conviction, while the worst
Are full of passionate intensity.'

The lines put me in a trance, and when I looked up she was standing there smiling, clutching her handbag and her shopping-bag and her precious sketchpad; looking old, but slim still and beautiful.

"We, you see, are safe. Our conviction is that we have love; it is unbreakable. We put our passionate intensity into frightful quarrels. But they are quite unimportant. Have you the keys?"

What, philosophy? On the autobahn? But she is a woman; she does not Deconstruct. I had been stewing, brooding; about Eamonn, and Love, and the IRA, and Mister Yates, and all around me Germans are throwing in food as though their lives depended on it, with passionate intensity.

Vera, while an excellent driver and much safer than I am, is not really good on the autobahn. It's a macho invention; keeping the rhythm depends upon cutting out brutally in front of pursuers; set upon brutal egoism. The women, in fact, are worse than the men.

She is far too polite! She will get boxed in, on the inside lane behind a big truck, and won't move out as long as the fast brothers are there overtaking. "Timid Granny", I say, getting cross.

"No," unperturbed. "A woman; a real one." That we should arrive twenty minutes later? I should gibber? I do, though.

I closed my eyes: I've had a solid German lunch and two splendid beers.

Why am I writing all this down? What importance can it possibly have?

But I think this "interlude" important. Everything I did, and thought, later on, I believe carried the mark of this day, on the road, through the heart of Germany. The autobahn, they say, are arteries, carrying the blood in sharp, scarlet spurts. I suppose that the parallel, physiologically, is accurate enough. The big Lastwagens: do not ask what is inside them. Do not look. When they crash, as they do sometimes, jack-knifing murderously across the chaussée, falling over the edge, lying disembowelled, it is always better not to enquire into the contents. They might well be and often are highly-toxic chemicals. Still more horrible are the dreadful by-products of the big modern hospitals, where we will be so kindly and so technically cared for, and where, inevitably most of us will die. I can accept this. There are women there and some of them are Veras; gentle girls with gentle hands.

I was stunned by the beers; I closed my eyes; I can hear Vera talking to herself in Czech. We speak "the European jargon": our shared language is French since her German is a lot better than mine and our "English" is literary. Czech is her private language; it sings, curses, speaks to tiny children. It "takes Czechs to really understand Germans". And "the French, the English, they only listen to themselves. They understand nothing; they never will."

"English public-school twits, talking about 'Czechos' as though they were the opposing cricket-team."

When we drove through England – "This is tripe. This is not the real thing . . . This is it" – we were in Wales. "Not that self-satisfied Cotswoldy bourgeois Britland."

Indeed I should understand this. Henri Castang was born and brought up to be French. But I hope he has learned better since, the prig, so smug and so vain.

I pushed the seat right back; I lowered the back-support; I stretched my legs. Vera is safe, past Mannheim and Darmstadt, down to Karlsruhe and the corner, where we won't follow the femoral artery down on to Stuttgart and Ulm and Munich: we turn off for Basel and Strasbourg; for Baden-Baden . . .

I was not really asleep. I was like the sailor in *The Caine Mutiny*. "Who's sleeping? I was sending Morse Code mentally." This book was popular with French policemen, all of whom had officers exactly like Captain Queeg. Are the police likely to know anything about love? Eamonn felt despair.

Coralie is young; she has not yet found it. A bleak prospect for my bold, my adventurous Lydia; for my timid, my vulnerable Emma. Who could be surprised at a girl imagining she will only find it with another girl?

Looked at in any terms it's hard, bitter. When I first saw Vera, the young, intense, sweaty Czech child . . . I thought then of the marriage of convenience: you give her your name, a consular document; it gets her out from behind the Curtain. You say "Good luck". Good God, I knew one old English journalist, delightful and civilised old-queen, who never even slept with his. "But it's the least we can do, isn't it?" I slept with mine; I lusted after that skinny little flat-breasted Czech gymnast. I wasn't to know that this would be "My Love".

Years and years later, I met an Englishwoman. Her name was Pearl. She had the most beautiful walk I've ever seen in any woman. Isn't that extraordinary! Big tall English girl and she was Tamara Karsavina! And what a lesson she taught me! She burst out laughing!

"Don't you know? My-Love won the Derby in nineteen forty-seven. Every woman in England had betted on him." Yes. I only got one, but it was the right one . . .

"We're coming in," said Vera in a soft voice. We were off the autobahn, rolling at a soft sixty on a country road with trees in their spring leaf; tender, young, green.

Baden-Baden, May

The place altogether different, and where the law does not run. Or, not as on the autobahn. Opportunism; brutality: here, things will be just a tiny scrap less crude . . . Certainly there will be no question of "police work" in the ordinary sense of the phrase. While dozing in the car, it is probable that Castang's subconscious was working on this. That here one could no longer be linear, male, materialist; deductive or inductive. Vera's presence introduced a different dimension, in which time and space, the mechanics of enquiry, take on a fundamentally different meaning.

Basically it is the same as many other little spa towns in central Europe. There is a cosy, sheltered valley surrounded by the steep but gently-wooded hills of the Black Forest; there is a favourable micro-climate. And one must remember that in May . . . this is the moment when every German says "There's nothing quite like spring in Germany," and it's perfectly true.

The "nobility" of central Europe came here to enjoy itself, on the pretext of drinking mineral waters which are good for a number of ailments affecting the elderly and the self-indulgent – and to gamble. There is still a casino, and one of Europe's best racecourses, in more seductive surroundings than Epsom or Ascot, gentler and prettier than Longchamp or Chantilly. In theory "Cheltenham" would come nearest, but alas the reality of Cheltenham is a poor affair. The public buildings are in the coldly neoclassical "Graeco-Roman" style of the nineteenth century, and quite hideous, but there are modern buildings in the town, some successful, while in the hills are delectable Lustschlossen of eighteenth-century baroque. They knew how to enjoy themselves: they still do. The Germans have taken great pains to make this a place where the harsh discords of the modern world will not jangle the nerves. It is full of elderly people, and all extremely rich. Castang would agree that this is a disgusting sight; and if you don't like it, stay away.

It has to be said that Vera, the austere, the often-rigid, even occasionally the fanatically-puritanical, falls in love with it all instantly. She has never been to her own delicious, Czech Karlsbad or Marienbad (she would not even wish to). If suffices that here she finds what in her imagination they ought to be, once were. In all the places whose names begin with "Bad" – there must be a good hundred of them – there's nowhere quite like this. Neither in Spa, nor Vichy, nor alas in Bath. Where architecture is not matched by ambience.

In a pleasantly old-fashioned hotel – large rooms, high ceilings, big windows and generous bathrooms – Vera showers, potters happily naked looking out at trees, lawns and parasols, revels, changes, says that she wishes to walk. Castang, though it can hardly be called unselfishly, is enchanted to give her pleasure: it is an emotion she habitually neither feels nor seeks. Self-indulgence, that male preserve to which he had given free reign in Lugano, in the Val Solda, conspicuously by the shore of Lake Como, she allows rarely. And when she does it is with a sense of fun, a childish delight, that touches him. She works hard and does not often unwind. He is struck by how badly she needs a bit of fun.

Along the valley, beside a skilfully landscaped brook, is a delightful walkway. It skirts clock-golf and tennis courts, hotels and homes-for-the-aged, cunningly trained trees and craftily-scaped bushes. No, the azaleas are not quite as rich as in Lugano, south of the Alps. The dwarf maples are not as thickly foliaged; the camellias are not quite as tall; the magnolias a little less obstreperous in their strewing underfoot of pale tobacco-shaded fleshy petal. But it's pretty luxurious. For the northern, gothic, Bruxellois Vera it's very grand indeed, and when she gets back to her hotel, oh yes, please do, and it's to be hoped that after a lavish dinner the effect can be repeated.

A little stroll, along the brook, before bed: the classic

breath-of-fresh-air; moonshadow casting patterns on the path. Careful German hands have arranged that the brook should have an even, shallow flow and shall make no noise. Stones are handpicked for fat, sleepy, bourgeois ducks to perch upon.

"Not very like Lake Como," said Vera jokingly.

"Not in the least like," said Castang, with such humourless over-emphasis that she was quite startled. "The Germans let them spread," he explained hastily, pointing to a Japanese maple stretching elegant fingers over the waterside. "Romantic garden. Classical-minded Italians prune them back to make the foliage grow thicker. I remember looking at one and thinking it was exactly like an ostrich asleep, on one leg and head under wing." A duck on the bank had chosen the same attitude. Helpful of it.

The next morning dawned pale and sunny, windless and effortless. The radio announced a low pollen count to reassure asthma sufferers. The breakfast waitress had a magenta bow in her hair and earrings to match.

"You have to work, don't you?" said Vera softly.

"I'm afraid so. And I hope I know how to go about it."

"I'm going to the Baths of Caracalla, to swim."

It is necessary to be a wolf. The slyness of the wolf is less despicable than that of the man.

'All taken in account I still maintain
That scelerate for scelerate
One would rather be wolf than man,'

remarked Jean de la Fontaine, who is full of sage advice for the police. To gain a footing inside people's houses Castang in his time has done a lot of imitations, including all the usual roles such as journalist, or earnest collector of statistics "conducting a survey"; the popularity of the Prime Minister is a reliable loosener of tongues. Useful too is the man from Gaz de France, "You haven't noticed any funny smells lately?"; everybody in France loves having a good sniff, and comparing the results with other experts. But the best of his imitations is that of police officer. The trouble with that here, is that he isn't German. Whatever the writers of sensational fiction may pretend, it isn't at all easy to do another language convincingly. Even if you have the accent right, the phrasing and the speech rhythms, the voice is produced from quite different areas of the mouth; beware of palatals, glottal stops and so on, if you happen to have been brought up in France. He had thought, true, of being the man with the Geiger counter, worrying about the high level of clicks around here. This goes well in Germany, where as it sometimes seems every childrens' playground has been built over a dump of toxic waste material, and the populace is ready to believe the worst of every innocent building site: it is quite easy to conceal a few harmless grammes of a radio-active chemical about the person. But he just isn't German enough.

A police impersonation will do, this close to the frontier. Indeed Castang has impudent pretences to his debit, right here, and if anybody were to call some real German police the computer would become alarmingly radio-active. It is a risk he must take. Not a great risk, since the most blameless civil servant with police on his doorstep will wonder what he can possibly be guilty of without even realising it. Nobody has a conscience so clear that there isn't somewhere a sub-paragraph D upon which he has slipped from virtue.

Remains the where of the interception, the timing. Some police villains prefer the home, in the evening (a wife can make for nasty complications of the where-were-you-last-night type, but she may too be thoroughly bloody-minded); others like the office, where Joe will be vulnerable to snide remarks from eavesdropping colleagues, for even where Joe is popular, office politics will always ensure that there's somebody happy to stab him. Castang isn't fussy, but notice that last parenthesis; he hasn't told his wife more than he had to. His "Well, there's a man whose traces I came across back in Bruce" may yet prove his undoing.

Does Mr Paul de Man, a.k.a. Thomas Lhomme, have a wife? Does an independent television producer keep office hours at the studio? Castang had decided upon a pounce early in the morning – well, fairly early.

Some preliminary reconnoitering was called for. People of good social standing live "up the hill", but would it be an apartment block? He was pleased to find a house, in a garden; both small, but bijou. This tells a lot more than any anonymous frontage. Hereabout it represents a lot of money. In order to make a lot of money you have to put a lot into it: he means that it takes money to make it; you have to juice a lot of people, and not just tipping the head waiter. You must juice your appearance; the car for example. Castang looked at the garage with pleasure. Snappy BMW – it would be, wouldn't it? But at home, meaning the chap wasn't off somewhere; and not locked away denoting a prudent mentality, but parked carelessly on the forecourt. No sign of a woman's car. Anything else one can deduce before ringing the doorbell? Garden, as well as house, trim and nicely cared for. Juice; a reliable cleaning woman, a probable contract with a gardening firm. But it could mean an interesting man; the fresh paint and clean curtains do not denote a squalid gangster. He gave a long solid ring at the bell; chap might still be in bed.

There was no great wait; the door opened and he was looking at a tall good-looking man with bright blue eyes, bright wavy blond hair, a trim forty and looking younger.

"Herr de Man? Police." It is important to get the intonation right, a lack of emphasis but without any note of apology. The eyes changed and the face frowned, but so would anybody's.

"Police?" Slowly, and thinking about it. "Where from? What police?"

"France. Or Belgium if you prefer." A line rehearsed, it must be said, to disconcert. Eyes surveyed him from head to foot. He was soberly dressed with a collar and tie, the shoes as always well polished; since coming to Brussels he has cultivated a respectable appearance and the anglophile jauntiness, a bit horsey, of former days (hacking jackets, whipcord trousers, Tattersall check shirts), has largely disappeared, but like a good cop he still insists on expensive and well-polished shoes.

"What identification have you?"

"Monsieur de Man," in French and smiling – accomodatingly. "It's very informal. I should hope perfectly polite. Nobody's being Military." The look of suspicion diminished without vanishing. "Do you know," still uninflected and with no note of cajolery, "why when it's judicial we always come in twos? So that two independent words can support each other. So that there can be no talk of improper procedure nor unfair pressure. So that there can be no threats, no considerations – and of course no opening for bribes. And I'm just here on my tod."

The face cleared. "I suppose you'd better come in then, rather than stand there nattering on doorsteps."

There was a pleasant living-room, furnished with plenty of civilised taste; nothing either too dear nor too cheap, and with no display of vulgarity.

Book-shelves and pictures, a table full of paper, the grey machines which take the place of typewriters but three times the space; the big tape recorder, but it would be the little ones he'd have to keep an eye out for. An attractive room; no doubt an attractive man. He wore a grey flannel suit, good if crumpled and certainly due for a clean; the shirt was expensive, and on its second day: clothes for a morning at home, and he hadn't shaved yet either. A bit red-eyed, as though he'd been up late the night before, but healthy-looking, confident; not about to get the heebyjeebies on account of police in the house.

"Talk French if you prefer. Belgium, did you say? Like a drink, perhaps?" in the hearty voice of a man who could do with one himself. He'd be feeling more anxiety than he showed.

"Do German cops take a drink, d'you think?"

"I'm not sure I know. Chivas all right?"

"Bit early. A beer if you've got one," pottering after him into the kitchen. Always accompany them; lean on them, it's a rule.

"Sure. Well, what's it all about then?" kicking the fridge door shut and tinkling with the ice cubes. "Let's sit out, since it's a nice morning."

"Oh, a number of little sins," pouring the beer carefully so that it wouldn't froth up too much. "Nothing to take too seriously. If Monsieur Lhomme is running call-girls to Italy it doesn't bother me much." That got home, he saw with satisfaction. "And I suppose if the Herr de Man had been dishing out cocaine at a party the Belgians wouldn't be much interested."

The mouth got small and hard. "But you seem to have been getting interested," over-carefully.

"Perhaps. What I came here for: know a man called Eamonn Hickey, do you?" and watched the mouth go tighter.

"Never heard the name."

"No? As the Brits say, 'I've 'eard different'."

"What have the Brits to do with whatever it is?"

"We'll come to that," lazily. "I'll tell you a story. There was an English general, field-marshal maybe. I don't know when this would have been. Nineteen hundred? And ten, maybe. He was in parade uniform, been trooping the colour I dare say. High boots, spurs you know? And going up the steps of the Foreign Office, or the Horse Guards maybe, some IRA men put a few bullets in his back. Interesting how instinct comes out. He faced about, and he tried to draw his sword. That's pathetic you'll say, and it's very English, and d'you know, I find it admirable. Tenacity as well as courage. They don't give up easily."

The man took small sips at his drink. "It would make good television," he allowed, "but what's it got to do with the price of Kodak shares?"

"I'll tell you that, too. What would the German government take seriously, among the activities of a private citizen? Being or having been a Stasi agent? Having Rote Fraktion connections? Selling chemical weapons to Libyans?"

"Or whatever. It wouldn't do, would it? It would be mere supposition. And if I found anything like that floating about, I'd reach for a lawyer, don't you know, and take steps to put a stop to it. There's such a thing as defamation of character."

"Then let's tighten it up a little," colourless. "In the course of shipping girls to Milano – no, don't interrupt – Eamonn Hickey appeared an inconvenient obstacle. Irishman, with a lot of odd acquaintances. I ought to know; I was one of them. So that a man said a quiet word to the Brits, that this acquaintance was worth looking into. And they'd take it seriously; tenacity is their middle name. They wouldn't be contented – you made the point yourself – with mere suspicions. Or anonymous denunciations. They'd want a little something, to carry conviction. So that this source, which was you – and don't attempt to deny it – was able to provide them with a juicy bit of bait. It follows logically that you know more than you should.

"No, I haven't finished yet, Monsieur de Man. These

Brits are pertinacious bastards. Scratching about in Italy, who do they turn up but Coralie. They aren't going to forget you. They're going to draw their sword, mate. I think then you might well find the Staatsanwalt after you, and not with a mere shred of suspicion. The IRA is also of interest to the German government. Good neighbour policy, let's call it."

"And who are you, and where are you, in all this haze?"

"Why, call it Brigati Rossi or Rote Armée or Libya, the IRA interests us too. And if we'd like a more personal motivation," ferocious now, "Eamonn Hickey was a good friend of mine and I'd like to know how he came to be dead."

"You make threats. Put a name to them."

"Is it a threat? More of a warning. I don't come here like the three witches, saying you could be deprived of your living , your comforts – the easy money. But I'm sure as hell saying that unless you tell me, and pretty quick, all you know, think, or guess, then the mortgage on this house is in trouble, and there'll be a severance up there at SudWestFunk, and when you read the small print Allianz aren't going to insure you any longer."

"Do you want another beer?" asked de Man getting up.

"No, I'll be on my way."

"I can't walk on only one leg," carrying his glass. "Tell me your name, Mr Uh, and where I can reach you. A business deal needs some thinking out."

"Agreed, but just until tonight. I'm only a bird of passage."

The biggest of stage settings? One wouldn't say that, thought Castang, since there are too many places in the world one hasn't seen and never will. In Japan, probably . . . Quito is said to be extraordinary . . . And what importance has "big"? It is meaningless to say "bigger than Disneyland" or "no, Las Vegas takes up more space". That sort of comparison is meaningless also in quality, because this is adult entertainment: that castellated assemblage on the other side of the valley looks, it is true, like a cardboad cut-out, but bears no relation to the palaces of Cinderella or Bugsy Siegel; it is by a long way more sophisticated.

Nor do any of the huge monuments of past time apply – Angkor or Cuzco, seen only by Castang between pages of the *National Geographic*, but empty, unpeopled, irrelevant.

If a comparison could be made at all (he is sitting on the terrace with a beer in front of him, waiting for Vera, trying to work it all out in his mind), then perhaps with a film set designed by megalomaniacs in Hollywood's palmiest days. Yes, of course – by Erich von Stroheim, with that lunatic, magnificent insistence upon the smallest detail being "real".

For it is real. These are not actors but ordinary working people and I am one of them. Yet it is all most carefully and elaborately staged – *ensceniert* since designed with a German breadth and executed with a German precision, every detail given a German thoroughness and loving care, and it all works perfectly . . . I am an actor here. I have strayed in from the squalors of the appalling world outside and here I am no longer my own man; I am trapped in the mega-production by Irving Thalberg and must accept the directions shouted at me through the megaphone.

Vera has walked down the hill from the baths (which have delighted her); has taken renewed pleasure in the shopping quarter. Never were there streets so lavishly lined with tubs of oleander, or with such orange trees in their white-painted *caisses-de-Versailles* – she has to reach out and touch the foliage, to be quite sure they aren't plastic. She has a vision too, quite different to that of her husband, indeed diametrically opposed since she sees it all as minutely small in scale. Little polished boxes of intricate marquetry; rosewood, satinwood, king- or tulipwood, palest, hardest lemon and the dark rosy flush of mahogany. Bunches of peonies from deepest crimson to sugar-pink, interlaced with white and cream – those lovely ones with the faintest carmine blush upon the petals, the exquisitely delicate veining of blood.

She hates the boxes! She feels momentary terror at being entrapped, airless and asphyxiated, within these spaces of veneer so hard and soulless, so very highly polished, so perfectly even. Here the real world has been so unanswerably excluded.

Or think of the slaughter of earth and of water. She has reached the little bridge across the Lichtenthaler Allée, where last night she had strolled with such pleasure, her arm taken by her man. So exactly engineered to be neither brook nor river, but a pleasaunce precisely three metres across and five centimetres deep, and her mind is filled with gigantic excavators relentlessly strip-mining an ore-rich landscape; with butchered forests, with hideous dead rivers and her nose is filled with the metallic sheen of toxic. deadly chemicals spilling their Sauron-reds and greens upon the helpless, innocent water. Her leg gives way, so that she has to hold on for a moment to the ornamental post-and-chain.

None of this here concerns us. We do not see these things, here. Therefore they do not occur. Just how thin the crust is, how easily broken through, how fragile our equilibrium and what an inferno of molten lava boils there beneath our feet; ignore it. Understand, once and for all: we don't want to know. She plods on past the stage where the orchestra plays on summery afternoons. Hundreds of people seem to be eating large Disneyland ice-creams – and then she sees her man sitting in a characteristic attitude, ludicrously engarlanded in window-boxes of petunias, of the waterfalls of ivy-leaved geranium, and she waves enthusiastically; there at last is a recognisable human being. We have destroyed in the name of ideologies, shouting about Pope or Marx or Führer. Now we plunder out of pure greed. It was not Satan that destroyed America. No more than never having enough money, from the first Conquistador to the last junkbond dealer; so *boring*.

"I only want something salady," said Vera.

"That's all right; we help ourselves inside, bring it out here and send the girl for drinks." How heartless he sounds: How inhumanly mechanical. Castang is enormously hungry, takes cold fish, cold meat, cold chicken. Queasy Vera is hungry too (has been, after all, swimming all morning) yet can still bear nothing but vegetables – and even the asparagus is viewed with distaste. Even an (excellent) German beer is refused on the childish grounds that, "Czech is better" and, "how dare horrible Americans pretend theirs is real Budweiser." Castang is reduced to saying, "I do see," several times in a conciliatory mutter. Gradually she cheers up, admits that the Baths-of-Caracalla had been immensely enjoyed, and takes a cigarette, which happens about once a month and is a gesture against intolerance.

"How did you get on? I'd like a small ice-cream please," and has a long argument with the waitress about passion-fruit.

Castang: one of his small post-prandial cigars. "Why d'you think Eamonn married a woman like Jane in the first place?" Vera psychologist, Vera theologian; both good, but at their worst both illuminating. "And as you know, I was good friends with ol' Jane."

But how about a good afternoon walk then? The post-prandial digestive stroll will extend itself into something more vigorous. I mean if one gets to the end of the Lichtenthaler Allée and then goes on – what happens then? But he must go back to the hotel first because he'd like to change his shoes. And there is that red light winking on the telephone meaning there's a call, but this can be handled while she's in the lav.

The call was from de Man, suggesting dinner together, saying there were things he wanted to talk over, naming a diplomatic sort of address. Oh, yes, thought Castang cheerfully.

And I think I understand Eamonn better since being in Ireland. A complicated Jesuitical Volk. Going to confession one day and sleeping with the curé the next . . . Which, inevitably, meant beginning to unwind a long and tangled ball of string, because yes, complicated and Jesuitical were two adjectives one would use about Eamonn. But why do people drink? Or pick their nose? Or gaze at themselves in the mirror? In Castang's police days one didn't ask oneself such questions. They came to mind, but one hadn't the time to pursue them, even if the inclination existed. That was a job for the examining magistrate instructing a case, and sometimes it would go on a long time, accumulate several kilos of paper, give employment to many lawyers, doctors, psychiatrists, and all the people who tell you that giving up smoking and eating margarine are the keys to eternal life.

Eamonn Hickey had wished to rid himself of some very notorious tangles in the persona of the Scotch-Irish. For one's father this had been a question of sheer resolution. Colonel Maurice Devaney dated back to a time as difficult as any in the traumatic history of a tormented land (Czechs would understand this – yes, or Belgians – better than the French or the English who had not the remotest clue).

"Let's see," counting on her fingers, "that generation, he'd be born around 1920 or even earlier; you don't know much about this but I read it up at the time I knew Iris . . ."

Partition, and then the civil war. Devaney decided where his loyalites lay, went into the army like so many of those northern Irish: almost a military caste, no? A nursery of professional soldiers. Even in southern Ireland there were many, many. And what a powerful magnetism is in that soil, that after the end of your active life you come back and live in Sandycove, with that view out over Dublin Bay and behind you those strange compelling hills called the Wicklow Mountains – which would remind Belgians of the Ardennes and that other odd frontier Volk, the Alsaciens, of the blue line of the Vosges or the Jura. Difficult enough for Colonel Devaney, but military discipline is a way through the tangle.

"But now imagine Eamonn, whose mother is southern Irish, and Catholic, and whose name is Hickey . . . When would he be born? Late 'thirties. De Valera time, all Ireland still had the most vivid memories of the Civil War. Collins was assassinated – another real tough called Kevin O'Higgins, shot coming out from Mass, I think as late as around 'thirty-seven, and this is all in your blood and it sinks into your earliest childhood. I'd have been perfectly ready to believe he was IRA. If I were Brit, and somebody came and whispered in my ear; Eamonn is an able and respected Community man, a good legal mind. But going back, he's a mind which belongs to the government in Dublin. They've an extraordinary appetite for legalism there; chicanery is in their every fibre. Oh yes, I'd be asking myself questions.

"Put it like that and it's as we know, he has this powerful sexual possessiveness, this hunt, this thirst after the kitchenmaids. All right, I'm not a man, I've no wide experience. I have to remind you that I'm – that you're the only man I've ever slept with. And you are a considerable sexual fascist. No no, I promise I'm not going to be tedious. But if you take this extremism of Irishness and all the political complexity of it, and you add the extremely devious nature of the character which is also so very Irish,

111

and on top of that you put the total madness of Irish sexual theology: then nothing will surprise me.

"I'd say that Jane was an enormous effort to counterbalance, to — to disinfect all that. I mean she's English, she's straight as a die, I happen to know she'd be burned at the stake rather than be unfaithful to the man she married, she has this intensely firm and tenacious English character.

"I ought to know something about this. I mean I never have, I mean I never would."

Eyes aflame.

"I'm incredibly old-fashioned? Or am I, I wonder, a few years in advance? That Spanish phrase — Sun, Sex, Seat? Well, the sun's already finished because it gives you skin cancer. Seat — unless we do something bloody quick about the private car, we'll be driven mad around the same moment we choke and roll over and die from the toxic metals. Remains sex, don't think I don't like it, I love it."

Out in that innocent German countryside (a never-ending stream of Mercedes cars, trucks and heavyweight lorries along the main road five metres to our right hand) Castang is falling about laughing.

"I enjoy it myself," said Castang. She is funny when she embarks upon one of her tirades, so that yes, he does get the giggles, but she is shrewd and he also feels respect.

"I wonder," she is saying, "whether a historian wouldn't find a co-relation. Perhaps even an equation? That when, like now, there is an exaggerated sense of sexual freedom it means that real, personal liberty has become much diminished."

There's always plenty of sex, says Castang copwise. Human beings are what they are. People didn't always talk about it so interminably nor, as you just remarked, display it so blatantly.

Perhaps you're right. Perhaps, thought Vera, love is there just the same but people don't talk about it. As though they were ashamed of it.

It seemed a good moment to tell her about Coralie, who to Eamonn had been more than just a kitchenmaid; so much more that he hadn't known how to cope with it. Love like the Loch Ness Monster, Surfacing when you least expect it.

"Have you seen her? What's she like?"

"Very pretty," colourlessly. "Remarkable eyes, a blue unusually brilliant and intense, and beautifully shaped. But hardly Greta Garbo, you know. Fine figure, fine features but otherwise I'd have thought a commonplace enough girl," wondering whether he was sounding too careful. Not already said too much? Vera didn't seem to have noticed.

"Being very pretty doesn't have to mean much. Look, here's a village. We can get a bus back; my feet are telling me I've had enough." A respectable, boring, rich and perfectly ordinary village, and who knew what went on in it? Plenty of sex: love too, no doubt. It doesn't show.

He didn't want to talk at a bus stop, nor in the bus: one doesn't know who talks French, or English either, nor whose ear might be hanging out. He had never learned any Czech; the children, to whom Vera talked Czech when they were tiny, can patter quite well. But in Germany one would be wary even of this. He has had to subdue a loose mouth; he has often been told how indiscreet he is.

Vera took her shoes off, lay on the bed and wiggled her toes.

"My man," said Castang, "my fellow here has asked me to dinner. I will take you, of course . . . that will disconcert him further."

"Really? I'll be quite curious."

"He's made a great fuss about it being a purely social occasion. Insists on the hotel along the road; the very grand one."

Vera sat bolt upright. "I've nothing I can possibly wear in a place like that."

"Your cotton frock will do very well," said Castang tranquilly. "Long and a bit bare on top, you'll look very nice. Place like that, full of whores and pop singers who go there because it's the most expensive, you wouldn't want to look like that anyhow."

"But why," alarmed, "insist on snobbish surroundings?"

"Two reasons, I think. First, that sort of place is discreet, there's lots of space and they're used to people being secretive about business deals. And I think he needs a show of luxury to give him confidence."

"I must go and do my hair," rushing for the bathroom.

It's a short walk and a fine warm evening. One wouldn't bring the car anyhow. Can't have a dirty Golf among all the shiny limousines. One isn't worrying about the people inside. Sure, a few very smart old gentlemen in panama hats, a few old ladies covered in diamonds, but businessmen look more loutish still in flossy surroundings and Vera is not in the least intimidated really, well aware that she looks very nice and even rather pretty. Probably, said Castang, he'll be wearing a white dinner-jacket; amused at the thought.

Very nearly! Silk and mohair, so that Castang was jealous. Brought up short by the sight of Vera, and covering it with the social manner.

"My wife," said Castang. "I told you there was nothing formal about our business."

"Of course. I'm delighted. I got them to give me a nice corner because we do quite a lot of television business here."

"Television business, that's exactly right," said Castang. "Nice and quiet."

"You'd like some champagne I'm sure. This menu's rather pompous; do tell me, Madame, when you've any special taste."

"Vera . . . when I was a child I longed to be called Magdalena von Dietrich. Don't worry about me, I like everything."

"Bordeaux d'you think?" fussily, "or Bourgogne?"

"We'll follow our destiny," said Castang. Candlelight and silken footsteps, but it'll be back to spaghetti and meatballs tomorrow. "We aren't in Brussels so I won't eat fish, and steak is all wrong in a place like that."

"I'm always a pest, being Czech, can I have fish, please?"

Plenty of good wine, Castang was thinking. Who cares what you eat in this kind of house – it'll all taste the same. But give Vera lashings of champagne and you'll be surprised. People fall in love with her simplicity, and when she's a bit pissed with her perfect honesty. Transparency. "Good like bread". Or as the Prince, the Leopard, says "like a true Sicilian", there's nothing as good as water.

Krug the man's asked for, and here's a magnum coming; television must pay pretty well. (One of Vera's favourite quotations: "Not that wine, dear, it's what we keep for the police.")

He holds silence. Vera, alarmed by this, talks.

Herr Paul de Man, not knowing quite what to make of either the silence or the volubility, orders a lot more wine (rather a fuss about Vera's fish). The men eat boring old veal, even if there's bits of lobster with it to make it more exciting. He's keyed up to the extreme, notices Castang, and there are fears, and there's emptiness; he'll drink a lot, and Castang will by God help him drink it. His own philosophical tenets are simple enough.

> When that I was a little tiny boy
> With a heigh-ho, the wind and the rain.

The rain it raineth every day; Vera is the theologian in the family.

"It's only elementary-school philosophy," (she isn't even noticing what she's eating: if it's white it's halibut; can't be salmon because it isn't pink.) "Roughly, a pleasure has to be paid for; but you have to want to pay for it. When you were a child you had to get up early to go to school. On your free day you could stay in bed. This is only a pleasure when it's agony on the other six days, but further only when you don't go on lying-in. After more than an hour the pleasure's no longer worth having. Right?"

Laughing, Mr de Man allows this.

"You understand because you are an artist, which is better than being an intellectual."

"It's possible to be both," he says, fatuously.

"The same with girls. You have lots and lots of them. Notoriously the expense is great and the position preposterous, but the point I'm making is they're no fun any more, it's like lying in bed all day. One good one is worth more than all the women in this room." Careful, thought Castang; you'll scandalise the waiters. But she doesn't raise her voice. "Haven't you found it so?"

"Yes," said de Man. "I have."

They sat on when the restaurant emptied, and the head waiter had to whisper tactfully that perhaps the Herrschaft would feel more comfortable outside on the terrace. Vera does not want any more to drink, and it's just as well, thought Castang (who does) that neither of them has to drive. That large puddle of brandy is going to tumble Monsieur de Man into a *vin-triste*. But he is coherent still; so am I, so am I, and which of us is now the more reckless?

Down at the end of the garden the brook, as tactful as a waiter, is just audible. Beyond, the lights of soft-voiced cars flit behind the trees of the park. Smile of the summer night. Around these three unimportant personages, courtesy of the hotel, is a pool of space. At a distance other men in silk suits, other pretty bare-shouldered women (but Vera wears no jewellery because she possesses none) are speaking softly: of love perhaps, or ten per cent; how much does ten per cent of love amount to? Paul de Man had wanted ten per cent of Coralie, and found it not enough.

A girl; no more. Nor was she Maria Magdalena von Dietrich: girls seldom are. But she possessed earth magic. Had Castang not felt it himself on just such a night as this on the shore of Lake Como?

Lake Lugano

A phrase could be found, thought Castang: he was lying on his back gazing at the ceiling; breathing shallowly since his chest hurt.

"Subsequent events interested him no more"? It wasn't quite that: he had not been executed. Though it had, as he was beginning to gather, been a close thing.

"Knowing he is to be hanged in a fortnight"? No, because his mind had not been concentrated. Nor had he "known". Wasn't he more like the man in *The Occurrence at Owl Street Bridge*? He had gone off with the rope around his neck. He had survived. Or was it that he had not yet reached the bottom of the rope? Why was his chest so tight, painful?

There was a legend about a man "they couldn't hang". Trap stuck; damp had swollen the wood or something; they'd tried several times – nice for the chap in question! There'd always been these legends , in France too, stories of the blade refusing to fall. Everyone struck dumb by superstitious terror; the machine had worked perfectly when tried out that morning, and the moment they took the chap off it worked afresh. Divine intervention!

He'd never believed a word of such stuff. As a young man he'd been like all criminal-brigade cops, blood-thirsty. "Pull the string myself," as they all said. Until he'd had to go on parade one day for the real thing, and that had cured him: he'd come away with the realisation that one could only survive this if dehumanised. So he'd survived now, and was he still human? He slept a little.

He woke, and his mind seemed preternaturally clear now, over the last few days: was that normal?

He had thought himself clever and had nearly lost his

life! By a number of shifts he'd wrung out that bit of information Paul de Man had had to give. It hadn't been much, but it was vital. Vera had done it by persuading a pliable, weak-natured sort of man (finally rather likeable) that he didn't have to be a total shit; not for his entire existence.

They'd done it between them, the classic technique of working in pairs; the nice one and the nasty one alternating the interrogations. Castang had done this before, had even done it with a woman in the other role: the novelty was that this woman was not a professional, she was his wife; she had not known. But there lay her natural force; in her truth, in her simplicity. It would not have worked, but for that.

For the man was frightened, both by Castang's threats and by Vera's persuasions to look himself in the eye (and they'd been helped, on both counts, by palace surroundings and a great deal to drink), but there was something of which he was a lot worse frightened.

Well, yes, . . . he'd been the cat's-paw, he'd been chatted into things; he had been charmed along the road of money and power – "all this" – and sometimes he'd been shown the razor held inside a silk glove. Being the literary type (seduced by Vera also being "an artist") he had tied himself up in fantasy scenarios. Be it the IRA, or the Mafia, the Red Brigades; all those lurid stories of private armies implanted by the CIA in order to Combat Communism. How often has Castang not heard them and damned those meddlers who had filled so many weak minds with phoney ideologies and Monopoly money!

The difficulty here is that some of these stories have a grain of truth in them. Far too many people in "secret services" had been paranoiac, and in possession of far too much money. Castang has known better people than this poor type, entangled in such tales. And he knew of clever people who fed these fears, and manipulated imbeciles to gain a heftier share in the money and the power and the leverage which both gave.

He was not surprised when the name "Lugano" popped up at last. "But be careful; be careful. This man kills people."

How much did de Man know, or guess at? He knew that

Eamonn Hickey had been killed. He did not know that "Margaret Rawlings" had been killed. Castang, who knows, guesses that he is only half a step in front of "Mr Rawlings" who will surely come to work this out, and soon. His guess is that it is the familiar problem of being too close and not seeing the wood for trees: he himself has the detachment of being no longer a police official but still having (rusted) police training. He has the great advantage of having a mandate only from Mr Suarez.

So that he doesn't give a damn about the IRA, save only that it blackens the memory of a colleague he had respected, a friend he had loved. One could guess indeed that Eamonn, the Scottish Irishman, had become unduly curious because the thing about the IRA (easily forgotten in the welter) is that it's Irish! Coralie then had been perhaps the second ingredient. To make guncotton, to make nitroglycerine, Castang knows just enough of chemistry to know that these are simple – even schoolboy – chemical manipulations. Well, let the Brits worry about the IRA (and so they did).

Paul de Man, paid off with (lavish) commissions on quite unimportant things like a call-girl agency, would be an ideal smoke-screen for obscurer and nastier sources of income (surely Eamonn had seen through much of this, had been over-curious, had been over-confident, had paid an over-great penalty. He'd been too clever, and too aware of it. Hadn't Castang, now, made the same mistake?)

The Irishwoman, "Shavana", and her friends; weren't they another set of marionettes? They much enjoyed the excitement of their little antiques fiddle, and had been well paid for the flow of funds into Switzerland. A "little picture". Worth "ten thousand". Nobody would tell that the real price was three hundred thousand ... But the Carabinieri could enjoy themselves with that one! To Castang it is coincidental, of a piece with a dozen such he recalls from his time in the "Beaux Arts", his "Carlotta-connection". But was it only sheer coincidence that Coralie had been a "girlfriend of Shavana's" and a part, however tangential, of this neat little network? What fate had decided that her parents should live in the Valtellina, that she should be happy to show her lover the home that she loved; that when "out in the hills", on some innocent picnic party, Shavana should have exercised her talent for amateur photography? That Eamonn should have kept those photos as a "souvenir" of a happy and an innocent day?

This is quite a commonplace; being "in bed" and for good reason, he felt sore and battered, glad to be there. Nice rest. His chest hurt – and itched. He explored this; elastic strapping. His right hand was bandaged, swollen, and felt mangled; he remembered some surgery being done on this, fairly minor but painstaking and lengthy. Tendons and things needing repair – troublesome. He was a bit woolly about this; they'd given him a shot of dope as well as antibiotics, anti-tetanus, unpleasant and a worry too because his left hand, while good enough for most things, had never been brilliant since the time his left elbow had been shot to bits. A long time ago now, but he'd be in trouble if there were two bad hands. Only a desk cop now, but one needed the hand for paperwork.

Irritatingly he felt quite fresh and active mentally, impatient with all this lolling about in bed. His mind was in a turmoil and he would do better to take deep breaths (but they hurt). quieten the mind, sort things out. Things? No, people. He'd have a bit of a sleep, first.

Italy

Yes, Italy, definitely. The shores of the Lake of Lugano are Swiss in bits and Italian in others. He'd floated about rather. But this was Italy.

Handicaps. To himself he thought that with Vera around he hadn't felt anxious to pursue the question of Coralie too closely. A hypocrisy, and it had done him no good.

Handicap for Paul de Man, driven silly by that same Coralie. Ready for dirty tricks, and extremely imprudent. Jealousy of Eamonn had led him to denounce this accredited agent of the Dublin government as an IRA "mole" in the Community. Other spirits had started to take an interest. Including one who already found Eamonn Hickey a thorn – and now something worse; a threat.

Handicaps to Coralie: every man she meets wants to get into bed with her.

This is just a chain of reasoning but it was sound; Castang has tested it. Eamonn became an object of curiosity to the British secret services, and they're a nosy crowd; the Spirit doesn't like that. To prevent them getting any closer, better suppress Eamonn. But damned bad luck, Miss Margaret Rawlings is unusually well informed about Italian doings, so she'd better be suppressed, too. Lucky, on the other hand, that Castang didn't get suppressed. Well for him, that he was thought a fool and a fortunate source of confusion. But when Castang arrives in this quiet and pleasant lakeside town, that's altogether too close for comfort. Never two without three, that's a piece of schoolboy wisdom.

There's been a telephone call back to Switzerland. No doubt the same busy little bee that had reported Miss

Rawlings' extreme curiosity.

The Spirit lived a quiet, comfortable life in Lugano, and wanted it to stay that way. And who was he, this spirit?

"I don't know what he is." De Man, on the terrace of the hotel in Baden-Baden, talking freely at last. Too freely.

"He's all sorts of people. One of those multiple personalities, perhaps, that American psychiatrists are fond of discovering. Three of them, six of them? A dozen of them . . .

"I've met him. Here. In the bar there. Business proposal, he says. You're a television producer, you get around, that's fine, I make a dollar for you and you make one for me, okay? I listened, fool that I was.

"He's called Pedro de Subercaseaux. Is that his name? I don't know. He could be French. Or Italian, or Spanish. Or South American. The lot, for all I know.

"He did indeed throw things my way. I've been doing pretty well. Professional – unprofessional . . ." Dully now; too drunk really to care.

"I wasn't to know I'd fall in love – what's that mean? – with Coralie. I realise I'd have done anything – for what? To get her? To make her love me? How stupid it all sounds now. I was insane. She was gone on Hickey, I'd have done anything – anything I tell you – to get him out of my light. I'd have killed him myself – happily.

"No, that wasn't his suggestion . . . I thought that out myself . . . maybe . . . you might be right . . . he did say that Hickey was IRA . . . I don't know any more . . . I thought only that the Brits would take him off my back. No, Hickey. I mean it worked and it didn't. I thought the Brits had assassinated Hickey. And then Coralie wouldn't touch me with a ten foot pole, though she can't have guessed.

"I've been pinning my hopes on these Brits. They aren't like us. I mean we might seem hard on top, and I suppose you think me pretty soft underneath. But they aren't like that. They have this big sentimental front of being sorry for birds or flowers, or the dear doggies, and underneath they're proper bastards. They'll take out Subercaseaux, if you give them the word. But am I to believe you? Don't be so sure yourself you're all that clever.

"He lives in Lugano. Very respectable citizen. You won't find it easy to get anywhere near him.

"Looks like? Hard to say. Looks like anyone. About forty I suppose. Tallish, looks good, hard condition, good skier. Looks like anybody round here – sort of man you find yourself standing next door to, having a piss here in the lavatory. You wouldn't notice him. Just don't ever let him know any information ever came from me. He kills people . . ."

One cannot say how much of all this Vera has taken in. She's surfing somewhere, by herself on a wave. She has a disconcerting habit of piecing things together quietly and reproducing the whole intact, days after one had forgotten it all.

Lugano

But that's easy. You go straight down the Karlsruhe-Basel autobahn. You follow the Swiss valleys. On both sides of you there are nasty jagged alps. Castang hates Alps. Down here it's all milk chocolate; prosperous little factories with acronym names: probably selling chemical weapons to Libyans, but it doesn't show. Ask, and they'll all be busy making your television screen ever wider and deeper, so that it ends by eating your entire room and you along with it. And then you bowl through the tunnel. Way up there above you is the famous confluence of passes, the Nufenen and the Gries, the Furka and the Saint Gotthard, but down here in the intestinal tract it echoes and booms borborygmically, you switch your lights on and suspend belief and suddenly . . . For up there it is Swiss and terrible but down here it's still Swiss but it's really Italy; it's the Ticino and it's Bellinzona and it swings away in the graceful speedy curves of the Autostrada and there's the lake and it's Lugano. And Lugano is only an Italian version, Swiss-franked, of Baden-Baden. They take their evening constitutional along the lake instead of the dear-little-brook. The Japanese maples are fuller and shaggier, for the Italians like to clip them to make the foliage thicker. Vera exclaims with delight at massive magnolias spreading carpets of petals for her to walk upon, at the towering banks of hundred-year-old camellias. But Castang rubs the heel of his hand alng an unshaved jaw and looks up at the Monte Bre. That's a fortress up there and how is he to crack it?

They crossed the little harbour, for Vera wants to walk, after hours stuck cramped in the car, and followed the coast road which winds along the base of the mountain. As far as the gates of Villa Favorita, hidden behind its wealthy screen of cypresses. There Baron Thyssen had had his splendid collection of beautiful pictures. They aren't there any more: to see them you'll have to go to Madrid, humbly ask permission of la Reina Sofia. It is with that sort of frustration that Castang looks upward at those very rich residences, clinging by their eye-teeth to the steep slope. This is not going to be easy . . . and he is rather silent, on the road back into the town. They have dinner in the hotel, that reliable, Swiss meal of veal escalopes chipped into fingers Züricher Art, à la crème, with rösti potatoes (surely the most genial of Swiss inventions) and rather bad local wine: and over this Castang mulls. "Thinks". One must try to outflank.

In the morning they will take that same coastal road which serpentines round the Monte Bre, and twenty kilometres along one passes the frontier, and here, so steep and narrow above the lake shore, is the Valsolda – where Miss Rawlings had taken him – immortalised by Fogazzaro (whose little house in Oria is no longer open to literary travellers, having been ransacked by people who cannot read).

It is hard to explain to Vera, but he still has the book, Miss Rawlings' book. She will like this book. The story of how Italy shook off the paralysing grip of Austria. Of how difficult it was for Franco the idealist to understand Luisa the intellectual. But they never stop loving each other, even when their adored daughter drowns in the Oria boathouse.

"Stop here," he says, (Vera is driving; she is safer on this narrow coast path; one would hardly dignify it by the name of road.) It is still early in the season. They have only expensive rooms, with a balcony, overlooking the lake. It is what he wants.

For it's a test, of sorts; nothing much; only a finger trying out the temperature; a finger licked and held up to test the direction of the wind: rather as the golfer will pick up a tuft of grass and toss it in the air. Only a few weeks ago he had passed a night here in the company of Miss Rawlings, and he was looking for that little blink and flicker of recognition.

He didn't get it, either from the desk (true, the room

had been booked, and settled, by Miss Rawlings) or from the chambermaid who in her "waitress" clothes was languidly clearing glasses from a terrace table. Yet in a place this small, and an occasion that recent, he would have expected – what? A word, a sign, a message? Perhaps they were simply being tactful, since he had come here with a different woman!

Here in this minute village Rawlings had a contact. She had gone out at night and talked to someone. It had been for a purpose that she had come here. Had he really escaped all observation? The customs post was only a few kilometres down the road, and in their Belgian-registered auto they had passed through without a glance. Hm. It was neither for the worse nor the better; he had had no great expectations from this small piece of coat-trailing.

It has been a hot afternoon; it is shading towards a beautiful shimmering evening. Vera, who is tired, has arranged herself with her book under a little tree on the terrace. The Valsolda is too steep to suit her never-very-brilliant leg. (He had been lazy too, eaten a large meal, drunk several glasses of wine, lolled about.) Behind the tiny square (little church, two shops and a pub) it is nothing but flights of steps. He climbs a bit but not seriously, perches on the stones of half-crumbled terraces full of oleander, cherry-laurel, populated by lizards. The lake, foreshortened, looks oddly small. Behind him are Alps, jagged and unpleasant. On the far side the hills are smaller but have a harsh, brooding look. Wooded, faintly sinister. And in between is the lake; magnetic, enigmatic. How deep is it? He knows from reading Fogazzaro that it is subject to violent winds, sudden storms. When he gets back he sits upon his balcony, smoking too much, fascinated by the water. They eat dinner, a mediocre and unmemorable meal. (Had it not been better, on the former occasion? Or had Rawlings been better company?) Vera yawns, says she is enjoying her book but feels no energy, will probably go to bed early. Tourists, round about, are noisy and drink a lot, discussing their day's doings and eagerly planning the next. Castang feels both bored and restless. Could he borrow a boat?

Why, yes, certainly; at the little landing-stage is a tatty punt-like craft kept for tourists to play with. The smart little motor-boat is private property, and so are the two or three sailing dinghies, but this is the sort of thing the locals use for a desultory bit of fishing and he is well content: he paddles himself out, lights a cigar just in case there should be gnats or mosquitoes, lets himself drift in the beautiful evening light: it is still day, but twilight comes sudden here in the mountains and already a light or two begins to twinkle across the lake on the shady side: the afterglow of sunset is still – delicately, subtly – lighting the Valsolda. Up towards Porlezza a couple of sailing boats are tacking languidly about; over at the far side a motor craft is bumbling with the engine scarcely above idle; fishing, one presumes. He has eaten perch said to be from the lake; he doesn't think there will be anything very grand to be found in it nowadays. Vaguely, he tries to recall the name of the great fish to be found – formerly – in other alpine lakes on the French side. You had to go deep for them. The "omble chevalier", that was it.

But what would you find here now? There are too many people, too many motorboats, too much sewage and fertiliser-nitrates and pesticides and God-knew-what chucked into the lake. It's ecology will be very fragile, and now, like everywhere else, so damaged as to be irrecoverable.

Castang watched birds. There was a kind of fish-hawk, no osprey, more a scavenging buzzardy type like himself. An osprey dives, no? Like a bullet. Comes up with something better than these trashy minnows or whatever they are. This thing cruises in languid circles, swoops negligently, comes up with small-fry, digests that at leisure. Very like himself.

When it happened, it happened damn fast: he was given very little time to react, even if he had been sharp, alert, prepared. *Bereit sein ist alles*, he said as he went under.

A terrifying sudden, hooded masked figure like something from outer space. Only a swimmer in diving costume with a snorkel, not even with air-cylinders on his back. From anywhere out along the shore this can do a just-underwater trudge. Nobody will notice wavelets or bubbles in the evening light. Least of all sleepy Castang.

The figure reared up, gave the punt-thing a violent toss. And he went overboard; it would have taken a miracle to stop it.

The idea was perfectly simple; once a man in trousers and shirt, dozy and unprepared, is in the water it will be very easy to hold him and keep him under. You are a swimmer, seal-like and slimy in your rubber suit that affords no grip. You have only to cling, holding him under in an enveloping asphyxiating grip. You will breathe, quietly, through your snorkel. It's all prepared; he is unprepared.

Castang fought. He is wiry still, the ex-boxer, the ex-gymnast. But all that is years ago; the seal is large, heavy, with strong choking arms and legs. Castang is swallowing water; he has no chance.

There is a name; its name is Laguiole. A French village; you pronounce it Layiole. It lives in his righthand trouser pocket. It was a present from Vera.

They are pocket-knives, of an attractively sinuous shape. They are fashionable; every lycée-student in Paris has one, for sharpening pencils and cutting sausage. They aren't like those stupid Swiss Army knives which will cut your toenails, pick your teeth, and saw up timber. For tourists they are sold with handles of horn, quite snazzy. But his has a delicate grip of ivory (quite illegal, now yellowing attractively). It has only three functions, since Castang is not in the Swiss Army. One is a marlinspike. One is a corkscrew, and this is useful too. Since – as is well-known – be you on a picnic or at home it is always the corkscrew that is lost, forgotten, gone – "Lost, lost, my precious", as Gollum remarked.

The third element is a blade. It has a sharp point, shark-like, and a razor-sharp edge because it was made from a good piece of steel. Castang had got into his pocket with his right hand, and is struggling now to get it open with his teeth. Between the two brass guards the eleven centimetre blade, narrow and fast as a barracuda, is tough to open.

Castang wrenched his fist free, loaded with the knife that is heavy for its' weight, and struck a clubbing blow at the mask. He was very nearly gone; it was nothing more than instinct; he could not say truly that there was training, or experience, behind it.

This was hopeless; he never had a chance. At the best of times it is a waste of breath to complain that one was taken by surprise, and he hadn't any breath. His lungs were full of water; he could see nothing, hear nothing. At the start there was a thought, that if he could reach the knife he might still touch land, again. But even with his feet on solid ground there would be no salvation, because of his fatally weakened, useless left arm which could be nothing but another dead, dragging weight like this great fat stupid thing which did not fight but which gripped him with all its heavy inert limbs around the waist and hips and bore him inexorably down. And then it cut his brain off and there wasn't any thinking any more: he was gone.

Who then was doing the thinking? It could not be his mind; that poor object, water-logged and blood-starved, was washing about in an Italian lake. *Entre deux eaux* but this phrase, "between two waters" is meaningless except in French, and if there is a next world and if this is it, do they then talk French there? Something is thinking for what used to be him, since it can't be that poor soggy lump that got drowned.

In this new world everything seemed to be very nasty. He could not see and he could not hear, but he was consciouss of pain, a lot of pain. Had the black men got him then, and were they tormenting him, as people in some remote former childhood had sometimes told him would happen? He'd never really believed it; that would be a bitter business were it really so. Would this be a circle then in the Inferno of Whatshisname? That appeared likely because now he seemed to be talking Italian. Dante, he said, Dante. Yes, that was his voice, he could hear it.

"Dante."

"Dante, who's that? Got the wrong number," said a loud voice and oddly jovial. That wasn't his voice, he could hear it wasn't. But this was him thinking! It wasn't a new world after all, it was the same old one as before and it was horrible and it stank too; he could smell the water, he could smell the lake and there were other smells at present unidentifiable.

"Stop that, it hurts," he said querulously.

"Oh good, that's very good," said the voice. Yes there were black men and yes they were tormenting him and he couldn't understand why they should wish to hurt him so, but then these odd telephone voices became confused and fuzzy.

"Stop shouting at me then." And then he didn't know any more at all what happened after that. Perhaps he fell asleep. That would be nice; he needed rest badly, and peace. And Vera. He thought that perhaps he said "Vera" before it all slipped out of reach.

When he woke up he could see. That was nice; he opened and shut his eyes a couple of times to be sure. Yes, eyelids and yes, they moved up and down when he told them to. A recognisable world because that is a ceiling. A familiar world; that is Vera. A great flood of happiness and love moved upward through his chest; this hurt but it was not horrible.

"Ow."

"Yes, try not to jig about; that's bound to hurt."

He thought about this for a while. "What's this, a hospital?"

"No, it's just a house. But it's true, there are hospitally smells. Alcohol, elastic strapping, you've some broken ribs. But that's good, you're coming round nicely. We were afraid of some brain damage because you didn't get any oxygen for a while there."

"Why have I got broken ribs?"

"Because you were in the water and they got you out and they gave you artificial respiration in the bottom of the boat. It got the water out of your lungs though."

"I remember . . . he squashed me. And then there were the black men. Beating me up, I thought I was a child, and in hell."

"There isn't any hell. What black men?"

"I think he might mean us," said a new voice.

Castang turned his head on quite a nice cool pillow to look at this new voice, and recognised his old enemy; the Carabinieri captain, but he was wearing ordinary clothes and looking distinctly more sympathetic.

"There were two of our boys in a motorboat. They fished you out, and well for you they did. I'm sorry about the ribs, their notions of first aid are fairly crude, but it did the job; you weren't without oxygen for very long. So we apologise, but you can still be grateful because it was quite a narrow squeak."

"What happened to the octopus? Which got me? Him in

the black wet suit?"

"You settled his hash. He didn't need any first aid. If you want to know he's in the morgue. Not talking, but we know who he is. Was."

"What happened to my hand?"

"The knife closed, and stuck in it. There was quite a lot of blood. The doctor has patched it up and thinks it'll be okay. No tendons severed. Rather a nasty cut but the arteries and stuff are all right. We see much worse, with broken glass." This professional voice was doing Castang good.

"Thank you," he said. "I'll thank them too when I'm up and about."

"He shouldn't be chatterboxing like this."

"No, I'm all right. Darling Vera."

"He's okay," said the officer briskly. "This is quite a time later," he explained. "We called the doctor of course, at once. He gave you a few shots, anti-tetanus and whatnot, and he put you out. You might have a residue of shock. He'll be in again. So will I. I'll tell you all about it, then. Your wife will stay with you."

"Yes," now pleasantly drowsy. "Think I'll have a bit of a sleep."

The sedative or whatever it was had been no stiffer than it had to be because he woke feeling quite good, and the hand was bandaged but could hold cups of soup and suchlike. One didn't just feel lucky to be alive at all: well, there was that, too. The doctor came, a bald round head, a pleasant giggly manner, and looked him over; tested his reflexes and was full of congratulation.

"You're fine. Some rest for the ribs, a couple of shots of antibiotic for the hand, your wife can give you those. Get up and do pipi if you feel up to it. Take things good and easy. Eat if you want. Let your own inclination guide you, as long as you don't exaggerate. No pretty sexy nurses needed. One look at your wife she'd show them all the door anyhow, from what I see of her."

"Darling Vera," said Castang, delighted.

"Where is this?" later eating vegetable soup with enthusiasm. "Not a clinic, doesn't feel like a hotel or anything."

"No, it's the doctor's own house, you're in his guest bedroom and I'm sleeping right alongside you."

"Oh good."

"He's awfully nice, he didn't want to move you until he was sure you were all right and then he said for these couple of days it wasn't worth moving you. He speaks good English and his wife's a poppet, we talk German in the kitchen. The Carabinieri brought you in the car, you were half-dead, then they came round the lake – you're here on the Italian side – and got me, I was in a fantod, but they were very sweet. The Captain fixed the hotel, he's a perfect lamb; you were an appalling pest, he said – but he was laughing – and exactly what they needed to rout out a nest of corruption and some quite sinister people. In fact," getting slightly worked up, "I'm jolly glad you did put paid to that fellow; I shouldn't say it, and God forgive me, but he tried very hard to kill you and he very nearly did," jaw extremely set and would be pulled apart by horses rather than cry. "But you worry me, you worry me, why do you insist on taking such risks."

"I didn't know there was any risk." Castang humble, Castang penitent, Castang clumsy clown.

So indeed the Captain would have said and not minced his words either, but for feeling rather sorry about Castang's ribs, busted by his own men. He came in that evening, uniformed but a bit five o'clock shadow. Como wasn't far away. Only got to cross the lake. Castang had had another little sleep by then, had got out to do pipi – "Easy does it. Lean on my arm" – and felt stiff, sore, but thoroughly alive. Had indeed asked, he hoped politely, Vera to take her clothes off. "Well well; the sap seems to be running inside the tree." She had cuddled him, complaining that the strapping round his chest did stink rather. He groaned at the idea of shaving; she borrowed an electric razor from Madame, put a lot of eau-de-cologne on his face, lugged him into the bathroom and washed him with a good deal of sploshing, but now he felt lovely. No sunlight, no Seat, but soup and sex will make a new man of poor-old-battered-Bibi.

"We took Joe down to Milano," said the Captain wearily, taking his cap off, rubbing his hair in a way Castang remembered, "to be post-mortemed; we fished him out of the lake. Once we had him on the slab we could put it together pretty well, what happened. Because of the knife. You don't remember anything at all, huh?"

"Not after he tipped me out of the boat. It was pretty clever. He rose up suddenly, gave that punt thing a bloody great heave and I went over, of course. I'd noticed nothing. He must have swum out quietly, just below water. There were a few boats, but quite far away. To make as little disturbance as possible his idea was just to clutch me tight and hold me under. Which worked, as near as possible."

"My men were in the motorboat. They recognised you – through binoculars – and were wondering what the hell you were doing out there. Had you got some bright idea? And lucky for you, they kept an eye open."

"I was watching birds," apologetically.

"That was bloody near your last bird," fairly snappish. "But you had the knife."

"Trouser pocket. First thing I thought of."

"Well for you. You knocked his mask crooked and that upset him a bit. Just enough, as it happened, because you got the knife open."

"With my teeth I think. My left arm's not worth much but he was only intent on dragging me down and holding me."

"Big man. Would have been a snip for him, but you slashed him. Across the chest."

"I did? I've no idea."

"Slashed his suit, slashed him. Nothing much, but enough to make him wince and slacken hold, perhaps, a moment."

"I recall nothing."

"Aha. That's interesting. One doesn't feel a superficial cut under water, but you got him on the nipple with the blade, and he felt it, he let you loose for one crucial, critical moment."

"I was gone by then."

"Well, thanks. Congratulations on a good homicidal instinct. Don't know whether you learn that in Paris, but I'll take pains not to hassle you in a swimming-bath."

"But what did I do?" blank; genuinely puzzled.

"Boy, you went in with the rapier. Knife-fighter, huh?"

"I'm sorry . . . I really don't know."

"In the gut, all ten centimetres," said the Captain.

"Jesus."

133

"Never mind about Jesus, you didn't stop to turn the water into wine, you went in there."

"You surprise me. This last ten years I'm gunshy."

"You didn't stop to think about the detail."

"I didn't know. But my wife will be grateful."

"*Piqueur*," with the respect of a professional. "Nix gunshy."

"But what happened?" totally bewildered and not even believing in it.

"He fought you. Knife in his gut, took the stuffing out of him, but he had some fight left. He fought your hand. That way, he closed the blade. On your knuckles. When we found you, the knife was in all four of your fingers. Quite something. You could have lost those, be a mole henceforward."

"I can't say the whole of my past flashed in front of my eyes," closing his, "but then I wouldn't have wanted it to."

"Past flashed in front of Joe's eyes all right," with some satisfaction.

"Who was he?".

"In the Customs' service. Handy for this leak in antiques we've been getting our fingers on. Drugs too, no doubt. Organised like a basketball team; you pass, I'll score."

"Pasott," thinking of the far from attractive character in Fogazzaro.

"You're still a bit woozy," said the Captain kindly enough.

Vera appeared shortly afterwards with food. "I phoned Mr Suarez."

"What did you tell him?"

"That you'd fallen off a ladder in the garden."

"Mm. Not bad. A wheelbarrow, underneath. Knowing that microscopically detailed mind, the scenario has to be complete and convincing. I could have been picking cherries, an activity he would denounce as both dangerous and unnecessary. But how did I cut my hand? Perhaps there was a cold frame underneath. Melons or something. But how did I come to be so imprudent as to fall off this ladder? It was an old one, a wooden one. A rung had rotted, unperceived. I'll get off with a lecture then, about the design and construction of aluminium ladders. I will reply that in Italy the people are both poor and backward."

The doctor, consulted, agreed readily that gardeners'

ladders were dangerous things, promised a medical certificate to satisfy the most tight-fisted of insurance companies, and added the picturesque supposition that Castang under the pretext of cherries had been spying upon the neighbour's wife, who was blonde, pretty, and given to bronzing in her garden with no bathing-costume.

Next day he was so far advanced as to lurch downstairs to the consulting-room, where he got a new and simpler sort of elastic strapping for the poor ribs and where the doctor, a keen student of the English language, was perplexed as many before him by the vagaries of colloquial speech.

"Now the English say, 'Doesn't amount to a row of beans'. Meaning, I take it, something trivial. I don't understand this."

"Nor do I," offering his hand for inspection.

"Very nice," spraying lavishly. "Fix anything with a bit of silicone. Don't put it under the tap; you'll just have to stink. I was hoping you'd help me. A row of beans is a lot, to an Italian peasant. I was wondering whether perhaps originally it might not have been a row of pins."

"What would they be doing, with a row of pins? Brits are capable of anything," gloomily.

"I thought perhaps some lady dressmaking, with the hem of a skirt d'you think?" Castang had been accustomed to "ask Harold" and still felt a sense of loss. Never mind, this beautiful medical certificate – Mr Suarez could bite on that, yes and break his teeth. But to gain a bit of time, anybody else would have faked it. Why does poor stupid Castang have to suffer the pains of real breakages, genuine duelling-scars? Not fair!

Lugano, May

Being led for a slow and stiff totter along the lake front –
no, this was not his style. A day or so had to be won. Being
put under the shower, and scrubbed by his wife; a plastic
bag round his hand, held in place by a rubber band; asking
a Swiss pharmacy for Bande Velpeau – so French, that;
Professor Velpeau dated from about eighteen-seventy.

"We're going to Bologna for a day," he told Vera.
"There are anyhow some loose ends to tidy up. We'll go
and see Bobby Bonacorsi."

"Oh good," Vera was fond of Colonel – now General –
Banditto. Who indeed greeted her with enthusiasm, kissed
her lavishly, said, "The hell with all computers," and took
them both out to lunch, and indeed a very splendid, very
Bolognese lunch. This is not, as Vera remarked, a question
of pouring a lot of disgusting mince over the spaghetti.

But Castang was shocked. He himself might be a bit
battered, groaning a bit at getting his stomach under the
table because of Bande Velpeau, a bit awkward with the
knife-and-fork because of Silicone . . . Bobby-the-Allegro
was thin now and Lobo, the old-grey-wolf. Everything was
the same and everything was different? Had he himself
changed so much, in under ten years?

There was still that tremendous crackle of electricity
when they came in. It varies with the personality; with
some it is the big blue flash, with others a great red glow,
but it's unmistakeable and it occurs around the really
exceptional man/woman. One doesn't say woman/man, as
Harold, who had it too, remarked: the cadence is wrong.
There were other differences: Harold had been demol-
ished by women in a thoroughly English-romantic way.
General Bonacorsi is more like the judge who, asked if he

136

were married, said, "No madam, no, but I maintain a loose woman in Edinburgh". Harold loved restaurants; Bobby said, "Sorry, no restaurants. I don't mind being assassinated since I live like Alan Breck by my sword, but they're crowded places and I must avoid taking too many people with me: they only came there to eat."

"Oh dear, are you on the list?"

"One must presume so; I find policemen in my lavatory and like General de Gaulle I complain at the absence of privacy."

"I'll travel with you in your bulletproof auto," they both said together.

"Of course you would. But my guards wouldn't let you. So we'll go to the roof-garden. One meets all sorts of amusing people up there, but I'm going to be selfish today and keep you to myself."

"Am I allowed to smoke or is that against the security rules?"

"You're not allowed. You're encouraged. If need be, I'll order it."

"Smoke in one of our offices, you're practically in the Mafia."

"Interesting remark. The two situations are very similar. Die and it's because you were smoking, or so gigantic amounts of phony statistics would have you believe. A tree dies. This tree has not been puffing at a surreptitious fag? Then it's certainly Mafioso. *Quod erat demonstrandum.* As the admirable Doctor Tage Voss points out, everybody dies, and then nothing is easier than to blame the cigarette. His splendid book should be on the table of everyone in the government."

"Which isn't all in the Mafia."

"No. Quite a lot of it may be, but to go about saying that it all is merely reminds one of the anti-smoking fanatics for whom tobacco has taken the place of Communism. We're hustled into fortresses and there we're obliged to accept a great many boring constraints."

"These are marvellous," said Castang spearing more baby artichokes.

"Yes, we live extremely well. It's because they feel guilty about the exploding cigar. They worried lest we might be attacked up here by a helicopter gunship. We all agreed we preferred green leaves to the concrete bombshelter."

And at the end of the splendid lunch the pretty waitress came with exceptional cigars.

"Take several and put them in your pockets – in your handbag, Vera – we're good friends with Fidel and indeed I often think of emigrating to Cuba; it's one of the few civilised places remaining."

"Is she a waitress, even?" asked Vera.

"No, she's an Army corporal. Waitresses would be frightened of passive exposure to cigar smoke. So now coffee, and you must both drink a great deal more, I'm waiting for the sun to go down, and then you shall tell me what you came for. Because I'm aware, Henri, that your affection for me is real, but I also know why you're a bit stiff when you sit, and about this plaster on your hand. Lets have that changed, I've a lovely Army nurse on call, travelling about with seventy-five pints of blood and nothing to do."

"Counsel me," said Castang.

"Yes," said Bobby. The waitress gave him his cigar clipped, and cognac to go with it. They had noticed his discipline about eating and drinking, and how easily his beautiful manners could disregard it for them; how he had signed to his aide to take the mobile phone away. "We'll talk about that here, and then down back in the office if we want the computer."

"Yes," said Castang. Oh, what a lovely cigar. This was probably the best restaurant in all Bologna, town of good eating, and they came up here longing for polenta. "I've the time; you've the money."

"My dear boy, you're not in Brussels now. Don't let's have any of this actress-bishop talk."

"You're quite right, it's just that I hate the way the air-conditioning swallows the smoke."

Vera is also an enthusiastic passive-smoker and is also curious about whatever her man does not tell her . . . They went downstairs.

"Tap out 'Pedro de Subercaseaux'," suggested Castang.

"I'm glad you didn't suggest phoning it, I hate its silly voice. Interpret, shall I, since I'm facing the screen? This is an interesting gentleman. Lugano, well-situated. Hm, very well protected. What does it mean, mafioso – that he smokes Davidoff cigarettes? He's a cool customer. You won't get him by any of the conventional means. Right; Miss Rawlings, Brit Lady, keen on flowers and butterflies, no trace exists. We know who did it. Fellow called Giulio, blameless civil servant, good God, a postmaster. No evidence allowing us – skip that. Mr Rawlings, oh dear, the machine's done its nut, refers us to a number of ultimate considerations all Foreign Office, the British Embassy in Rome will be Most Offended if we pursue matters further, oh, all right.

"Empathy," said General Bonacorsi. "One bad turn that Americans have done us is to empty perfectly good words of all meaning because imperfectly understood. Scientists, otherwise impeccable but who boasted that art and language were without meaning for them; infinitely pathetic, do not allow me to ramble, empathy, good German word which at present escapes me."

"*Einfühlung*," said Vera.

"Just so. Not that soppy feeling-with but the genuine feeling-into. The stepping, if need be slipping, into another's skin. Here's what we need in this instance. The feeling-into." He left the machine alone, picked up his cigar, looking at Castang and the cigar alternately as though either might offer an answer but neither a particularly good one. "Perhaps, Henri. Who knows after all. You have the necessary cheek. You're better on your own perhaps, than in a group. Without trying to get into the boots of my colleague in Milano, we've discussed this sort of thing occasionally. An open kidnapping, plainly impossible; would create an Incident with the Swiss; out of the question. A surreptitious snatch has been thought of and rejected: frankly it's too difficult. No European country is willing to – no no, too many special interests at stake. Failing something new, untouchable . . . as for the USA" he put a query to the machine and made a face at the answer. "Categorically rejected. Sorry to be of so little help."

"Your thing there," said Castang colourlessly, "can it tell us what became of that girl Coralie?"

"If we ask it the right questions," pulling on his earlobe and staring past Vera at the window. "What was her name, again? Mixed up in that affair in the Valtellina, a suspected traffic in antiques wasn't it? We can ask Milano," keyboarding with the cigar getting in the way. "Here we are, mm, protective custody; they were keeping her out of the way. Wait a bit, here's more. Released on the authority of the instructing magistrate – she was no longer at risk – no subsequent trace. Query, left the country. That seems to be all. Hold on, there's a note on this, coded reference, what the hell is that?" trying a few more keys with his head on one side. "I thought as much, it's a reserved area, a Secret Service thing, it won't tell me any more without an authority I can only get if I go to some trouble; does that explain things to you then?"

"I might make a guess and say Brits."

"You see now for yourself."

"So your view of the matter in general, Bobby?"

"This is really what you came for, isn't it? . . . Let me think . . . On the whole, Henri, I'd say forget it. Nothing to do with your having no official status; that's an advantage if anything because the French government . . . but in Rome, the political will wouldn't be there. This fellow's got a lot of friends in Germany as well as Switzerland – you follow me? In Milano, your little misadventure on the lake, they took trouble because of cleaning out a spot of corruption – there was an official involved. But it was what in France you'd call an *opération ponctuelle*. A one-off, not part of a determined tactical sequence. If it singes the Italian wing of your friend in Lugano, so much the better; tells him they aren't totally supine. It might set him back for six months, before he thinks up another bolthole, but as you know antiques, while juicy, are just one of the rackets – so that looked at all round, I'd have to say you're on your own. I envy you; I'd like to be in Brussels myself. *Abrazo?*" opening his arms.

When it was Vera's turn she hugged him. "Bobby, Bobby – how long still?"

"Ten months, to the extreme limit on age grounds. Will I last that long?"

"You could go now."

"I could and I should. But one always tells oneself there's that little business to be cleared up by next week, in order to hand over a clean table. One will go when one's pushed. And one wonders in turn about the manner of the pushing. You won't catch me though, down in Palermo. Children – don't leave it so long next time, okay? Bye . . ." So they left him there laughing. Next time – next time?

Lugano

Convalescence well advanced, and a twinge from the ribs only when picking things up off the floor, a too over-enthusiastic morning exercise. One went to Locarno or one went to Isola Bella, and Italian lakes begin to look the same after the first three. Vera said nothing. Was he catching, there, a reflection of his awareness that he could do nothing? He now wore only a small plaster on his hand. Almost healed; almost forgotten. Why not finish with a weekend in Venice? If it were not for the Monte Bre looming there above this ridiculous Swiss toytown; the reminder that Roberto Bonacorsi stayed at his desk, did his job, with his life at risk.

Castang had his own job in Brussels. He felt ashamed of it too now and then – they all did, protected as they were by every bureaucratic safety-cushion. One could be reminded of other grandiose projects which squared their projected costs for piffling results. The Shuttle Programme, whose rubber band was not resilient at freezing-point, as demonstrated by Professor Feynman on television with a piece of elastic and a glass of ice-water: he needed no maths, he needed no physics, he needed no Nobel Prize, and naturally, he was instantly drowned in a tidal-wave of Patriotic Rhetoric. Exactly the same happens to us in Europe: the remotest gleam of common sense will be shouted down by a horde of overpaid economics experts.

Wasn't I of more use, thought Castang, back in Picardy, trying to use some common sense, some elementary humanity, in applying the codes of criminal law and criminal procedure? I arrested people; I turned them over to a judge of instruction who had to decide, an unenviable job, whether there had really been any crime at all . . . But my job was useful too; I was the biblical centurion, under orders and with men under me; I said "do this", and they did it. And now I tell myself "Do this" – and I don't do it. I don't know how. I am not Richard Feynman. I am looking for something very simple.

In fact, a rubber band and a glass of water.

Until he met – rolling along the lakefront like Bollocky Bill the Sailor – a figure remembered for its way of walking (where are your spurs?). This personage wore perfectly ordinary clothes and attracted no attention, but to Castang's eyes, and was that really very sharp, would be in any surroundings unmistakably British. To be sure, Miss Rawlings had also looked unmistakeably British, and could never have pretended to be anything else, but she also looked completely at home and comfortable in European surroundings.

The figure was a hundred metres off and getting closer quite unhurriedly, so that Castang waited for it and – himself observed by an eye as quick as his own – studied it. The conventional business suit, quite possibly Austin Reed in Regent Street, would attract no attention whatever in London and would practically cause a crowd to gather in Frankfurt. There is also the military look – the real business men are a lot more round-shouldered. It was so much easier to imagine him in a khaki bush skirt, with parachute wings sewn on above the breast pocket, and perhaps a purple-and-white striped ribbon. Was this why they sent Miss Rawlings in the first place? Only the elegantly curling, slightly greying hair was just a scrap longer than when last seen.

"Come and have a beer," said Mr Rawlings mildly.

Ensconced in a terrible pub, where even the *tagliatelli al burro* costs twenty Swiss francs and they say "Carlsberg or Tuborg?" Mr R Britishly stretched a leg (tearing the carpet with his spurs), and enquired "Ribs all right?"

"Nearly. I swim, I paddle little boats."

"You gave our Carabinieri friends a fright. They staked you out like a goat; couldn't really blame them. I admired your cheek, sailing across there in your own car. Monsieur Castang never can resist a bit of fortune-tempting? Well, here's to your good recovery."

"Cheers."

"This isn't a very good place to talk."

"Nowhere is," said Castang. "We're both out in the open, aren't we?" Mr Rawlings fished a pencil out of his pocket, twiddled it absently, allowed it to point in the direction of the mountain, and said, "This part of Switzerland is very respectable. One would need to be elsewhere. I just popped in on the chance of a word. I was expecting you to be in Brussels. I've a bit of business there, as it happens."

"But you might just tell me about the Valtellina." Mr Rawlings cast a circular glance. The pub was nearly empty. The waiter was languidly serving coffee to two fat ladies in shorts.

"It's safe to drink the local water," said Castang. It drew a smile.

"Come come, no hard feelings. There was a gentleman called Giulio, postmaster by profession. Mm, Italian posts are a disgrace. Perhaps because he was a Nimrod, a mighty hunter before the Lord. But other people can carry a hunting rifle. Other people can shoot straight too, once they know what they're aiming at. It was felt that this might be appropriate, since the local people have this in common with Corsicans: when somebody has a hunting accident nobody ever questions it. We were, you see, rather attached to her memory."

Castang was impressed. Brits can appear pathetic. They show up there in St Moritz, on the frontier with the Valtellina, and apologise for being last on the bobsleigh piste. But it shouldn't be forgotten that they invented these games. Odd Victorian survivals persist here and there: Castang had a sudden vision of Mr Rawlings with a Norfolk jacket and mutton-chop whiskers, unexpectedly deflating Norwegians who thought they knew how to Curl. It's a Brit game. The slider is still built of a piece of Scottish granite, shaped and polished as decreed by Brit chieftains. He recalled an affair from many years ago which had delighted Adrien Richard. The Brits had been diddled by a fast financier. They sent two business men, utterly ludicrous. Round-shouldered and their bottoms stuck out of those English jackets with two flaps at the back. Everybody was sorry for them until they pursued the peculator to New York, opened his safe by God-knew-what illegal means, secured therein the evidence they wanted, told the NYPD to fuck off, and nailed down a pretty little conviction in the New York Courts. And for God's sake, when they started out they looked like Chico and Harpo at the races. It's very strange to think that these were the original Know How people. Traces of it still exist.

The Brits had sat there in St Moritz remembering how to Curl, and just down the road they rounded up friend-Giulio, brought him out on the hill with his pretty Mannlicher, and blew him to pieces.

Gut-shot him, likely as not, just to remind him.

"Perhaps we can do a deal," said Castang.

"All ears."

"You'd like to know the identity of a chap in Bruce. I could save you a bit of trouble there. You know where Coralie is?"

"Yes."

"Like to do a swop?"

Mr Rawlings thought about it and said, "No."

"All one to me."

"Look, Castang, you've been inconceivably lucky, twice. The gentleman with the rifle thought you no more than a stooge. The swimming chap wasn't good enough for the job. You don't imagine you bear a charmed life, perhaps? Third time pays for all, or some such phrase? Leave all this to the people whose job it is."

"I'm grateful for the good advice."

"You don't mind my telling you something, Castang? You're a fool. More to the point, you're a harbinger of disaster. I don't want anything to do with you. The beer was on me," putting some money on the table. "The johnny in Brussels – if you can find that out I'm damn sure I can. Have a nice day now."

Well, of course, he's right, thought Castang idly, and rather fancying another beer, decided not to; let's go up the hill instead.

What's it all for? Do I in fact deserve to be in the cemetery? Am I giving myself so much importance as to imagine that if I'm not, that has some sort of meaning? Castang has not felt "idealist" since he was quite a young boy, wondering what point there was in going to the university – in order to learn to be another mediocre schoolmaster? Early days in the police soon knocked the nonsense out of him. Because if you weren't cut out to make a professional, you didn't survive at all. It would be brought home to you very rapidly that you were in the wrong business: can't stand the heat, then stay out of the kitchen. And even when it made him sick, or tired out of his mind (not to speak of the flagrant Injustice of it all) he'd gone on liking it. Became, even, a good enough pro to do quite well. He'd got his feet on the ladder, climbed some way up it. One didn't think about being "good". Time to time, one made oneself useful. At one of their early encounters he recalled Bobby Bonacorsi saying much the same thing. One had a few odd talents, like the (poisoned) gift of imagination, which the others didn't have, and this was painful but, dammit, it was useful.

There'd been the setbacks. Like getting shot in the elbow, meaning downgraded physically; getting on the wrong side of superiors. The sense of humour, at last, of the Director of Police Judiciaire: this chap's a pain in the ass but too good to waste altogether. Send him to Brussels; brilliant.

Yes, it is a job worth doing, even when nine-tenths of it is shuffling bumf around: one maintained that against all comers. His chief complaint was that it was all much too easy: why the hell should he be paid – pretty well – for this? One was useful, yes, but stuff like a Criminal Code, one had to get that past Parliaments and one would always get defeated (one wasn't defeated, one was just fatally watered down) by the nationalists, the Jelly-bellied Flag Flappers. One went on, but it's kind of boring. One was stimulated by a good chief, like Harold Claverhouse, and then one found oneself instrumental, highly so, in his downfall: it had been a sore blow. And then Eamonn, another valuable man. Come on, Castang, what's the matter with you? You got the curse or something?

Eamonn, yes, and Miss Margaret Rawlings, yes, and this – chap – Castang, a comically near-miss. An old crim-brig cop isn't going to just sit there saying it's-no-business-of-mine.

There aren't any sentiments involved. As Vera says, a child has feelings. One is sentimental in adolescence.

Adults have emotions and they can be tough to handle, because one is forever making the commonplace mistake of applying rational standards. One remembers the words of an old street-wise cop. 'Oh, if you want to know what's right. As opposed to Right. It's the one you don't want to do. The one that's all against the rational considerations."

This is a wonderful house. And a clever one. Go up the Monte Bre on the cable car and you'll miss it altogether. The roads – and the paths – up here go in odd zigzag patterns. With a car you could wind to and fro for twenty minutes without finding anything at all. Castang has done his homework, and it's still of no great help.

Bits of it are built out over an area of sheer cliff. The Royal Marine Commandos could scale that, given a few ropes and things. But you'd hear them coming. Round the back there are high walls, and they'd be scaleable too, but what's the point of your platoon of toughs, of number sixty-two indecent-assault unit? A famous wisecrack of Bismark's applies. "Suppose the British Army were to invade Schleswig-Holstein?" "It would be arrested by the police."

The front door is along a narrow passage, with clipped cypresses on each side. There is room for one person at a time. There's a blank wall then, and a door, and a bell. There's also a way in at the back for autos, but you've got to be able to say an Open Sesame. Open Long-fields-of-barley-and-of-rye won't do it.

Suppose you were out on the lake. With a boat and binoculars and let's suppose a high-powered hunting rifle. You'd see the windows. But they'd appear as a blank sheet of bronze: they wouldn't tell you anything. What are you going to do? Put a gunboat on the lake, let fly with the twin twenty-millimetre? Zoom in like Biggles with a torpedo?

Puffing from all the climbing; the Monte Bre is not high but it's steep in patches; Castang addressed himself to the speakbox.

"Good morning; can I help you?"

"Calling on Monsieur de Subercaseaux: Castang, Henri."

"That would be business, Monsieur Castang? I'm afraid that Monsieur only receives by appointment. I'll put you through to the secretary, if you wish." A very polite voice with a Swiss accent.

"It's personal business. Can you deliver a message?"

"I can."

"Put it that it's in code, just a bit. Could you say that it's the gentleman who nearly had the swimming accident?"

The voice was too well trained to giggle. "I can try. Monsieur Castang. So will you be patient, please?"

So he was. He had a week. What's five minutes? The voice came back unfailingly polite.

A buzz said he should push the door. Three paces further there was another door; he was in the "sas" between two worlds; looked as is his habit for the English expression, found only "decompression chamber" which was not quite right. He stood still, aware he was being scanned. Recorders, transmitters? Guns. Photographed too, perhaps; there was a blink as the second door opened. There was his knife – but they knew about that, didn't they? He approved of all this, it was business-like. Beyond was a hallway and a black man in a white jacket, owner of the polite voice saying, "Monsieur is pleased. But since this is unexpected he asks for a moment more of patience."

A library. Books to the ceiling on all sides. No windows. A diffused ceiling light and a faint breath of air-conditioning. Chairs, a fine table with cosmopolitan magazines – the *Connoisseur* – very nice too for anyone in the antiques business. A globe, very fine. He remembered these magazines, working tools in his days with Carlotta Salès. He put on a light, sat down and began to read. There was a total, perfect silence. Perhaps very expensive dentists would be like this.

A panel with fake books opened with a small click. The man he had come to see stepped in and paced slowly across the room smiling, saying, "Don't get up." Castang had the feeling it was contrived, that he had been watched through a spyhole. But did it matter? He was at a disadvantage to be sure, half out of a deep chair and dropping the magazine. But that was the case anyhow. A strong handclasp feeling like a chamois leather glove. A tall figure in a tobacco-brown track-suit of some soft jersey material. A formidable face with a wide thin mouth and wide-apart greenish-grey eyes. Oyster-shell hair slicked close to an impressive head. He sat down and took his time studying Castang, who was doing the same but more woodenly. He broke into an easy, comfortable laugh.

"Cigars on the table there, in that box. Now what can we offer you – coffee, a beer? – no, I know, white wine about half and half with Perrier," picking up a microphone. "Good idea? Two nice spritzers, Jo, please. I'm pleased you've come to see me. That shows a straight, clean mentality, something I see all too little of. I'd like you to find the same in myself. Be as open as you please, and we'll understand each other. I had thought you one of these constrained French officials – narrow, rigid, inflexible – and now that I see you – are you in fact French?"

"I've always understood so," choosing quite a small claro and clipping it with the cutter in the box," but I knew little of my parentage. One grows up in France it makes one French," striking a match. "Later on in life one finds differences. My wife's Czech. Does that alert one?"

"It does indeed and certainly it alerts me. Thank you Jo, on the table there if you would. May I drink to an expression of my apologies? 'Here's looking at you,' as we might say. This is a lesson to me. I should never have tried to have you killed without seeing you. That was stupid of me, and I loathe being stupid. I hope that you'll accept this apology, which is embarassing to mouth. I sent an ass to do the job and now I'm glad he was an ass; I don't have to apologise for him since you took the matter so well in hand. I hope by the way that you're quite recovered."

"Not quite tip-top yet," said Castang, "but mending."

"Oh good!"

"But will you start again?"

"Splendid! No. Not unless I judge you to be a grave threat to my interests. In my present view that is not the case."

"We can talk about this? I have felt embittered."

"We can indeed. And if it lies within my powers I'll make honourable amends. I qualify, because my powers are wide, but they have limits. It is well for me to know and understand these limits."

"Keeping to essentials, Eamonn Hickey was a close friend. Dear to me."

"Ah. Now I understand. Good, now try and understand me. Your friend was a highly able man. He loomed large;

does that answer you, at all? But then — eccentric, unpredictable, Irish. That's a threat. Indeed an awkward customer; you presented a parallel. When I protect myself, I tend to be radical — *pour encourager les autres*? Cliché I'm afraid, but dead they tell no tales. He knew much too much about the financing of the IRA. The idea then was to help the Brits by persuading them that one less will lighten their burdens. I'm truly sorry. I didn't know you then."

"Clear. You used an imperfect and unreliable medium. Paul de Man aka. Thomas Lhomme."

"You cover me in coals of fire." The remote and lipless smile. "Hit me a shrewd one. You see, he was simply burned up with sexual jealousy. So you worked your way through that. You were, you are, a skilled police officer. I didn't know this. Do you begin to see why I agreed, when that donkey rang up saying he proposed to make an end of you? *Ay de mi*, that little business in the Valtellina was a good one until first Hickey and then you . . . no point in dwelling on that; I can't blame you. And now you've got on to one of my German boys. Oh dear . . ."

"Don't hit him. I frightened him and if the Brits get on to him they'll be pretty vindictive. There's more. Miss Margaret Rawlings."

"Too many bright ideas. That's business, I'm afraid."

"Business," repeated Castang. "Yes, I suppose."

"I raise little trees in my garden; oranges, lemons. I speak to them. You'd find that perhaps sentimental?"

"No. My wife does the same."

"When the young shoots grow long and straggling they must be cut, for they weaken the young tree."

"Trees are not human."

"Correct; they can be ruthless but they lack human vices. They have not meanness of mind. They are not paranoiac. They are not hypocrites."

"They don't kill people either at long distance."

"In your police career you have met business men. Things go poorly and they lay off employees. But so doing they condemn others, often to protracted suffering, now and then also to death. The fact does not occur to them. You in some innocent gesture, drinking a cup of coffee, contribute unwittingly to the death of a peasant in

Colombia. That is the human condition. There are a great many millions, and they kill one another. People prefer not to know. I am clearer-sighted."

"You're beginning to talk philosophy. I'm ill-placed here to argue and the time's wrong."

"Most of philosophy," paternally, "is elementary biology. Birth and death. I must try and find an opportunity for you to think more clearly. Meantime, would you like to see my garden?"

"Very much indeed."

They went out through the salon and Castang commented on the pictures.

"Yes, I have many; I designed this house to hold them. I deal in them, of course. I keep some, occasionally for many years. One or two I do not part with."

And one or two, Carlotta Salès would know about, and there wouldn't be a damn thing she could do about it. Just like him . . . still, he'd got this far.

"I spent some time in the fine arts – Fraud Service, back in Paris. Not long enough to acquire knowledge. I've just eye enough to tell that these are very fine."

"An excellent business, when one only handles the best. As I grow older I think of divesting some of my holdings, to put more into this. These also I talk to, these also I love."

They reached French windows. The garden was surprisingly large and made larger still by the skilful use of different levels; in places very steep, following the contours of the mountain. Filled throughout with sun, up to those walls . . . plenty of shade where one wanted it. He saw a gardener. There would be a driver perhaps, beside the houseman, the cook? They would live on the premises; they would be armed. A maid? There had been no sign of a wife.

Towards the end there was a grassy space and a small, pretty swimming-pool. A naked girl lay on a mat, slipping into a robe as they came nearer. There was a bit of his question answered. She sat up, politely turning towards them, and he recognised Coralie.

'Good morning,' she said. The voice was soft, warm, with no trace of either spite or syrup. She gave no sign of surprise, fear, or gloating: she was poised, and that was that. "How are you?" she asked with a friendly simplicity. "Better, I hope."

Castang did not do badly. He kept his self-command. They continued their tour. Subercaseaux was saying that the water for the pool as for the fall and pond in the "wild garden", the stream and canal and fountain close to the house, was sometimes "a difficulty". He did not display his possessions. He spoke of things in the same level tone of detachment and affection.

It had been a trap, and a demonstration. But done without sadism.

They got back to the house; pleasantly cool.

"Apéro?" politely. "I won't ask you to stay for lunch, since your wife will be looking for you."

"Thank you but no. I enjoyed that. A bit rich for my blood. I'm a man of the north, and a simple man."

"I understand. I like the north myself. But here is where I belong."

"I've learned a lot. I'm grateful. I'd like to knock you off your perch, but I see there's no chance of it."

The man smiled at that. "We're on a better business footing. I've apologised. I do so again, on account for your friend. I can't apologise for Brits; my IRA connections are good, and I won't compromise them. I won't tell you more, because I don't wish to find myself embarrassed by you. Now when do you think of leaving?"

"Pretty well any day. The ribs are okay and they'll be looking for me, back in Bruce."

"Why don't you come to dinner? We can eat on the terrace, a rarity in the north. Bringing your wife, naturally. I like Czechs." Rather as though he owned them, but no matter. "Why not tonight? If, of course, you have nothing booked. I dislike large parties and I don't entertain here, since I value my privacy. But a small informal foursome, what d'you say?"

That was a challenge, and Castang's weakness is to accept them. And what will Vera make of Coralie . . .? And this is not the Hof in Baden-Baden. The contrast will tickle Vera. And won't she just love the pictures . . .

"I'll accept. I believe I can speak for my wife. Can I ring, to confirm?"

"Of course. No special clothes. No grandezza."

It had not been a glass of watered wine that made him reckless. Nor the beer, earlier. What had possessed him? This was not in the least like the no-account man in Baden-Baden, where going out to dinner was a routine piece of police work. This was a risky enterprise. Here was not a man to be bluffed with food and drink and a mix of threats and promises, where an innocent woman could be used to mask both: yes, the word was appropriate, for that had been a masquerade.

Here we have an unusually skilled and cool operator in a position of effortless superiority. And dangerous: Lhomme had warned him; Rawlings had thought him crazed: Roberto Bonacorsi had shaken his head and told him to leave well alone.

It is not of course the occasion which is risky. One wasn't about to be offered poisoned mushrooms by a Borgia Pope. One wouldn't disappear through the trapdoor to be discovered in a Swiss sewer. But this man has a long arm. If he wishes to arrange a traffic accident in the streets of Schaerbeek – there's no doubt of it, he knows how.

So far, Castang has got away with it. In fact it had been a good move, a scrap of imaginative temerity to appeal to such a man: indeed they had come to an unspoken agreement, Castang getting a paternalist "pardon" in exchange for the acknowledgement that there wasn't a damn thing any once or future police official could do.

The sensible thing to do now is to murmur a polite excuse and make tracks out of here.

Within these few days, Vera had imposed her personality upon a horrible hotel room. She had come to mysterious agreements with the chambermaid, the porter ate out of her hand; even the falsely-genial concierge broke into beams of delight when he saw her coming, with sage advice about junk-shops, reliable pizza-joints, or inexpensive hairdressers. Without ever being untidy (even the bedclothes were put to air in ways helpful to the staff – indeed he complained that she barely stopped short of making her own bed) her clothes, smelling marvellously of herself, aired everywhere and splendidly upon hangers. The bathroom, always impeccable, was unmistakeably her property; he even found her earrings in his tooth glass. Leave it to me, she would say, and managers gave her discounts, scribbled personal recommendations on cards: they loved her.

Why? Because shé is straight, simple, without pretence or affectation. But were these qualities likely to bend a cynic as ruthless as Monsieur Pedro de Subercaseaux? Forgive me if I doubt that.

He found her very cool to his proposal.

"Who is this? The capo-mafioso? This is the man who kills people? Eamonn? This Englishwoman who was with you here? You, as near as makes no odds. How can you suggest anything so horrible?"

"I quite agree. It's one of his little ways of showing me that I'm nothing, that I don't even exist."

"I don't see how you could even consider it."

"Right, right. I think he only intended to humiliate. But it's easy enough to make a phone call, get the butler, Miss Otis regrets."

"It's absorbing though that you were actually there. Tell me more over lunch; I thought something salady in that Greek place, Lebanese or whatever it is." Vera's Mediterranean geography is often sketchy.

To hit the nail on the head, after some graphic descriptions to stretch Vera's eyes, "Just to show me he can do anything at all if he puts his mind to it, who should be sitting there by the pool but the girl that Eamonn went overboard for."

This virtuous disassociation has an opposite effect to that intended, and is a mistake.

"Really? The one you saved from a fate worse than death – or did you? The one that so upset Jane? I'd be interested."

The moment he shows reluctance she becomes enthusiastic. He knows this quite well, in the ordinary course of things. "Well, it can't do any harm, I suppose. Here in Switzerland he takes pains to be most respectable. He's anyhow Sicilian enough to be a Man of Honour, and in his own house he shows himself an excellent host. I do admit, my first reaction was to think it would be funny. What d'you want to wear? – we could buy something for you."

"Man of Honour is he? Needn't think I'm going to dress up for this cheap mafioso; I'll go in jeans."

"No look, this is a beautiful house and there are some marvellous pictures, let's get you something pretty and I'll wear a suit."

"Pooh."

"Please be serious. This isn't a comic occasion like Baden. Not the moment to get drunk or be tactless."

"I don't want anything new. Like a provincial housewife at a wedding. Take me as you find me or not at all."

"As you wish," and sure enough she stopped in front of a dress shop murmuring, "No stiff Swiss snobberies, but I might find a frock."

"That's pretty." Two-piece in cotton, jade-green, cut rather low in front.

"Too dark for me. Might just see if they have a better colour. You go for a walk." Which he does because this will be agony; the vendeuse saying, "Lovely, made for you" and her going, "no no no, ghastly." She reappeared of course exhausted.

"Must have a bath, but must just get the girl to press your suit." He sighed and slumped on the sofa with an Edgar Wallace book, only to be found in Switzerland and very exciting. Oh God, female caprices. She locked herself in the bathroom too "because you distract me so".

And having bought "something nice" in a pretty plum colour which suits – he agrees – her fair hair and pale complexion much better than the jade-green, she appears in jeans after all.

"It was much too dressy," she explains. "I can wear that in Brussels but not on the lakefront."

Better not upset her any further. In fact she looks very well because she has kept her slim figure, has a comic top on, highly naked and known as "the modesty-vest", and he feels proud of her, as against all the Coralies in creation. What does it matter anyhow? – and wears an open shirt himself. Not a Sicilian evening party! No doubt that the instinct "not to let oneself be impressed" is the right one.

Castang had no faith in all those little one-way streets. The taxi-man said, "I know the address," and brought them in a rather smelly Mercedes to a totally different entrance, a shadowy porte-cochère where "Jo" gave them a warm Caribbean smile, took Vera's jacket, and, "Oh the lovely pictures," cutting the ground from underneath

Coralie (rather overdressed, noticed Castang happily, in a long skirt and too much lipstick).

The Master made one of his entrances, sliding silently in from behind a door (open shirt and a silk scarf), pacing tigerishly gentle to where Vera is paying respect to Monsieur Matisse, kissing her hand and saying, "You go well together," which would normally go straight to her heart.

But she is a bit knocked out. "You know I know this, but I thought it was in Moscow."

"I've had it for some years. I won't let go of it. But I've allowed it to be reproduced because it is really very good indeed and one must share these things. The one in Moscow is a variant. No — I must be honest — mine is the variant."

She turned around then, as tigerish as himself. "You like, I believe, straight talking. You are the picture collector. I am a painter, a very small one. You are a murderer. You came within a hair's breadth of killing my man."

"My dear Madame Castang—"

"That will do very nicely. But I'm your guest; I'm in your house. You may say Vera."

"Pedro. I have apologised; I do so afresh in front of you."

"Thank you. But it's not quite good enough, you know."

Good God, thought Castang. But the man is unscratched.

"I accept your reproof. I acted in ignorance, and since that is culpable I feel due shame. But may I in turn put you to the proof? Here on this table is paper. Here is a pencil. Will you make me a drawing?"

"Yes," said Vera. "I will." Jo intervened with glasses. The *apéro*. The magnum was swathed but it was Krug thought Castang, accepting a small cigar; or something as good "which he gets from the grower." Pray, Heilige Maria, that Vera is not about to get pissed; she did promise but in this mood there's no holding her.

She took a small drink without noticing, the pad on her knee.

"I don't guarantee this. It's Jean Cocteau isn't it? Sergei Diaghilew on a menu card." Her hand moved in quick lines. So he has seen her a few hundred times. Even at a hundred and twenty kilometres an hour on the autobahn, a building . . . It is her training, her five-finger exercises. And she has the whole room paralysed. Castang makes meaningless conversation to Coralie: they have nothing to say to one another. The room is full of static electricity; it is as though they were all standing under one of the high-tension pylons that carry unimaginable quantities of current across the Rhine, over the Pyrenees.

"There," tearing it off. "May I do Jo? Will you allow me, please?" as he stood, a little taken aback, by his serving table. "You are perfect so. I beg you not to feel put upon."

She is full up with the charge. In fact she could be underground, in the linear accelerator near Geneva. She is being bombarded with particles at extremely high speed. They bounce when they hit a bit of carbon like in a pencil. They make remarkable curves when they hit. Very simple, very beautiful.

"This is most remarkable," Subercaseaux was saying. "No you mayn't see it. I don't quite know even whether I can send it to be framed. No, I'm keeping this, you can all look at the other. Jo, my boy, tell yourself that a girl one day in this house was looking at Matisse, took you on at a speed-game of chess; you're a pretty good chess player but I think you'll agree that she has astonished you."

You turned it nicely, thought Castang, but you were hit, weren't you. He's not showing the drawing, he's putting it away. And that-is-my wife, that-was; bravo Vera.

"May I kiss your hand, Madame, to thank you?" said the well-trained butler. "May I keep this?"

"Give it me back then a second," and wrote, *For Jo from Vera. Lugano '92.* She signed *Vera Castang* and he felt enormous pride and went to pour himself another glass, because goddammit, the company is transfixed.

"You talk to pictures," said Vera. "But what do they say back? Who talks to you? My man tells me you talk to trees. They too are metaphysical. They talk only to those with ears to hear."

Coralie looked puzzled, understanding little of this. She would like to say "Draw me" and doesn't dare. She is accustomed to being the centre of attention.

Vera finished her glass and said, "No more, thank you."

Castang who would have liked more, a lot more, hardens himself. Subercaseaux put down his glass and said mildly, "I think we can move to the table."

The table was outside on the terrace, under an awning. From here there was a very fine view, downward to the lake and the roofs glimpsed behind their screen of cypresses of "Favorita" at the water's edge. From this height of anonymity, prudence, a little at a time, did the perfectly-successful man at the peak, surely, of material achievement look down, very quietly, upon Baron Thyssen? "You have more pictures. Yours are more famous. Yours were more easily acquired. But I'll match you. Yours was a nineteenth-century world. Mine is the twentieth. All this is mine, mine, mine." Or would he never be satisfied? What is there to do now but go on living and moving towards the end? Like old Maugham all those long and weary years in Cap d'Antibes. Westward one looked along the lakefront. The angle cut off, naturally, the "poor" quarters of Lugano huddling up the slope; the railway station; the autoroute. One went as far as the other mountain at the opposite end of the town, and one only bothered with that because of the sunsets, which are spectacular and romantic.

It is most remarkable and one will have to say so to the Master of "all this" who has heard it so many times and receives the most extravagant praise with utter impassibility. Castang has been wondering whether a boat out there on the lake would provide a solid enough platform for a marksman with telescopic sights over a really high-class rifle. An extremely difficult shot, across the deceptive distances of water and up the rocky hillside. One would start with a bit of elementary trigonometry; a three-point fix from the shoreline, to begin. But there would be those to be found who would attempt it, and a good few more ready to pay for it, and pay well. It was too obvious though, wasn't it. A case long foreseen, and an elementary defence: don't go too near the edge, and above all don't stay there. This careful, controlled man – how do you get him to the edge? He occupies a lot of terrain, but there are edges to it. Castang wonders where.

The sunset duly displayed – my lake, my sunset, my rather tiresome little town (the noise scarcely above a murmur, this high, the stink dispersed by pleasant on-shore breezes; Italy, over there, a back-drop, just scenery) — everyone's attention was called to the serious business of eating. A round table, large enough for six, and since we are four, quite informal, two men and two women, there are no precedences to be considered. Master will sit next to Vera and Castang to Coralie and we're all perfectly cosy. Nor is there any nonsense about pompous grand-hotel food which looks good, but tastes of nothing at all. This was home food, simple, beautifully cooked, plentiful, and startlingly ordinary. Rich people are very often mean. You are invited out, looking forward to this, and you get deep-freeze shepherd's pie and Jugoslav Riesling. Here one could have confidence. Whatever he was — a great deal and mostly pretty dreadful — he wasn't mean.

Nor pretentious. The plates were good Limoges porcelain but no gold-edged Sèvres. The soup-tureen was certainly silver but plain and of a shape to please even difficult Vera. The soup was cold without being icy and tasted quite delicious. A little cream, a few chives. Country bread. There was only one kind of wine: admitted, a very good one. Jo came and showed the label to Master (Castang craning but in vain from opposite, trying not to crane and getting caught) with a very faint smile and the murmur, "I think, Jo, we'll need another of those . . . Are you skilled?" wickedly, to Castang. "Do you want to guess the year?" (Castang properly crushed.) Coralie, wary, says nothing; had Vera even looked at her? What is one to make of this thin, plain woman, who must be close to fifty and looks it, too?

"Yes, I will have a little more soup, please."

"Castang?"

"Decidedly." Becoming uncrushed but the more wary. A pause.

'I like to smoke, between courses. A Russian habit, it's said, but I don't wish to hurry my cook."

"We will be Russian," said Vera "but not Gollivud — Nabokov's name for La Houssaie." A chuckle, from Master.

"Have you ever been to Los Angeles?"

"No. No occasion. Don't think I'd dare, anyhow, not at

least without Swifty Lazar to represent me." Gradually, the dinner party begins to warm. Conversation, he said this morning, he wanted. Not too much to eat, and plenty of time to digest it.

Duck, plain, in the "Tours" style, served like underdone roast beef; Jo expert with the very sharp knife. Four different vegetables, at which Vera expands like the wine in the big glass. She has not noticed that she is the dominant personality around this table; she is not self-conscious and said only, "I wish I could cook," when the second duck appears and a plain lettuce salad follows. Master eats duck, but like her prefers the vegetables.

"There's only cheese to come, so don't hesitate. Or is there pudding, Jo?"

"A little, for the sweet tooth, or will it be teeth?"

"Me, anyhow," said Coralie.

Vera smiled and said, "You tuck in while you can." Ambiguous expression.

There is only one cheese, but what a beauty. Vera took a cigarette, she's been smoking all evening; the occasion demands it. Master smiles paternally upon "the child's pudding".

"What is it?"

"Sort of vanilla cream, bavarois is it? I really don't know. And wood strawberries, yum."

"Tempt you, Vera?"

"Yes, but no." She has had a perfect dinner and now that has to be put in proportion. "Suppose I'm dead. Do I look back, and count on my fingers the times I've had a good dinner? Would I be any the less happy if I were a Beduin and got a very hard scrap of cheese, and perhaps a raw onion? She put her elbows on the table.

"You – you kill people."

"Does that shock you?"

"I don't think it shocks me. It affronts me."

Castang who had – ridiculously – held his breath, let it out and pinched his nose, the bridge of which now hurts with an effort not to laugh. A Vera-word! Dates from reading Beatrix Potter to a five-year-old Lydia. Odd, the memory! Mrs Tabitha Twitchet had been affronted by the kittens taking all their clothes off . . .

"I'm rude, am I?"

"Not rude . . . I don't mind greatly if you are."

"I'm not a bore?"

"No, you're not a bore."

"This is important to me. No, it's vital, I can't keep it in."

"Then you must let it come out, mustn't you." He has decided to treat her as a "silly woman" – which, thinks Castang, is a mistake.

Jo had brought the cigar box. Castang took a slimmish R & J but Subercaseaux took a big one, and was listening to it, clipping it, holding it for Jo to light, but he didn't take his eyes off Vera.

"To kill people is so very poor a human response – at such a very low level."

He was turning it, had it burning evenly now. "You know that I won't do you any injury."

"Not here, no. Probably not even in Switzerland. But we'll be going home in a day or so. To Brussels and there of course you had Eamonn killed. You have an instrument there, just as you had here, along the road." They were sitting in the open air, or Castang might have thought "the room was holding its breath."

"What did my man say to you this morning? That he felt affronted too? No, he's polite, he might have expressed himself as a scrap aggrieved about having his ribs broken. That tickled you and you chuckled at it and said you liked people with courage, you liked things put direct, you don't like a picture with too much varnish on it – you asked us to dinner because you were bored and it would amuse you. But now you've got me and that's different. You can throw me out of course, that will be easy. Rather languid – 'See these people out Jo, because they affront me.' " That gentleman had put the coffee things on the table and vanished. Knows when to be tactful.

Subercaseaux had pushed his chair back, leaned back in it. He was still not quite satisfied with the way the cigar was drawing, giving it quarter-turns, the face still, the eyes level.

"You were bored because you're always bored. You've everything have you? Or is it nothing at all?" Vera is sitting forward with her elbows on the table. The painter's hands make swift decisive movements, as they did when she was drawing, as sharply professional as a butcher cutting up meat on the block.

"Can you even go down to the village without making it unforeseen and unexpected, because fear will always accompany you?" Other people talk about the "village" meaning Greenwich, or Highgate; this village girl would use the word about Manhattan. "Since you never know, do you? Maybe the Company, or the Kahjaybay or the Stasi have taken a dislike to you, people who are quite as good at killing as you are. I don't speak of your friends; there's no possibility you would ever have any. I'm probably as close as you can get to a friend, because I don't hate you at all, I only remember that Eamonn was a friend of mine. I've nothing to do with any Secret Service. Nor has my man. Eamonn was a friend of his too. I probably haven't understood but as I see it he got exploited by the English, who were anxious to find out whether an Irishman might not have been in the IRA. Believe me, I'm not trying to insult you."

She took a cigarette from the crystal box at her elbow and smoked it nervously. There was a crystal ashtray at her other elbow; everything had been so beautifully arranged before Jo left. The coffee pot sat on a silver lamp, waiting for a hostess to pour it out. The other three sat there in silence. Remarkably, the Master didn't budge or utter. She was aware that her voice had risen, brought it back to conversation level, to her normal soft contralto.

"Mostly you stay here, in this house. It's a wonderful house, I admire it. I've never seen anything like it, no doubt I never will again. It isn't very likely I'd be invited into Baron Thyssen's house down the road, is it? That's conceivably grander but I shouldn't think it's any better. But a house can be a palace and you still judge it by the people who live in it. The Queen's got a palace, hasn't she, and she has better pictures even than you and she's richer. But nobody envies her and probably nobody's even looked at the pictures since George the Fourth; it's all a nothing.

"So now I have to come to my point, it's taken me long enough, hasn't it.

"What have you got? Nobody speaks to you, nobody contradicts you. You speak to the pictures, to the trees. What do they say? You've a girl here. Do you love her? Does she love you?"

Coralie said, "Vera . . ." A soft, even timid voice. But she had to say something, didn't she?

Vera stabbed the cigarette out and took another without thinking.

She turned a little to face Coralie, looked directly at her for what seemed the first time that evening, but without anything harsh or bitter in her face or voice.

"Yes," she said. "You. I know you. Eamonn loved you. Poor Thomas Lhomme loved you. Ah, it's one of these tricks of the Belgian language, schizo at best. Paul de Man ... I know about that, you see; an acolyte, a German acolyte, of this gentleman here, my host and yours, because you're not going to claim him as a friend, are you?" still perfectly gentle.

"You know my man too, don't you? Yes, I knew that also. How do I know? I know many things, I am a magician. How is that? Because I love. You should start learning about love, because you should have felt it, that's not something one learns from the intellect but out of the heart. Do you remember in Mozart, Cherubino sings about love, and everybody thinks oh, silly girl, she falls in love with absolutely everyone in sight, what can she possibly know about it? But she's talking to the Countess, and she says 'You – you who know.' Because the Countess, she knows all about love and has suffered for it. And out of her instinct – does it matter at all whether it's a boy or a girl, the singer or the song? The water, or the wave? That is the magic, isn't it?"

Vera's voice is in a low register but she has sunk it too to a near-whisper.

"Look at this house. Who could ever sing here? Who could ever be happy?"

Subercaseaux had never said anything at all and even now, consciously or unconsciously, he avoided the slightest drama. His chair was pushed back already and did not grate on the tiles of the terrace. He got to his feet; the cigar was in his mouth, giving an immobility to the lip, the jaw. The eyes had gone blank. From a standing position they did not dwell on any of the three persons present. He put his hands in his pockets. None of his movements lacked dignity, but he did little. No smile, no frown. He walked away across the terrace to one of the inside doors. It was not a "tired" walk, it was not expressive of anything at all. Simply – he walked away.

"We've stayed too long," said Vera to the paralysed Castang. "Come on, we'd better go home."

Coralie stayed sitting at the table because she found nothing to say. Castang got up, automaton. Vera walked back through the salon to the "lobby" doorway. Jo was there, polite and impassive, holding her little jacket for her.

"Would you like me to call a taxi, Monsieur? I can have one within five minutes."

"I think we'd like to walk."

"Isn't it rather a long way?"

"I think so, yes. But downhill. And walking, it's a nice night. And one needn't bother about the oneway streets, am I right?"

"If you like to walk," impassive, "you need only follow the contour of the hill. Thank you Madame, good night to you; come safely home."

It was not late. The town hummed and glowed beneath them. Sometimes the road turned at acute angles and the world below could be seen. Twinkle; the distance seems greater than it is. Up here is quiet, with the quietness of Swiss wealth; there are restaurants and nightclubs, bordels and gambling-houses, but it is understood that they shall not be noisy. Behind walls people are drinking, fornicating and planning to get richer; swallowing pills in the pursuit of joy and power, wit or energy, and also to relieve constipation or tiresome little problems with the prostate. Others look for oblivion. What did Lady Dedlock do, all those years in London? When she went to Paris, she was just as bored. What was there to amuse her?

A Swiss Lady Dedlock is also querulous, for this sniffing or snorting of little lines (not very ladylike) which used to be an amusing game, grows tedious and is too much trouble; she has been told moreover that it does things to one's nose (and hers is ladylike.) Spikes are likewise a bore. One has to go picking at one's veins, which is not recommended and altogether it's the sort of thing slummy people do outside railway stations. Men of course always have it easy; they can smoke opium or something. Hash one has smoked, chewed, otherwise ingested; altogether much too Turkish-immigrant. She's forever trying new sorts of pills and they all make one constipated and with that she's quite enough trouble as it is. People get AIDS, rather working-class of them, like a sour stomach or farting. A lot of people – even those one knows – get cancer. Sex too, all those different positions, not in the least comfortable she can only think of three really that are at all tolerable and doesn't even enjoy those much. Why are there such lots of ways of making music (assuming one knows how) and so few of living?

In the blandest and Swissest of towns one can get mugged and this, thinks Castang, is a pity, since to walk, of a summer night, is among the greatest of pleasures and used to be free. Vēra has no diamond rings and even my watch is a beat-up old Longines but the urchins don't know that and would when frustrated kick one's teeth in, so that the price to pay now is a shadow of fear; nasty thought of hospitals and insurance companies, so that really one would prefer the plastic bomb at the moment of turning on the ignition. And there, one will have to put up with whatever's in store. In science as in art there are no certainties. A pity, that the world is full of sad people, not right in their head, bitterly unhappy – which comes to the same thing. Young girls are at risk and so are old men, and so are all the others. They're all carrying guns and knives in every variation, they've loud whistles and little bombs of tear-gas, a pile of silly junk sold to the credulous, to the cowards who are frightened of everything and the blusterers who claim to be scared of nothing. Is there anybody left at all ruled by anything beyond the fear which puts paid even to hope; let alone faith or charity? Stay at home, dear people, behind as many bolts and bars as you can muster; watch horror movies on television.

These two characters are well past their best. The woman, who hurt her spine many years ago, limps still when attempting any distance, takes the arm of a man whose elbow was shattered by a gunshot. Surgery patched them up and they learned to manage. His legs are sound and her arms. If one could put them together, discarding the damaged or unserviceable bits, one would have a talented, experienced, fairly efficient human being. And one is put together, thinks Castang happily. By love. It just looks like a passably battered middle-aged couple. And the world is full of them, which might be a hopeful thought.

They may be seen in railway stations (like Frau Dedlock's junkies) thinking of one another, helping each other. Which is why railways remain nice while autoroutes stay horrible.

"Are you angry with me?" she asked. "Isn't it pretty, the lake front, from here?"

"Yes, it's far enough one can't see any greasy food fragments. Nobody has vomited on the pavement. We remain unaware that they haven't washed much lately. Angry? What does that word mean?"

"That I could have called down hideous retaliations."

"Ach – I hold pretty loosely to this life of mine. One learned that in the police, because one had to. So did you. Now we've comforts, and they dull us. But the equation stays the same."

"Oh that," said Vera. "When you were nearly drowned I wsan't frightened. Got over that, years ago. Remember when you got shot? It did worry me when the children were small. I thought of the pain to go through. It would be so harsh and bitter. The woman needing her man, the girls needing their father. And by the skin of our teeth, we come through, don't we?"

"One had to think of the others – the enormous majority which faces and has to overcome worse." Yes: Castang thinks of the trains, which carry away, and which leave behind.

"Not the cancer, the gunshot," said Vera, her voice growing stronger. "Being burned alive. Starving, slowly. Torture, and knowing one couldn't face it. But perhaps worst of all never having known love. So many people haven't. While we have given and taken so much, and do we know, what it is and how to value it?"

"Suppose," said Castang, "that the retaliation were against the children? Since cruelty also knows no limit?"

"Wouldn't we have to say that they'd had happy lives? They've known love. And that then, like us, they need know no fear. It's unthinkable. And so many have lived it. You have to think, I'm afraid, of the young girl in the line, in the camp. Hair cut, dirty, but beautiful, sixteen years old, a virgin. I do not want to die. No, dear, come out of there, come behind the shed, I'll look after you. I've thought of that . . .

"I'm sorry. We're down, pretty well." The lit and neatened boulevards of Lugano; swept, trimmed, and dull.

"Tired?" asked Catang.

"Yes. I'd like a rest. Come to that, I didn't eat much, and didn't notice what I ate."

"What a pity!" said Castang laughing.

"Would I be very silly if I said I wanted a pizza or something, somewhere cheap and vulgar? Noisy music, and a shot of Valpol?"

"Not in the least," laughing harder. "And then we'll phone for a taxi. It's a long way still." Music – hard rock and acid rock, but who needs definitions; salsa-reggae-caribbean-samba? A zither, a cymbalom, gypsy squawks and slithers? An eighteenth-century gavotte, a Chopinesque polka or the seventh-symphony's-slow-movement . . .?

"A pizza," said Castang, "would go down a treat." The place was full of children of the same age as their own. It was stuffy, noisy, and smelly.

"Just what was wanted," said Vera gratefully. A margarita, a half of Valpol, a disgusting ice-cream, and a racket one-can't-hear-oneself-think.

"So do you want one of my lines of poetry? I have them for all occasions but this one's a hotty if banal nowadays, all about how the glacier knocks in the cupboard and the desert sighs in the bed?"

"Go right ahead," screamed Castang, with his mouth full.

"Jesus how did Auden manage to be that good?

'Where the beggars raffle the banknotes
And Jill goes down on her back.' "

"Well perhaps that's not altogether fair," said Castang mildly.

"Though I like it; isn't that the one about the crack in the teacup, and 'Time coughs when you would kiss'?"

"What?"

"I said it's too noisy in here to talk." Vera's smile has an edge to it. Sarcastic, sardonic, sly? Not quite but something beginning with an s. Sinister, maybe.

Unfortunate thus to find Coralie in a corner when he

asked the night porter for the key, making herself small on one of those sofas. Vera caught a corner of her lip up, on her teeth.

"We can't discuss this in a hotel lobby. I'm very tired, and I'm going to bed. Don't let me get to hear of her any more. I'm not Jane, you know. I won't run away, but . . . Make it under ten minutes." Pushing the button for the lift. Castang stood his ground.

"Do they know where you are? . . . They'll guess, though . . . Do you need any money?"

"I don't want any."

"Eamonn died. We'll all die and so will I, but I'm not in any special hurry. You've plenty of living left to do."

"Do you think he'll come after me?"

"I doubt it. Not his style, which is that nothing is important – not even you.

"But the advice I'd give you would be to get out of here. Not the autoroute this late, that's a needless risk. But take the first train out, in any direction. And forget him, me, Eamonn. I know that sounds easy but you're young, you know.

"I don't believe you're at risk from him – but you remember the Englishman? There at Como? He might get on to you, try to use you, for purposes of his own; that might be a danger.

"I'd go home then, but I wouldn't stay. You've clothes and stuff there – a car perhaps? Start a new world.

"I know; I don't come out of this well. But remember what my wife said; that fear paralyses us, so that one has to walk up to it. One feels better then. You have to walk out of that door and keep going."

The sapphire eyes looked at him, steadily, but there was nothing to read there. She got up. "Goodbye," she said, picking up her bag. She had one of those pouch affairs, made of pieces of parti-coloured leather, in which girls keep all sorts of junk. She slung it over her shoulder.

"So I'll just say thanks, shall I?"

Castang's mind had gone back – back – to a young French boy with whom he used to share patrol duty at night, on the streets in Paris. He used to talk enthusiastically about an Italian girlfriend who caused him tribulations. Neither of them knew any Italian. The boy – what was his name? –

spoke of her always as *La Bella Iocchi*.

He turned and went upstairs. An idea came to him in the lift.

Vera was in bed; her eyes didn't turn.

"I've got a quote for you – a philosopher. If that's what they call them at Harvard University. 'I think for scientific or philosophic purposes the best we can do is to give up the notion of knowledge as a bad job'. "

She said nothing; didn't move.

"I'm just going to do my teeth."

When they took the room the reception girl had put the usual question "Twin or double?" Vera had said, "I'll go and look", and when she came back, "Double, it's the better room". Castang doesn't comment; it's a nice big bed. He got into it, saying mildly, "I hope you sleep. I'm a bit stirred up; I'll have a cigarette still. Did you think of the window? Oh, good," turning out the little light. He stretched his legs, coming to terms with fatigue. That's a little "police" exercise, an alternate contracting and loosening of the instep muscles. The woman beside him stayed absolutely immobile. He put out the cigarette, stretched his neck muscles, breathed slowly, as near down to the bottom of his lungs as he could get.

A small, chill, uninflected voice said, "My whole body is one solid block of ice. Warm me."

It's a hot summer night. But women are like that. He knows very well that it does not mean "Make love to me"; simply "Show solidarity".

Lugano, a dolorous call

A good conductor will tap for a stop, say – mildly – "But it isn't just Ta-tum-ta-ta-tum, is it?" And the next time around – for the Wiener Philharmoniker has done this several hundred times too many – "Let's leave out the nostalgia, gentlemen, please" (women hornplayers are still a comparative rarity but in Wien, even more so). "Let's forget my imperial Hapsburg sentiments. Leave in the pain." Because the *Schöne Blaue Donau* is not just *Grand Valse Noble*, and nor is it the inevitable encore done for the Japanese tourists at the New Year Concert, before we all have a glass of champagne and the drummer settles down to the Radetsky Marsch and hoorah, we can all clap in unison on the back-beat. It has – it used to have – its place in the best of symphonic concerts simply because it is Noble. So let's forget the Wiener Pallawatsch of so many bad conductors, shall we? Those opening horn-calls echo Leonora's. Dolour.

Music, damn it, is so much more economical than words. What a poor thing prose is. And what an extraordinary thing is a waltz. Look again at the finale of *Casque d'Or*. She has her two hands clasped lightly behind his neck. With his right hand he guides her behind her waist. His left arm hangs straight down. Since Castang's left arm has no strength in it, this detail has always struck him.

Breakfast. This function took place in a gloomy room, facing north, illustrative of incompetence, widespread among modern architects who forget essentials and have to cram them into odd corners at the last moment, which is why you find yourself of a summer morning, in quite expensive establishments, eating by electric light in the basement.

The management will retort that you have a nice bedroom, facing south and the lake. But Vera hates breakfasting in her room; far too much mess and never enough coffee. She wishes to be showered, dressed, lipstick on and hair done, before anything as serious as breakfast; has anyhow the acutest dislike of being found in her nightie by waiters. She seems in quite a reasonable state of mind but is silent, peeling a peach, with a tendency to break off and stare at the coffee pot. Whereas Castang, quite brisk, is eating cholesterol.

"Monsieur Castang, I have a call for you. I'm sorry, I have no phone to bring to the table; will you take it over at the desk?"

"I suppose I'd better."

"Tell them to ring again later." said Vera, pretty crisp.

"It'll be business . . . Castang here, but I'd better warn you, in the middle of a crowded room."

The voice comes unaltered, quiet and level. "I should like to see you."

"Sorry, I don't propose to climb the hill."

"And you think about leaving today, perhaps?"

"I hadn't given it thought."

"Buying little souvenirs? Picture-postcards?"

"Look, my coffee's getting cold."

"You'll get more. I am serious. You know what I'm talking about. I incline to view it as a hostile act, which would tend to annul the agreement between us."

"Come, that's nonsense."

"Not good business, Monsieur Castang."

"I'll choose my words carefully. I had, have, no means of persuading – the person in question – to any course of action whatever. It must have been evident to you that I had no foreknowledge. Seeing – it – took me by surprise. I had no communication between the morning and the evening. Indeed how could I?"

"Precisely what I propose to determine."

"Could be described as an impressionable person. Likeliest I'd say is that last night's conversation – this is an open line, right?" A dry chuckle.

"I'm aware. My contacts with that hotel are excellent. I have no rancour towards your wife. On the contrary, I feel respect for courage and I do not make threats. I do not need to. But I am going to be sure that you have not abused, I'll call it a latitude."

"Then say what's in your mind – if you're not bothered about it being recorded."

That dry little laugh again. "No; throughout this town I have good relations. You were noticed in company with an English busybody. I don't lay claim to having your every movement observed and dissected. I ask myself, as is natural, whether you have shown weakness of purpose. I know these English; I don't under-estimate their talent for conspiracy."

"Now I understand. I could give you my word, which you'd respect, but I think I can do better. These people you speak of – they've no opinion of my methods. They think me a fool and they wrote me off."

"What are your methods, Castang?"

"I'm like Maigret, I haven't any."

The chuckle. "Come up here; we'll talk about it."

"No. I've two good reasons for refusing."

"Don't be afraid to speak out." A busy moment, at breakfast. Waiters arrive, write enigmatic little chits, leave again in a hurry. The hell with being cautious.

"You might say I'm frightened of being offered a big bribe and being tempted to accept it. But my better reason is that I've nothing to say, beyond what my wife said already, last night."

"Fine words. I'm a businessman; I'll say put it to proof."

Castang looked across the room. Vera's eye was on him. She stood up, shrugged, picked up her bag, walked towards the door.

"Sorry, I was thinking . . . that's your privilege."

"Prettily expressed. I'll give it a little thought. Say, I'll devise a test. Are you courageous, Castang?"

"No more than my wife."

This time, a genuine laugh. "Stay within reach of your telephone. For – it might be an hour. Will you do that? I hesitate to say – you'd better."

"I'm quite used to having my arm twisted."

The connection broke and he felt no appetite, but he ordered some fresh coffee and lit a lovely post-breakfast cigarette.

He found Vera brushing her teeth.

"I may have a bit of business, still. Over by lunchtime with any luck. Will you check on the train times? Anything at all we can bring home, for the girls? Meet you for lunch, downstairs? We might have to stay one more night – I'll tell Monsieur Suarez the doctor had to check me over." She spat, rinsed, spat, nodded. Business? I won't enquire; I never do. Just don't piss me about, okay? But the phone rang sooner than expected, and women have always little chores to occupy them.

"I've a meeting. So you're on your own this morning, okay?" Chill look, and chill nod. And what can he do about that?

The message had been short, simple.

"You'll need to be fairly quick; you haven't much above fifteen minutes. Your wife must stay behind. You go to the landing stage, the one called Paradise. There'll be a boat making a tour, round the lake. You buy a ticket – one. You walk to the after-deck. Open, but you wear your raincoat, you separate yourself from any tourists. There won't be many, it's a cloudy day. You stay there at the back and wait.

"This is your test. Disregard it and you must accept the consequences."

She has ostentatiously not listened, not asked, doesn't want to know: he is on his own. Her *buté* look of sheer obstinacy; the word means to butt one's head against the classical brick wall.

Yes, but one must do what one has set out to do. Because one has to. I, you, he or she.

He had better not tell her, because she wouldn't be at all long in picking up the thread. These tourist boats, tuff-tuff-tuff. On the afterdeck you're a sitting target. Duck? Pigeon? But that is "the test". Or the first part of it; there will be more to come.

"I have to buzz," Did this jauntiness sound hideously artificial? "See you at lunchtime."

She started to speak, decided against it. Speech is useless. Or unnecessary.

On the lakefront he had a minute to work it out. The mechanics of this are straightforward. The little ferries from the shoreside here cross over to Italy. But the "round-the-lake" thing is pure tourism, and Swiss. It goes as far as the frontiers, invisible on the water. But it does not cross them. Potters about and nobody has to show a passport. No Customs men come aboard; no police. Subercaseaux has chosen this as a meeting-place.

Castang had to admire the simplicity, the economy of the device. It is discreet. Even had he wished it there was no time to arrange any accompaniment. There is even privacy for anything that has to be said. These boats are bigger than the little ferries and less primitive: the midshp section is glassed in and one can get served with drinks. Few people stay out here at the back where it's draughty. And these boats do not leave Swiss territory . . .

There was nobody he recognised at the landing-stage. But there was a timetable. This was the terminus, but there is a stop – the last – at Favorita, and in between there is five minutes of open water. A passenger standing alone can be seen, and identified, from anywhere along the shore. He had been right the first time: if the occasion demanded it one could be very simply and neatly potted. Castang looked at the ducks with sympathy; the lake of Lugano supports a large population of them, and they get fed plenty of cake too. Sleek look they have, and thoroughly pleased with themselves.

Castang is called a brave man by ordinary standards. The police in France loses perhaps thirty men a year through violence. He has lived through twenty-five years of this. Hit by cars, most of them. Deliberately? That is for a tribunal to determine. These cars will be travelling at illegal speeds but the most you'll get, as a rule, will be a charge of homicide by negligence. The violence arrives suddenly for the most part, and is not anticipated. You can also get shot at. You are wearing, of course, a pistol, but even if you lay your hand to it you're supposed to put that in a written report. Ninety per cent of cops have never even fired theirs. On a range, yes, during training. Oh sure, as a plain-clothes, criminal-brigade officer he has sometimes had to shoot at people. Hit them, too. Furthermore he has been shot at – and hit. He has never stood like a ninny for seven minutes, in full view, waiting to be shot, at the caprice of a professional assassin. As Eamonn had been shot, standing at his own front door. As Margaret Rawlings had been shot, standing on a hillside in the Valtellina, looking out there with her bird-watching binoculars, curious to see whether anybody was taking an undue interest in the movements of Bibi.

He himself had been very near to death on this same lake, drowned, asphyxiated, since that is silent, accomplished without fuss; would pass for an accident under the superificial examination which would be normal. Tourists get killed falling off mountains – thirty or more yearly in the Alps. They fall overboard from boats. They go swimming underwater with aqualungs in Lake Constance, and get tangled in some pretty tricky hazards down there, too.

That great big lumping cliché about the cold sweat is – he discovers – no exaggeration at all. His shirt feels drenched. His socks are wringing. His chest feels as though caught in a vice and that isn't his now-healed ribs. His pulse and heartbeat are roughly those of a Tour rider; say upon the last kilometre of the Col du Galibier. Which is three thousand metres high, and try that some time on your own bicycle.

People do, too. Not here. Castang is willing himself to stay still. The screws thump, the boat churns out backwards, the tourists are all at the shoreside edge pointing their Nikons. Steadies, goes ahead, crosses the harbour area, plooters round the big, heavy promontory of the Monte Bre. Begins to inch in with a flurry from the motors. The Favorita landing stage is tiny. Above it the hillside goes on up, from here looking nigh-vertical. Some very fancy residences, up there. The deckhand shoves the little gangway out; there is space for just one man at a time.

One man comes aboard. Conventional, unobtrusive. He has large-lens dark glasses, and so do many tourists. He has a cap in a soft greenish tweed and a short auto coat of dark blue, both of which Castang envies, for it is chilly on the water. A wealthy tourist then. He walked all around the boat, satisfying himself, before coming to rest near Castang. The boat has been Swissly cleaned since being used the evening before, but he takes out a handkerchief and wipes the wooden bench and table, before sitting down saying, "Well done," in his quiet way. "Rather a – pretty view," as though he'd never seen it before. It is a grey day, hazy and the colours have gone Irish. Almost

Castang could think himself back in Killiney and looking out on to the hills of Wicklow. A cold air off the mountain has disagreed with a wet warm wind from seaward. A mist blurs the outlines of the Italian shore. Wisps of cloud, ethereal and transparent, cling to the hilltops, light as a Kashmir shawl round an old lady's shoulders. Moisture above the water has a muted sparkle. All the distances have become deceptive. Look upward to the sky and one sees a glow neither gold nor silver, but saying that the sun will break through. Perhaps this afternoon. Had one looked at the two men sitting together one would take them for friends – perhaps colleagues, in the same line of business. They have that look of experience shared, of a similar outlook. Well, one wouldn't be that far out. Not perhaps two civil servants, who would not dress like that. But two men of the same age group, let's say the other one from Milan and the one from Turin, attending the same conference here in Lugano. There's a bit of business we can do together. We understand each other. We're in agreement on the broad outline, let's look at the loose ends. Let's look too at this lake they talk about.

"I see a rose," said Castang. "I look at it, I breathe it in. It has a lovely smell, I hope so anyhow. Just coming out of bud – dewdrops on it, in the photograph at least, in some damn nursery's catalogue. Warmed by the morning sun and beginning to open its heart. I'm lyrical, huh? Yes, because I want to look at it as though it were the last thing I'd ever see. Seeing – anything – ever again. At times, one wonders."

The boat is going ahead again now, a soft beat at reduced revs, down towards the foot of the lake, but one knows it will stop at the frontier. Just before Oria and the Val Solda, the country of Franco and Luisa.

"A girl too, it's the same. Ah yes, you wondered, whether there were some conspiracy. No, I walked back, with my wife, last night – didn't hurry. Stopped for a rest. Got back to the hotel – there she was. Having made up her own mind she didn't want anything you could offer her. She was shaky of course. Cold, frightened. Nothing I could do there."

"And what sage advice – good, I make no doubt – did you feel able to offer?"

"None. Oh, to point her nose, east south or west and then keep walking, but that conclusion she'd come to already. She was simply tired and confused, terrified of you; as well she might.

"I'd gone to see her, as I imagine you know already, at her parents' house, up there in the Valtellina. I gave her the same advice then. To get out of there, make herself a new world. Young, very pretty, full of juice. She can, mm?

"I took her down, to the Carabinieri in Sondrio: I'd have been too far out of line to do anything else. They'd be interested since she knew a bit about that little network of yours, up there."

"Yes," said Subercaseaux gently. "To be sure. I've you to thank, for that."

"Right; the English woman, killed a few paces off – yes, that impressed me all right; deeply. But it went back too, further.

"The man you killed in Brussels. No, Namur or nearby, but the detail isn't important. To you, neither. Man unexpectedly sharp, got in your way.

"Why? That was my big stumbling block; couldn't make that out."

The boat had reached the frontier. It marked time, gently, turning slowly, giving everyone time; photo-stop. Not that there's anything to see: a shed, the Swiss and Italian flags; the landing stage and the little grey Customs launch peacefully at anchor. Along that steep shoreline five metres above the water runs a little fiddly roadway. Lots of people go to and fro; Italians content with the higher level of Swiss monthly-payments and putting up with this awkward and nerve-racking shuttle along the narrow – you could say even dangerous daily run. Of course, there's a bit of low-level smuggling. Who could possibly control a few cartons of cigarettes, a bottle or two of grappa, a packet of butter or a pound of ham? Heaven's sake; taxes cover these petty little traffics a hundred-fold. So that this is not at all the place to worry about narcotics. Or antiques either. They take up so little space.

"You saw a way of putting the man Lhomme – de Man, it has no importance – in your pocket. Just the kind of chap you find useful, and like to use; smart in the head and weak underneath; a good-looking house but with no foundation.

"But I'd got on the train a bit earlier. I was in Ireland, wondering whether my friend really had been in the IRA. On the way back I saw his wife. Who'd left him, on account of this girl — yes, this same one. She's rather more formidable than either you or I took her to be. Attractive? More than that. She has a gift one does not meet so often. That men fall in love with her; deeply, with the entire heart. It happened, fatally, to my friend. It happened to de Man, poor bastard, and was his downfall too. It could have happened to you — I wonder? But you wouldn't recognise it, would you, because you are incapable of love."

Subercaseaux listened, impassive. A good listener and one must make no mistake, thought Castang; a highly gifted man.

"I can't tell what may have been in her mind. She may have had some idea of getting close to you. She could have thought of planting a knife in you, some moment when, let's put it tactfully, you were off guard.

"She was looking, still, for someone to love. She does not love only herself. She wants to learn.

"But I revert to my friend — he loved her. He was a man who physically found all girls irresistible. This one, he thought he'd take to bed like all the others. He found out, too late, that she had other qualities; that she had a grip on his heart. The wife sensed it. She cut her moorings, she left him. He went to Italy with this girl — he loved her, she may have loved him. Unhappily for him he came across traces of an IRA network — you know about that, it makes money for you. Added leverage from the political potential. That interested him. He was just another civil servant in the Communauté in Brussels, but he ate the bread and salt of the Irish government. He found out too much and got under your feet. Too bad for him. And perhaps his death has saved my life — who knows?

"I got on to it by accident; I found some photos in his house. The Brits got a sniff of that wind; they're interested in the IRA and it seemed to bear out some suspicions of theirs. And that, mister, is how I came to be up in the mountains with an Englishwoman.

"He loved her. Perhaps she was learning to love him. You killed him."

178

The boat had turned, was pacing in a stately manner down the middle of the lake, along the line that here is an invisible border, as well as the frontier between Italy and Switzerland. The passengers had got a bit chilled; had crowded into the cabin, where the waitress was kept busy running for coffee, beer, Coca-cola. She had come out on to the afterdeck, seen the two men talking together. Neither had lifted a finger nor caught her eye: she'd gone away again, glad to have that much less work.

"Women, that's your vulnerable area, isn't it, your blind spot? Did you feel, I wonder, pure contempt for me, and think of sticking a splinter up my arse? It wouldn't have been difficult for you to find out that I had been to bed with her, over there in Como – you have such good informants among chambermaids. Or no, I have no importance and am no conceivable threat. More likely it was simple vanity; she'd – to your mind – made a fool of two men you squash like flies: you could pick her up and wear her a while – on your wrist, like a watch.

"Since you've concentrated your life, an entire existence, on male cleverness, trickeries, astuteness, where women play no role at all. I suppose the shrink would be curious about your mother. Since like the rest of us you had one.

"Girls are just decorative. Exactly like caviare and foie gras, champagne and lobster, all that stuff which bores you, tastes quite good but it's so facile . . . So that you've never understood anything about women at all. You take them to bed, just to show that you aren't homosexual.

"My wife shocked you, didn't she? You, hadn't expected that . . . It's possible that Coralie shocked you; she has the potential."

Castang lost his temper with that impassive, bored face.

"Have you even any grasp at all of the quality of women? Of course not, because you've never had one. The strength, the tact, the patience, the endurance? The thinking? We go, us men, on our little linear way and we comprehend nothing. But women think round, they think with the body and with the womb and we despise that because we cannot grasp it. We do things and we imagine them to be important. We even think ourselves brighter if we're homosexual, poor asses. That we might be a good poet or painter, physicist or biologist. Waste of time. When it comes to anything important we are helpless children."

He wanted one of his little cigars. The draught blew the lighter out. He had to make a tent, with the collar of his raincoat.

"Poets have some grasp of metaphysics. I've learned that from my wife. Truth is in poems, one wonders where else because there's a different world.

"I'm ignorant. And I'm totally uneducated. I've a law degree, and I've twenty-five years with the cops. Might as well have been the Massachusetts Institute of Technology for all the good it's done me. Equations . . . I understand nothing."

A line has come into his head; a line like many more taught him by Vera. "As kingfishers catch fire, dragonflies draw flame." He was talking to himself, making no sense, unaware of it.

"She taught me that, what does it mean? Painters' colours, painters' movement. Kingfisher, *c'est le martin-pêcheur*, I looked that up in the dictionary, I don't think I've ever seen one. Got pretty rare, nowadays. Dragonfly, *c'est la libellule*, I've seen them, what does it tell me?"

Aware of a sudden that he was talking nonsense he looked up at Subercaseaux, who was staring stonily at the background. The boat was heading for the "head of the lake", passing under the bridge which carries the autoroute across to Italy. Working for a specialised police area, fraud repression in the fine arts, where Carlotta Salès had insisted that he learn something about Renaissance Italian painting, he had done a lot of dreary homework.

Vera, giggling at this, had said he ought to have a shot too at the poets who got romantic about Italy. Byron say; or Robert Browning. Why not,

Hark, those two in the hazel coppice –
A boy and a girl, if the good fates please,
Making love, say –
The happier they!

Well yes, but there was a lot more, and a couplet which had also stayed in the mind.

As a man calls for wine before he fights . . .
Think first, fight afterwards – the soldier's art.

Rather good advice in the circumstances.

He caught at his drifting mind, looked up in a fright.
The face of stone was examining the lake and the
mountains as though they had never been seen before,
attentively studying the recessions of the picture he saw
every day.

"I should think I can sum it up out of police
experience," said Castang. "It's Brecht. 'Who does not
recognize the truth, is an imbecile. But who recognises it,
and names it a lie – that is a criminal'."

He got no answer; hadn't expected any. Back where
they sat, the screw rumbled, a soporific noise of churning
water. Marauding seagulls hung about, squawking. A hard
and a greedy eye; out for what they can get. Beautiful
beasts but you couldn't like them; far too human. They
brought him back to Lymington. Along the Solent. He had
walked there with Jane, with Vera. Across the water the
island. Nothing much in the way of a parallel; that had
been a wintry day, with the wind which made one's eyes
water.

Jane and Vera, women who understood one another,
had talked of a book he had not heard of. *The Good Soldier*;
man called Ford. When it was, kindly, explained to him, he
understood. Wealthy man, estate owner, distinguished,
much respected by all. A just man, and kind. Good
landlord, good magistrate, the perfect gentleman. And
the Hollow man.

Yes, Jane had been right, this was like Eamonn:
delightful man, valued friend; good at his job; a fine mind,
open, balanced, illuminated by history, detached from
politics: a good man. And then this fatal flaw. Inability to
love. Or is one convinced that one cannot be loved?

Eamonn had come to terms with his failures. One
cannot call criminal this desire, pursuit, acquisition of a
great many girls. Quite an innocent sort of compensation
for the absence of love. But this man sitting next to him:
this man had needed more. Wealth, but above all, power.
A right of life and death over everyone with whom he

came in contact. Behaved like a good soldier, and wasn't one.

Without thinking Castang spoke out loud.

"You cannot love. I suppose, because you never have been loved. I can see now that Vera was right. You do not love; you possess. You think you love a picture, a tree, a girl? They refuse. They withdraw. They have nothing to say to you. You are dead, and you don't know it."

Shocked at his own wandering absence of mind he brought his head round to look at Subercaseaux, but the man was paying no heed; he was still, staring at the water. The boat had been hovering, tacking to and fro in the narrow gulf at the head of the lake, moved over close enough to the Italian side so that tourists could snap yet another picturesque village. Now the boat had had enough, had done its job, the passengers were all slack and sleepy, turned for the last time to lumber off home.

Had the man got what he came for? What had he come for, what did he want, unless it were to make another little demonstration of his ability to make fear, to show Castang his impotence? A little touch to restore the balance, to show that Vera's home-truths of the night before did not penetrate, slid uselessly off that armourplate.

His own sweat had dried in the open air but he felt uncomfortable in his clothes, pulled his shirt distastefully away from his armpit.

"If you wanted to frighten me, you did. Coming out here, I was scared enough I sweated a bucket, boy, out of the wind I stink. If I kept hold of my own sphincter that's not much to boast of.

"But underneath I'm like my wife, since she has taught me everything I know and that includes police work, the job of running shits like you down, and in the male world we can't, we know that well enough, that you're untouchable and that you and your friends will assassinate us, as you did those like dalla Chiesa or Falcone, who have tried to pursue you. But maybe you've caught a glimpse just the same of how you are nothing, of why no woman but a whore will ever think twice of you – since why kill Eamonn? He was no threat. Those people in the Valtellina are small fry, and couldn't even involve you, as the Carabinieri very well know.

"So why kill him? Because you got a glimpse, as he did, of what a woman can mean to a man? And that is the one unbearable thing? You have to kill, then?

"But you'd have to kill the whole world, wouldn't you?"

Castang slumped again into his pit of fatigue and frustration; aimless thoughts fluttered away into the wind. The seagulls are beautiful, but they have on purpose except to be greedy.

"You're exactly like the Pope," he muttered foolishly to himself. "Stupid Polish prat, sitting up there in his castle mumbling that women don't exist. But nobody listens to him, nobody pays a blind bit of heed, his own troops don't believe a bloody word of it."

He tried to shake off this idiot lethargy. They were nearly back in, they were no further than three hundred metres out from dear ol' Lugano, and Vera is waiting for him: he'd like a cigarette. He looked up.

There was nobody there.

Castang stood, as though propelled by the pilot firing the charge on the ejector seat.

Stop the boat! Where's the Captain?

No, there's no point in that, is there?

He blundered forward across the desk – into the cabin, where the tourists are yawning, stretching, feeling about them for the bag, the camera, the purse and the discarded scarf. The waitress has tidied her bar. She has gathered up the dirty glasses, got her payments in, mopped her tables down. The washing-up to do, still, but within three minutes they'll be gone, the stupes, and she can finish her work in quiet. What's that fellow then, standing there with his mouth open looking excited?

Castang decided he would say nothing. What would be the point? The skipper wouldn't even believe it. Are you trying to tell me we set out with twenty-nine bods and come back with twenty-eight? Not possible.

Castang went to the gangway. Not the first by any means, but he could look – he could see . . .

Oh, dear Jesus – no no, the Pope can't help you here. Boy, you better get yourself organised. Questura, Polizei Praesidium, what name do they give it here in Switzerland where they have four languages and speak all of them worse than he does, no, that's nonsense, they speak Italian but okay, his French, even his German, will suffice; the story isn't really complex, in fact it's extremely simple, but I'll have a lot of tedious explaining. Nobody's going to believe this. Ring up Vera, have you the number of the hotel? Ring up Roberto Bonacorsi, the Swiss police won't listen to me but a Carabinieri General, that'll bring them up standing, won't it? Better ring up Mr Suarez, I planned to be back tomorrow but we've run into a bit of bureaucracy here, there are going to be forms-to-fill-in. I might, I'm sorry, be delayed for twenty-four hours.

And this has often happened to Castang. He – Vera too, one can't leave her out – long before coming to live in Belgium, noticed how the most complicated things in life became simple. Like dying. One must take responsibility for this too. As one must for the job of living.

"Tell us it again," says the Swiss police officer. "Slower."

Classic interrogatory technique. We're dim, we don't catch on fast. Tell it three, four, five times, while we listen.

French bastard, dear Jesus, ex-PJ-officer, Smartyboots.

"What did you do, push him? Stick a needle in his thigh? Expedient demise huh? When we fish him out we'll know, remember."

Leave out all the crap. Music, poems, stick to facts can't you? We have male, linear minds. If we can't understand it we won't accept it.

Jacques Brel had a comic song, starting in ordinary three/four waltz time. He plays with it, accelerates it; what about a twenty-times four then, a hundred times, a thousand. We are waltzing, but now there are three of us. *Il y a toi, y'a l'amour et y'a moi.* You, me, love; the rest is a right muddle.

God, for example; who's God? Is that the old man with the beard, of our child's imagination? No, you can look him up in the phonebook.

Celui qui est dans l'annuaire
Entre Dieu m'en garde et Dieu le Père.

But this long list, of Smiths, between God-made-the-world and God-keep-us-from-harm – it's all men!

To get a few women in, back to the singing in the pub.

'Hallo Patsy Fagan, you can hear the girls all cry.
Hallo Patsy Fagan, you're the apple of my eye.'

For the police Castang has a piece of police reasoning.

"This fellow – one kept on hearing 'he kills people'. They exist, we've known a couple like that. They end up killing themselves? One way or another? Life ceases to have any meaning? But nobody's going to blink an eye, are they?"

Never mind all this rubbish of music and poetry.